Slaying at Stanway

ACF BOOKENS

VINCI
BOOKS

By ACF Bookens

The Stitches in Crime Series

Crossed by Death

Bobbins and Bodies

Hanged by a Thread

Counted Corpse

Stitch X for Murder

Sewn at the Crime

Blood and Backstitches

Fatal Floss

Strangled Skein

Aida Time

Needle you Mind

Vinci Books

vinci-books.com

Published by Vinci Books Ltd in 2026

1

A CIP catalogue record for this book is available from the British Library.
Paperback ISBN: 9781036707798

The EU GPSR authorised representative is Logos Europe, 9 rue Nicolas
Poussion, 17000 La Rochelle, France
contact@logoseurope.eu

Chapter One

_____

I'VE ALWAYS DREAMED of inheriting a grand old house since I was 7 years old, after reading a novel about a young woman who got such a thing. I imagined a sprawling house with comfortable rooms and lots of space, both inside and out, for roaming. Space was what I craved most.

Growing up in a small cottage in a university town with my two parents, three dogs, five cats, and a parakeet, I always longed for more space, especially when my mother set up the stray cat rescue out of our front, screened-in porch.

Critters were always everywhere – in my bed, in the kitchen, sometimes even sleeping in the shower. I loved them all and had sweet nicknames for each of them. But sometimes, I just wanted to not have to take care of anyone but myself.

When things had gotten too hectic with fur and fangs inside the house, I would go outside. I started by simply tidying up the neglected flower beds in front of the ranch house my parents had bought when they were first married.

Even at 7, I knew that most of the green plants growing under the azalea hedge were weeds. So most afternoons after school, I'd tuck myself into the growing shade of the shrubs and pull-out ground ivy and clover and even wire grass.

Then, as I got the yard into good stead, I started asking my parents for money to buy flowers. With my few dollars in hand, I'd ride my bike to the hardware store on the Square and pick up four packs of whatever they had, usually pansies, petunias, or impatiens. I'd plant them in front of the azaleas.

By the time I was a teenager, the lawn in my parents' front yard had gradually been removed, and I had replaced it with an elaborate and tidy cottage garden with weaving paths, a bench for seating, and even a small arbor that bridged the walkway from the mailbox to the front door. Everyone in the neighborhood loved my design, but no one wanted to do what I had done. I knew because I had tried to convince them to give it a go. But the most they ever did was add some petunias to the bed by their mailboxes.

Eventually, I realized that my interest in flowers and landscaping was unique and that most people didn't have the time or didn't want to put the effort into maintaining anything but grass. However, everyone loved flowers, and when I found that I could enhance my parents' yard with lilies and irises, even an English rose bush, I started my first business, selling cut flowers to my neighbors.

When it came time for me to go to college, I went off to North Carolina to study horticulture at NC State, and when I came back to Virginia, I started working as a greenhouse supervisor for a local garden center, a center I was managing the day my world upended.

If you'd asked me six months ago what I thought my life

would look like 180 days later, I would have told you that I was looking forward to harvesting zinnias and making tabletop arrangements to sell at the garden center. I might have said I hoped to be able to add that money to my savings and maybe, if all went well, be able to buy a little craftsman cottage in the mountainside town of Crozet in a year or two.

I would not have told you that my parents would be killed in a tragic car crash one summer night when their car hydroplaned off a mountainside. I wouldn't have told you that I would, as their only child, inherit everything they owned, including the ranch house with the neglected front garden and the dozen stray cats on the porch. I wouldn't have said that I would soon discover, when going through my mother's papers, that I actually owned a house in the English Cotswolds, a house recently inherited from my aunt and the woman after whom I was named. I wouldn't have said that my entire life would be entirely different. I wouldn't have said that at all.

And yet, here I am, a woman in my early 40s, never married with no children, about to set off into an entirely new life in an entirely new country. I've lived one of those lives that often seemed so ordinary as to not be worth noticing, at least to myself. I've done all the usual professional things – college, of course, and my job at the garden center. I have friends, good friends from college, women I talk to often via text and see maybe once a year. I've become friends with some of the folks from work, too, and on a weekend, I usually go out with them to see a movie or get dinner, sometimes take in a concert or play. But no one in my life is my person per se. No best friend. No husband.

I was a bit lonely but not because I didn't have friends. No, I was lonely because I didn't have that special person to talk about my day with, someone whose hobbies I could learn to understand and maybe enjoy myself. Someone to cuddle up to on cold nights. But after a decade or so of on and off online dating, I'd given up and decided that the man of my dreams was just going to have to find me. I was done trying to find him. "It's my power position," I told my college roommate on the phone one night. "I'm not exactly trying to manifest him because I don't really even know what that means. But I'm trusting that if I live my life on my terms, he'll find me."

My old roommate had been more than a bit skeptical, pointing out that no one was going to break into my house, in all likelihood, to date me. I admitted she had a point but also reiterated that I was so weary of online dating. "Short of finding a matchmaker, he may have to," I'd said. "I just cannot do online dating anymore. It's too demoralizing."

I had really tried at online dating. I'd done the flirty thing, the question thing, even the first date thing itself. And while I'd met some nice people, I found I was spending an inordinate amount of time trying to pry interest out of men – "Hi. You're cute," seemed to be a pretty standard response to my "Hi," and I didn't really know where to go with that – or to deflect the inappropriate photos or commentary that came into my inbox. As I figured it, I was about 1 for 20 in finding men I might actually want to date and that was after whittling out all the guys with no profile pic, who posed with a fish, or who shared absolutely no information about themselves in their profiles. At this point, I was more likely to hit it off with a burglar than any of the men on the dating sites.

Thus, when I found myself more or less family-less, without any good friends nearby, and without any prospects on the dating scene, I decided to take my new property inheritance in England as a sign and go there. I had nothing to lose by moving to my mother's hometown and doing what I'd started doing back when I was a teenager – running a flower farm.

It was relatively easy to get the business set-up, even from Virginia, so while I had a lawyer at my disposal for the execution of my parents' wills, I asked him to do the necessaries, using my new address, to create my flower farm and be sure I could get work as soon as I arrived.

Then, I checked in with the lawyer of record for my great aunt's property to be sure I could access it when I arrived, booked airline tickets, and gave notice at my job. All that was left was to end my lease, arrange an estate sale for my parents' belongings, and rehome the dozens of plants I had babied for years. The plant placement was by far the most difficult part of the process since, of course, I had to be sure they would go to good homes. It wasn't just anyone who could care properly for a banana tree, after all.

I was not delusional. I knew I'd need to grieve sometime, but with all the arrangements for the move and such, I didn't give myself time to do so. The loss was too great to deal with immediately, I told my friends. I needed time to let it sink in, to come to terms with the fact that I was, with the exception of a few cousins I had met once or twice, alone in the world. That realization was too much for me to carry in the midst of what had to be done, so I tucked it away and plowed ahead. To England.

Thus, three months after my parents' death, I was on the way "across the pond" to begin life anew and, I knew, to grieve. As hard as that was. And it was very, very hard.

. . .

WHEN I STEPPED off the bus, er, coach in Stow-on-the-Wold, the first thing I saw was the town square with its small monument that reminded me, probably quite intentionally, of the much larger-scale one I had just walked around at Piccadilly Circus in London. In an attempt to ease my transition, I'd taken a layover in the city to take in the National Museum and a few shows. Surprisingly, it had been *Back to the Future: The Musical* that I had loved best. Maybe it was homesickness.

My new life now before me, I brushed my long dark hair off my neck, straightened my calf-length puffer jacket, and strode into town, my suitcase splashing mud against my jeans and booties. I hoped my aunt's house had a washer and dryer.

Still, now that I was in my new town, I was eager to make it my own and immediately asked directions to Nigella Smith's home at the local pub, The Pig and Cane. The woman behind the bar had turned to the man cooking fries in the back kitchen, and they had talked for a few minutes as they tried to parse out which Nigella Smith this middle-aged American woman with the huge suitcase might be looking for.

"Reckon it's the one with the leg thing?" the barkeep asked.

"Nah, she hasn't gone by Smith since she married that Scottish fella. Could be the one down the lane with the sheep?" the cook said.

The barkeep seemed to consider this option and then shook his head. "Nah, she's a Sutton now." She turned back to me.

"We need a bit more information if you please. Why are you looking for her?"

I might have been put off by this question if but for two

things. I was an American and, therefore, used to personal questions asked by strangers, and I had just watched these people try to help me and felt the least I could do was give them a bit more to go on. "She was my great-aunt. She died just a couple of months ago. Does that help?"

"Oh yes," the barkeep said. "You'll be meaning Auntie Jelly then, won't she, Mick?"

The cook nodded. "God rest her soul."

"Thank you," I said. "Could you point me to where she lived?" I felt a bit abrupt repeating my inquiry to people who had, apparently, known my aunt well enough to call her Jelly, but I was exhausted and just wanted to put down my suitcase and put up my feet.

"Definitely, but let me take you up there. It's a fair piece, and with that suitcase, it'll take you far longer than you'd like, I expect," the cook said as he hung his apron on a hook by the door to the kitchen. "Be back in twenty, Margaret," he said as he hefted my suitcase and led me out the door.

It turned out that the cook was named Michael "Mick" Harper, and his family had lived in Stow for, as he put it, "near on 1000 years."

I had expressed my awe and slight disbelief at that fact, but when Mick pointed out that the town had been founded, by most accounts, in the 1100s, I reminded myself that America was just a baby country in comparison. Mick went on to explain, with a jovial lift to his voice, that the first residents here were monks but that "my people were definitely not of the cloth unless you count wool."

I was charmed by this very English and apparently VERY local man, and I grew more so as he talked about his wife and kids, about how the children were obsessed with rugby at the moment and so he never knew who would have what bruise when he got home, and about how he hoped I'd come into the pub from time to time to relax and catch up. He said "catch up" as if we'd known each other for decades. I liked that.

"You been here before?" he asked. "You know, to visit your aunt."

I smiled at the memory. "Once," I said, "when I was seven. We came for a few days, but all I can remember is a tire swing and an old lady with boots."

"That'd be Aunt Jelly then," he said. "And that tire swing is famous round these parts. All of the neighbor kids played on it. Now that I have kids of my own, I realize that was Jelly's way of giving the parents, especially the mums, a little break. Sort of like the neighborhood granny, I guess."

The image of my aunt as the neighborhood grandmother gave me a ping of joy. "Maybe that's why she left me the house then?" I mused aloud. "Maybe she remembered me swinging on that swing?"

"Aye, I'm sure she did," Mick said. "She had a memory like a steel trap." Mick glanced over at me out of the corner of his eye. "Forgive me asking, Miss, but do you have a family who'll be joining you?"

My throat tightened just a bit. "No, it's just me." I took a deep breath. "But maybe I'll invite all the neighborhood kids over to swing." I smiled over at my driver. "Maybe save your loves from getting a few bruises."

Mick laughed, and by the time he pulled his ancient Mini Cooper up at the door of a lanky farmhouse that seemed to spread, like a kid making a snow-angel, across the gravel courtyard, I knew I had made my first friend. "You come on down to the pub anytime you need anything," he told me as he pulled m suitcase out of the trunk, something he called a "boot." "Me and Margaret are always happy to help our neighbors."

I smiled. "Thank you, and forgive me asking. Is Margaret your wife?"

Mick's face went a bright shade of red under his dark hair. "Oh, no ma'am. She's my sister."

A flush to match Mick's spread over my body, but I smiled and said, "It was nice to meet you both. Thank you so much." I held out what I thought was a respectable tip – a five-pound note – to the young man, but he looked at it and turned away.

When he put out a hand and waved through the open car window as he pulled away, I decided I was going to like Stow.

MY OPINION FALTERED A BIT, however, when I unlocked the heavy iron lock on the front door of my aunt's cottage. It was colder inside than it was out, which was saying something because the damp air had already chilled me to the bone and was starting to drift with flakes of snow. Inside, though, the air was even more damp, and from what I could see, there wasn't a heating vent or even a radiator in sight.

Fortunately, I had long ago learned how to build a fire in a fireplace, a skill my father had insisted I perfect just in case the power went out. So after testing the chimney to be sure it drafted, I had a warm fire glowing in the hearth of what was the most delightfully old-fashioned kitchen I had ever seen, never mind the chill and damp. In the center of the room was a long farm table, gouged and scraped by what I thought must have been decades of wear. A long counter spanned one side, and on it, I found a deep farm sink with built-in dish rack and what people would now call a pot-filler faucet but was, I knew from a quick search on the internet, just a practical set up in farmhouse kitchens. As the article said, "One never knew when one might need to rinse a bucket or bathe a chicken."

The walls were a yellow-beige plaster that mimicked the color of the stone that the coach driver had told me was the true marker of the Cotswold architecture, and in one corner, I found a short refrigerator that looked like it was vintage but turned out to be brand-spanking new with a classic look. A little further investigation found that there was a modern dishwasher, a double oven, and even a microwave tucked discretely behind a cabinet door. Aunt Jelly had clearly appreciated old-warm charm *and* new-world amenities, and I really loved the combination too.

The fire going steadily and the kettle by the sink warming water for what I hoped would be a fine English tea soon, I made my way through the rest of the house, crossing the hall into what was clearly a living room with another fireplace, two arm chairs, a table with a half-finished jigsaw puzzle by the window, and a comfy couch facing a small flat-screen TV at the far-end of the room. Further down the hall, I discovered what must have been my aunt's office with a desk, bookshelves, and three filing cabinets, and just beyond that, a half-bath with, again, old-looking but clearly new fixtures.

After lugging my suitcase up a solid set of wooden stairs that ran half the length of the central hallway, I found four bedrooms, all decorated with four-posted beds, antique dressers, and lamps that sat on wooden nightstands. Here, I saw radiators tucked beneath the windows and gave a sigh of relief. Each room also had a fireplace, but I didn't relish making up quite that many fires every day.

At the back of the house, off one of the bedrooms, I located a full bath complete with a steam shower, a soaking tub, and a view out over the Cotswold country-side that left me practically breathless. I could see the rolling pastures for miles around, and the piled-stone walls gave the landscape a gentle gridded pattern that somehow combined both the natural world with a very human one in a way that felt both just and sound.

I decided this view was going to be mine every day and slung my suitcase up on the bed before going down to make that cup of tea to carry with me on the rest of my tour. As I passed back up the hallway, I saw there was another full bathroom, not quite as well appointed as my own but very lovely, in the middle of the hall and was grateful that my guests, should I have any, would have their own space and leave me to mine.

After figuring out how to use a tea diffuser to steep a cup of Earl Gray and adding three teaspoons of sugar to make up for the lack of milk, I made my way back out into the courtyard in front of the house, curious to see what the splaying limbs of the building contained since they didn't seem accessible from the living quarters proper.

Sure enough, as soon as I turned a corner, I found a low-flung building made from the same stone as the house on three walls but open but for a massive wooden timber in the middle on the fourth. The space was full of clean hay, and at one side, I saw an actual manger like the kind Jesus always laid in at the living nativity things at Christmas. Beside it, a black basin full of water stood clear and seemingly cool in the chilly air. "A stable?" I said to myself.

"Yes, ma'am," a man's voice said from just behind me. "This is where Bramble, Clover, and Thistle spend their evenings."

I turned, fully startled, and stared at the rugged, handsome man holding a pitchfork behind me.

"You must be Ms. Hunt," he said. "Sorry to give you a

fright. I'm Graham Whitfield, but most folks call me Gray." He started to put out his hand, but when I stared a second too long at the dirt encasing his fingers like gloves, he withdrew it, a slight blush rising to his cheeks.

"Nice to meet you, Gray," I said. "Please call me Nell." I shook off my hesitation and extended my own hand, which he shook firmly without pause. "So I have, what, horses?"

Gray beamed. "No, missus. Miniature donkeys. Want me to show you?"

A kick of delight rose in my chest at the idea of donkeys of any size but especially small ones. "Yes, please."

"Follow me, just watch your step. With the snow, it's a bit mucky back here."

I kept my eyes on the ground as I made my way past what looked to be a sturdy, busy chicken coop that flanked off behind the house, a large patch of freshly turned earth that I took to be a vegetable garden, and out to a wide pasture where I saw three very small animals with very large ears. As soon as the donkeys caught sight of us humans, they began to trot over, braying all the time, and I decided that the sound of a donkey braying was my new favorite sound.

"This one here with the white spot on his nose is Bramble. This girl here is Thistle, and this feisty one is Clover. She'll take to you soon enough, but until then, don't get behind her."

"Because she'll poop on me?" I said with a raised eyebrow.

"Well, that too. But she's a kicker, that one," Gray said as he scratched Thistle's nose. "Feed her some apples though, and she'll soon become your best guardian."

"Guardian?" I asked, confused about what exactly that meant. Was it some English country term that I didn't know? Maybe some old-world legend about protecting the house or something?

"Oh yes, these donkeys guard the chickens. Most days the birds are out here with them, but because of the snow, I kept them in today. The donkeys keep the hawks and other predators out of the pasture." He reached over and rubbed Clover's head. "Haven't lost a bird yet."

"Well, good job guys," I said as I patted first Thistle, then Bramble, before letting Clover sniff my hand, which I pulled back just in time to avoid getting a nip on the finger. "Oh, she is feisty."

"Told you," Gray said. "But you don't need to worry about them, Missus. I've got it all under control."

"Oh, well thank you, Gray," I paused and looked around. "Forgive me. I'm still figuring things out. Do you work here?"

"Oh yes, ma'am, I'm your farmhand. Been working for Aunt Jelly for going on 15 years now. Took over my chores when the farm work got to be too much for her." He smiled and waved at the patch of turned ground behind her. "She kept herself busy in that garden until the day she died though. Said weeding made her feel calm."

I felt the same way about the work of gardening and let a wave of loss and warmth spread through me as I realized that I and my great aunt shared that love. "Well, the place looks wonderful, and I can tell the animals are well cared for." I paused. "But I'm afraid I can't afford to pay you. I'm just getting set up, and my budget doesn't account for a farmhand, I'm afraid."

Gray nodded. "You don't need to worry about that either, Missus. As I understand it, Aunt Jelly took care of having my salary taken care of, that is if you want to keep me on."

"Oh, well, then, great," I said, not sure how I actually felt about having an employee right away but very certain I wasn't going to fire this man, at least not immediately, if he could help me make this transition. The animals were a delightful addition to my expectations for the place, but I didn't know anything at all about caring for chickens or miniature donkeys. "Maybe you can teach me some of what you do. I'd like to help."

"Of course," he said. "But you get yourself settled first. Then, we'll make you a farmer proper."

"Graham, um, Gray, can I ask you a question?"

"Of course, Missus," he said.

"Did my aunt tell you why she left this place to me?"

Gray studied me a long moment. "You don't know?"

I shook my head. "None of the paperwork was personal, and my aunt didn't leave a letter or anything. I only met her once when I was a kid, so I have no idea why I was her heir."

With one grimy hand, Gray rubbed his chin. "Well, as I understand it . . ." he paused and stared at his feet, "well, missus, I don't know quite how to say this, but she thought you might enjoy the garden." He looked up at me sheepishly.

"Really?" I said. "That's why she gave me this entire house and land, because she thought I'd want the garden. Wow."

Gray looked at me carefully. "That's what she said, missus, was I wrong?"

"Oh no, no. Not at all." I smiled and scanned the property again. "I love to garden. I've always loved it. I just didn't know my great-aunt knew that about me."

"Definitely did," Gray said. "She even said something about your wanting to have a flower farm."

At this, tears sprang to my eyes. "She knew that, too."

Gray nodded.

My mother must have told her sister about my dream. Just the fact that my mom had cared enough to share that information with someone made the grief that I had been holding so carefully at bay threaten to break over my carefully constructed walls. I needed to change the subject.

I turned and studied the garden patch again. "Did, er, Aunt Jelly grow vegetables here?" I asked.

"A few, yes. Some lettuces, rhubarb, and strawberries," he gestured to an unturned patch of brown-green leaves at the far corner of the garden. "But mostly she did flowers. Dahlias and sunflowers, lilies, and irises. Her pride and joy, they were."

Tears sprung afresh to my eyes. "She had a flower garden?" My throat grew tight. "For her own pleasure?"

"Mostly, yeah, but she also did arrangements for weddings and such. Nothing big or fancy, but people loved her flowers." Gray stared affectionately at the garden. "I'd be happy to help you keep up a garden like hers if you'd like, Missus."

"Please, do call me, Nell, and yes, I'd like your help very much." I glanced down at the near empty mug of tea in my hand. "In fact, if you have a minute, I'd like to tell you about my plans, see what you think."

"Your plans, ma'am?"

"Oh yes, as my aunt told you, I'm hoping to open a flower farm here, selling cut flowers and doing arrangements for weddings and such." I stared at the garden patch. "We might need a bit more space, though." I looked over at Gray hesitantly, afraid that maybe he would find my eagerness to alter my aunt's space rude or invasive.

But he was grinning from ear to ear. "Aunt Jelly is probably dancing a jig right now at that idea." He leaned his pitchfork up against the pasture fence. "Let's get planning."

Gray was a wealth of information about not only the growing conditions for flowers here in the Cotswolds but also what the traditional flowers for funerals, weddings, and other celebrations were. I had known the region was known for remarkable flowers, particularly through the nearby Cheltenham flower show, but I had no sense of what people might expect in the arrangements they might order.

He'd also suggested that I might consider a flower CSA so that I could have a steady income even when events were fewer, like in the winter.

"I like the idea of having a subscription for flowers, but what could I possibly have for subscribers in the cold months?" I asked him as I made notes about options for price points and flowers each month.

Gray sat and thrummed his fingers on the table for a long minute, and then said, "Well, what if you did some seed pod bunches for November, packaged so that people could place them out as food for the birds."

I loved that idea and told him so. "I could even save up my own lard and make suet batches to give them."

"Aye," Gray said. "And then how about swags of yew and boxwood with some berries?"

"Do we have yews and boxwoods here?" I couldn't recall seeing any on the parts of the property I had visited as of yet.

"Not many," Gray said and then waggled his eyebrows, "but loads of people in the area do, and if we asked them to prune just before December, you could help them out by taking away the clippings for your own use."

I could hardly write fast enough to keep up with these ideas. "And the berries."

"Let's plant a bank of deciduous hollies around the pasture. It'll take a couple of years to get enough fruit, but then you'll have plenty." He smiled at me. "Until then, I'll convince my ma to give you some from her bushes."

"Oh yeah, that's just great. 'Mom, the new American woman who is my boss wants to know if I can have some of your plants?' That'll make a great first impression." I laughed.

"Well, you've got a few months to warm her to you, haven't you?" Gray said with a wink.

"I suppose so," I said.

By the time Gray left just before dusk, the two of us had planned a full-on subscription series, and I had even felt bold enough to tell him the name for my business: The Statice Symbol.

His chuckle at the pun had warmed my heart, and as I made a bowl of soup from the can I found in the cupboard, I let myself feel right at home.

Chapter Two

WHEN I WOKE the next morning, I knew two things: I needed something besides soup for breakfast, and I needed to get warm. Despite the fact that I had a radiator in my bedroom, I hadn't been able to figure out how to get it to work before I'd gone to bed. So I'd slept in a full sweatsuit, two pairs of socks, and a hat. And when I discovered that I also didn't have hot water for a shower, I decided it was time to find coffee – or, if necessary, tea – and get some hot food in my stomach.

Plus, I knew the walk into town would be good to not only help me get warm but also get my mental juices flowing. I had a lot to do, and I was eager to get to doing it. But I also needed to have a plan, not just the great subscription plan Gray and I had dreamt up yesterday but a full-on business plan that would make the most of both my time and the money I'd gotten from the sale of my parents' house. Such thinking required not only warmth but protein.

By the time I'd walked the half-mile into town, I was equal parts warmer and hungrier, so when I saw a tea shop with a neon "Breakfast" sign in the window, I hadn't even slowed my pace as I walked in. Inside, I was met with a warm blast of delicious air and the site of the most charming shop I'd ever seen.

Each antique round table was surrounded by mismatched chairs, some ladder backs, some wingbacks, some actual stools. Nothing matched, but everything aligned from the mix of modern light fixtures hanging on the ceiling to the framed pieces of wallpaper or fabric – I couldn't tell which – that adorned the walls. And the woman behind the counter with her mohawk afro, cheek piercing, and long broomstick skirt looked like she fit right in.

When I walked up to the counter to place my order, the woman greeted me with a hearty "howdy," and I felt a piece of tension I hadn't known I was carrying in my shoulders melt at the sound of the woman's American accent.

"You're American, too," I said. "I just moved here yesterday."

"You must be Nigella Hunt," the woman said as she put out her hand to shake mine. "Jasmine Jenkins. American by birth, English by choice," she said with a smile. "You, my dear, look like a woman who could use something filling and hot. Traditional English breakfast? Cup of coffee?"

Jazz phrased those two sentences like questions, but I somehow knew they were strong suggestions. "Yes, please. As long as the breakfast has sausage or bacon."

"Yes, ma'am, but here when people say bacon, they don't mean that delightful fried food we know from home. They mean what those of us from the American South call *Canadian bacon*. That alright with you."

"As long as it's from a pig," I said, remembering my grandfather from North Carolina and the way he'd rip off a piece of tough Canadian bacon with his teeth and savor it while he chewed. I wouldn't make a habit of eating the stuff given that I also had my grandfather's tendency toward high cholesterol, but today, I was all about the joy of this new place.

"Take a seat," Jasmine said. "I'll bring it out."

"Oh, thanks," I said and made my way to a small wooden table flanked by two massive wingback chairs. I took the seat with the best view of the room and settled back to take in what would probably be my new favorite hangout spot.

Within a couple of minutes, Jasmine brought out a huge mug of coffee, a tiny silver pot full of what looked to be heavy cream, and a full shaker of sugar. "I took you for a sweet and creamy girl," she said as she set the items in front of me. "Did I get it right?"

"You did. Impressive," I said as I began to pour what was definitely heavy cream into my mug and followed it with the three spoons of sugar. "Thank you."

"Mind if I sit for a bit?" she said as she looked over at the empty counter. "I have a lull."

"Please," I said. "I had no idea I'd find another American so quickly."

"Well, if you hadn't found me, I would have hunted you down later today. We ex-pats have to stick together." Jazz lowered her voice conspiratorially, "after all, we're the ones who call soccer by its correct name."

I laughed. "I expect the rest of the world would disagree with you on that point, but I'm with you. So what brought you here?"

"Actually, most of my family is here. My brother took a job down in Gloucester a few years ago and convinced my parents to come too. They all live on a sort of compound like thing in the countryside. I visited a couple of times and decided I didn't want to be left out."

"So you live at the compound, too?" I asked with a raised eyebrow.

"Oh no, no no. I didn't want to be left out of life in the Cotswolds. Daily life with my family I'm completely fine missing out on." She grinned. "But actually, that's the other reason why I was going to track you down today."

"Not just so you could encourage me to hold on to the word *soccer*. What, are you tired of the metric system too?"

Jasmine laughed. "Well, yes, but no, really, I kind of need to hire you."

I stared at my new friend. "Hire me? For what? Do you want help here?" I couldn't figure out why it would be important for me, in particular, to work in the coffee shop, but I couldn't hazard a guess what else Jasmine might be talking about.

"No, but if you're looking for work, I could probably find a way to give you a few hours." She looked at me sincerely.

"Oh, goodness. No, that's kind of you. I'm all set. But what *did* you want to hire me for?"

"I know it's totally last minute, but my brother's florist just backed out on his wedding this weekend, and Gray tells me you are opening a flower farm."

"Will be opening a flower farm," I said. "I don't have any flowers yet, so I don't think I can help. I'm sorry. I wish I could."

"Oh, we have the flowers. They've all been ordered and will be in from London on Friday. What we don't have is someone to arrange them." Jasmine grinned at me. "You up for a job this weekend?"

I stared at her for a long minute and then threw my

hands in the air. "Why not? Might as well jump in with both feet. Tell me what we have going on."

For the next few minutes, Jasmine described the theme of the wedding – Spring Magic – the color scheme – pastels – and the location, some swanky manor house to the South. She said they'd need to do center pieces, boutonnieres, and bouquets and told me I'd have a gorgeous array of roses, orchids, and other pastel flowers to work with.

"Okay," I said as I began to wish I'd brought a pen and paper. "And when is everything being delivered?

"It'll be at Stanway House at Noon on Friday. If you're free, we can ride down together on Friday morning and stay through Sunday. I have a room with two queen beds if you don't mind sharing."

"A chance to be part of a top-tier wedding and stay a weekend in an English manor house – count me all in."

"Not just any top-tier wedding. The most extravagant wedding of the year, if the tabloids are to be believed. And not just any manor house. This is the house that inspired *Peter Pan.*"

AS I WALKED BACK to my aunt's house after meeting with Jasmine and getting a promise that my new friend would email me the details about the event, including a full list of flowers they'd have to work with, I pondered my good fortune in having not only a mortgage-free house to live in, but also a garden (with a part-time gardener), two new friends, and my first job in flowers in England. I had to resist the urge to imagine an impending disaster as my anxious mind was wont to do, but I was determined to take this joy, even if temporary, and live it big.

When I got back to the house, I took a walk around the

yard and found that Gray had been by already to let out the donkeys and, apparently, the chickens. The birds were wandering all over the farmyard and the pasture, pecking and strutting as if they owned the place, which I supposed they did in a way that was more firm, certainly, than my own ownership.

Remembering Gray's wisdom about Clover, I detoured back inside the kitchen and picked up the three apples I'd seen in the bowl on the table and made a mental note to add apples to my shopping list. As I approached the pasture, the chickens moved a bit away, but the three donkeys repeated their routine from yesterday and brayed their way to me as the chickens scattered around their feet.

"Good morning, you three," I said as I smiled at the trio. "How is the morning? Anything exciting happening? Have you had to fight off any marauders yet?"

Thistle and Bramble stared at me with what I thought might be a blend of happiness and dopiness, and I carefully held out an apple to each of them, which they pulled from my open hands with their wide lips.

"And you, Madame Clover, how are you this morning?"

Clover's expression could only be described as acerbic, and even when I presented my patronage to the crochety donkey, she could not be bothered to take it from my hand, a fact that she made clear by very slowly but deliberately turning her back on me.

Thankful to have the fence between me and the surly donkey, I was not to be dissuaded from my mission to win this heart and mind. "Clover, I can see that you are clearly the leader here, and I applaud you for your caution. You don't know me. I may very well be a threat, although I assure you, I am not."

The donkey turned halfway back toward me. "Also, I

can see how you might be offput by my accent. Americans are notoriously bad tourists, as I understand it, and perhaps you have run afoul of some of our less kind citizens. I can promise you, though, that while I am American, I will not be running my country's flag up any pole here, and we will not be adding bugles to the morning schedule."

Now, the donkey turned all the way back around. "I will not force you to like me. I can see you're a woman of strong will and mind, but should you wish to have it, I will leave this apple right here for you." I balanced the remaining apple carefully on the lowest rail of the fence and took a few steps back.

Immediately, Thistle trotted forward to take the gift, and before I could even process what was happening, Clover had shoved him out the way and taken the apple for herself. Clearly, she could hold her own. I admired that.

I headed back toward the house, stopping briefly to gaze at the garden and then out to a small area beside the pasture, where Gray had suggested we could expand and add more of the hearty, deer-resistant flowers behind an electric line. "Between the shock and the donkeys, I think most of our woodland friends would stay away," he had said.

The space was ample as it was for annuals, but I knew I wanted to put in some perennials, like peonies and dahlias, that would have permanent space. I'd have to dig up the dahlia tubers each winter, at least I thought I would because it would be a bit too cool for them here, but I still wouldn't be able to put much in where they belonged. Maybe I could use that space for cold crops like lettuce and carrots and then put the dahlias in when I harvested those.

My mind was going a thousand miles an hour when I got back to my kitchen, my hands itching to get my colored pens and graph paper and start plotting the garden out. But first, I realized as soon as I opened my computer to consult my favorite sources on cut flowers, I had to plan the flowers for this weekend's wedding. The list that Jasmine had just sent over was extensive, and I wasn't just going to be able to whip up casual bouquets given that the bride had requested elaborate flower and ribbon patterns. This job was turning out to be quite extensive, even without providing the flowers themselves.

"She wants intertwined white and silver ribbons that drape exactly seven inches off her bouquet and five off the bridesmaids'," I said to myself. "Whew, they made reality shows about brides like this one."

Still, I reminded myself, I was glad of the work. I had sizable savings, but past experience had taught me "sizable" wasn't really that much when it came to daily life. I was going to have some big start-up expenses for my business both in terms of flower supplies and marketing. And I was really hoping to build a high tunnel somewhere on the property to help me propagate at least some flowers during the winter months. Even with Gray's good ideas about subscription options for winter, I knew that events would still require flowers of the more traditional sort.

By the time I had sorted the flower order information that Jasmine had sent over into the various "buckets," for the wedding, I was pretty tapped out and decided to take a nap. I had only recently become the sort of woman who took naps, but I found that fifteen or thirty minutes of rest on the couch usually rejuvenated me enough to get me through the rest of the day, a situation that was preferable to my earlier choice to simply turn on the tv about 2pm and watch it until bed on my days off. I wasn't going to have that lounging privilege here, even with Gray's help, so I figured I might as well get my body accustomed to the new schedule right away.

The sound of clucking chickens and the occasional rooster call turned out to be just the right noises to help me fall asleep. Unfortunately, they were not the sounds to help me wake up, and when, two hours after I'd first closed my eyes, I awakened to the sound of someone knocking on my door, I felt as if I'd emerged in another universe. It took me a few moments to realize, first, where I was and then, what the sound was. But as soon as I did, I sprang up from the couch and opened the door to find Jasmine standing there, a smile on her face and two cups of something that looked blessedly caffeinated in my hands. "Thought you might need fortification if you've seen my future sister-in-law's demands?"

I smiled and held my tongue. I didn't know Jasmine that well, and even though my new friend had just tipped her hand about her feelings regarding her future family member, I knew better than to speak ill of family, sometimes even with the closest friends. "She is precise," I said instead.

"That is one way of putting it," I said. "Us Americans, we aren't always known for our tact, but you seem to have it covered." She handed me the cup of what I was now sure was coffee. "Have time to plan for Friday?"

I nodded. "I just woke up from the most wild nap, and aside from feeling like I might need to go right to bed, I'm good to go. Thanks for the coffee."

"It is decaf," Jasmine said. "I figured you are about my age and could use with not being up all night."

"Yes, indeed. And sometimes just the idea of coffee is enough to power me through a few more hours. Thanks again." I held up the cup in mock toast. "I did get some planning done on the flowers. Want to take a look? See if I missed anything?"

"I wouldn't even begin to know how to tell you if you had, but maybe you can give me a preview so I can actually be of some help on Friday?" Jasmine smiled and batted her eyelashes. "Unless, that is, you'd prefer to work directly with the bride instead."

Too quickly, I said, "No, I'm happy to show you. Have a seat." As Jasmine laughed, we sat side by side at the dining table and looked through my charts for the way I was going to sort and begin arranging the flowers.

"So when you say *buckets*, do you actually mean buckets? Like plastic things with handles?"

"Exactly," I said. "The flowers will likely be delivered in boxes. Unless they're coming from very close by, and even then, most people don't want buckets of water in their vehicles. So that means when they reach us, we need to put them in water immediately."

Jasmine nodded as she pulled a small notebook from her bag and began jotting things down.

I smiled, pleased that my friend was taking our project seriously. "We'll simply put things in some buckets to get them into water asap, but then, as soon as that's done, we start sorting using my list here." I spent a few minutes going over the various collections of flowers and telling Jazz about how we'd prepare the boutonnieres and corsages for the mothers. "I'll do the bouquets because, well, because . . . ." I gave Jasmine a small smile.

"Because Bridezilla, yes, good plan. And maybe you can coach me on the aisle hanging things?"

"Yes, I can do that," I said. "First bit of coaching – they're called aisle markers."

Jazz made a note. "Got it." She glanced one more time at her list. "Feel like we're good to go?"

I nodded. "I do." I put my notes into the purple folder I'd scavenged from a drawer and closed it up. "Now, to just get the rest of my business going."

Jasmine stood up and slapped her hand on the table. "Your business is going," she said. "Tonight, we're going out for fish and chips."

"We are?" I said as she pulled me out of my seat.

"We are. A few friends and I are giving you a proper welcome to Stow. You ready?"

I glanced down at my sweater, jeans, and the muddy work boots I'd found in the front closet. "I have no idea. Am I?"

"You're perfect," Jazz said. "We're taking you to our favorite pub. We'll be the youngest ones there by like two centuries."

I laughed and grabbed my puffer jacket and scarf as Jasmine pulled me out the door.

Chapter Three

WITHIN A FEW MINUTES, the two of us had pulled up in Jazz's smart car and parked outside a pub that looked as if it had been there since the town was founded, and maybe it had. The Fox and Compass's door was set into the middle of a long building that looked to hold apartments or hotel rooms above. The door was arched at the top and painted green, and from what I could see in the evening light, the wood was thick enough to help secure a castle.

Inside, sconces donned the walls, and there were exposed wood beams that appeared, to my untrained eye, hand-hewn. As I scanned the patrons, I saw exactly what Jasmine meant. Everyone in there was at least 60, maybe older, and they were all men. Well, all men except for the dogs who seemed to be drowsing under every other table.

"This place is so, so . . ." I fumbled for my words.

"So English," Jasmine said. "It is. It's been here for hundreds of years, and it's the locals place. You won't find summer tourists in here, not if these lads have their way." I glanced around at the men drinking their pints. "We've won our place here, though, because of my wife, she's a star darts player. The guys are convinced that at some point they're going to best her." Jazz looked over at a tall, willowy woman with a dart raised over her shoulder. "They aren't."

I watched as the woman threw a dart right into the center of the board, and I smiled when the man sitting next to that woman dropped his head to the table and handed her a coin.

The woman glanced over then and when Jasmine waved, her entire face lit up as she made her way over to us and bent down to give her a quick kiss. "You must be Nigella," she said as she held out her hand.

"Call me, Nell," I said. "Nice to meet you."

"You didn't tell me to call you Nell," Jasmine said with her bottom lip sticking out.

"You haven't yet, as I can remember, said my name or I would have." I teased my friend. "Are you going to introduce your wife?"

Jasmine blushed. "Yes, of course. Danielle, this is Nell, my new fellow ex-pat in Stow."

"Blimey," Danielle said. "Two of you. We'll never hear the end of your ridiculous talk about 'real football' now." She gave her wife a gentle elbow in the ribs. "Unless, of course, Nell, you're a more reasonable sort than Jazz is."

"Jazz, is it?" I said with a raised eyebrow at my friend who had just teased me about not telling her my nickname. I turned back to Danielle, "Afraid not. Feels disingenuous, like a betrayal to my heritage or something, to call soccer *football*. I'd feel like I was putting on airs."

"Or just getting it right," an old fellow behind them said.

"You tell them, Rogey," Danielle said. "You tell them."

I was already beginning to feel completely at home in the pub, and when Jazz suggested I go to the bar to order them both a cider and black and a bag of crisps, I was practically giddy with the Englishness of it all. The barkeep didn't even bat an eye at my order until, that is, he asked what kind of crisps I wanted.

"Barbecue," I said confidently.

"Jazz, help your American out," the barkeep called over my head. "She wants barbecue crisps." He said *barbecue* as if he was holding his nose, and it took me a minute to realize that was his imitation of my accent.

"Be nice, Jim," Jazz said. "Just give her options."

Jim sighed and then looked at me. "We have salt and vinegar if you like those. I hear they've made it across the ocean."

I was feeling a little brave, so I said, "We do have those, but I'm here for the real experience. What else have you got?"

Jim seemed to like this answer and said, "Tomato. Cheese and Onion. Prawn."

My eyes went wide. "You have shrimp-flavored potato chips?"

"We have prawn crisps, my love. Want to try them?"

I shook my head. "I think I better ease my way into that. How about cheese and onion?"

Jim handed me a bag and said, "Good choice. Here's your pints, too." He set two huge glasses of a reddish pink liquid beside the chips, er, crisps.

"Thanks," I said and tucked the crisps against one of the glasses to carry them back to the table. "What exactly did you have me order?"

"Taste it, first," Jazz said. "Then I'll tell you."

Still riding that blaze of bravery, I took a sip and found it was a sort of tangy and sort of sweet, fermented drink. "Okay, the cider part I recognize – hard apple cider, but what's the *black*?"

"Black currant juice," Danielle said. "Sort of an easy drink around here. We'll work you up to oatmeal stout."

I looked at her. "Stout made from oatmeal."

"It's a thing," Jazz said. "But an acquired taste for sure. Cheers." She held up her glass to mine and they clinked.

"I'm sorry," I said as I just realized Danielle didn't have a drink. "I should have gotten you something."

"Oh, thank you, love, but I don't drink. Three years sober last month," she said casually. "I'll get my ginger ale soon enough." Then, she turned to Jazz. "Who else is coming?"

"Just Jay and Ollie, I think. Oh and Gray said he might turn up," Jazz said.

"Gray as in Gray Whitfield?" I asked, even as I wondered why I felt a little excited by that idea.

"Yep, your farmhand, that's the one," Danielle said.

"Well, I wouldn't exactly call him *mine*," I said. "I mean, he's his own person."

Jazz and Daniel exchanged a quick glance and then nodded in unison. "Right, okay," Jazz said. "Well, his own person is here, so look alive."

I sat up a little straighter and pasted a bright smile on my face as Gray joined our table and took a seat right next to me. "Hey," I said, trying to sound casual.

"Hey," Gray said. "Thanks for inviting me," he added as he turned to Jazz. "It's good to get out. They doing trivia tonight?"

"Why? You want to be slaughtered again?" Danielle said.

Jazz looked to me. "The old dudes here may appear laidback and easy-going, but start quizzing them about the films Meryl Streep has been in and they get outright cutthroat." She drew one finger across her neck.

"And do not, whatever you do, suggest you can do the YMCA dance better than they can," Gray added.

"Don't ask," Danielle said with a wink. "But no, it's not trivia night. Just hang out with the Americans night." She bumped against her wife with a smile.

"Hey, you married one of us," I said, letting myself slip into the familial tone of the group. "You've made a permanent alliance."

"You bet I have," Danielle said as she gave Jazz a huge wet kiss on the cheek. "Wouldn't trade it for the world."

I smiled at my new friends. I loved seeing people in love. If you'd asked me ten years ago if I'd had that experience of love, I would have said definitely. But now, a bit older and bit more aware of myself, I wasn't sure I could say that any of my previous relationships were really loving, at least not in the way I had hoped for.

To be honest, I wasn't sure I even wanted to hope for that anymore. I wasn't feeling sorry for myself or closed to the possibility. I just felt like, at this point in my life, it was probably better for me in all ways to focus on myself and my goals and enjoy what I had instead of pining for what I didn't.

Still, it was fun to see people enjoying each other, and I was certainly enjoying myself, even if there wasn't anything romantic involved in the night for me. And when Ollie and Jay showed up, I found myself quickly swept up in the teasing, quick-witted banter of my new friends.

Ollie, it turned out, was a police constable over in Cheltenham. "He'll be the man on call when we're out at Stanway this weekend," Jazz said.

"Let's hope you don't need the police at a wedding," Jay said, "but knowing your family . . . "He turned to Ollie. "You might as well book a room."

Ollie rolled his eyes.

"And what do you do, Jay?" I asked.

"Jay, here" Danielle said, "is the Stow pr guy." She smiled at her friend. "If you need publicity, he's your guy."

Jay blushed a little. "Not really. But I do write press releases and such for the town." He took out a business card and handed it to me. "If you need any help with marketing or such."

The card read "Jay Patel" and featured the same crest that I had been noticing all over town. "Thanks, Jay," I said and slid the card into my jacket pocket while also making a note to ask Jay, once I knew him a bit better, for his suggestions about marketing my new farm.

"And you, Nell, what do you do?" Ollie asked as he returned to the table with another round of pints for everyone.

I glanced first at Jazz then at Gray. "I'm actually starting a flower farm out at my great-aunt's house. You may have known her. I think everyone called her Aunt Jelly."

"You are Aunt Jelly's family?" Ollie's already warm face took on an extra depth of joy. "That woman made the best strawberry rhubarb pie I have ever tasted. She was a gem."

"Leave it to Ollie to always mention the food first," Jazz teased. "But seriously, she was an amazing person. But you already know that, Nell."

I shook my head. "No, I actually didn't know her much

at all. I met her once, when we visited when I was 7, and she sent holiday letters every year. That was it."

Danielle leaned across the table toward me. "So your great-aunt left you her house and land after meeting you just once when you were 7."

I popped my lips and nodded. "That's the gist of it. She and my mother were close, but Mom hated to fly so we only came here that once. I remember, um, Aunt Jelly, but only as an old lady who gave me cookies and let me swing on my tire swing."

"Remember that tire swing?" Ollie said, turning to Jay and then back to me. "We used to swing for hours on that thing. I lost my first tooth there in fact."

"I remember that" Jay said. "Smacked your whole face right into the tire and came up with one less of these pearly ones."

I laughed. "Did you get the tooth out of the tire for the tooth fairy?"

"Of course," Ollie said. "Had to borrow my dad's pocket knife and gouge it out, but that beauty went under my pillow. Got a whole pound for that one, I did." He rubbed his knuckles over his collar in mock pride.

The conversation turned from there to what everyone got under their pillows when they lost teeth. The variety was mostly in types of money until it came to Jazz, and she said, "When I lost my first one, I got Miles Davis's *Kind Of Blue*."

"Your parents gave you CDs when you lost teeth?" Jay said.

"Not CDs, man. Vinyl. Still have it. And all the other ones I got," Jazz said.

I studied my new friend for a minute. "Is this how you came to be Jazz?"

"Oh no, I got the records because I already had the nickname," she said.

"I thought it was just short for Jasmine," Ollie added.

"Well, it is, but my parents started calling me that because from the time I was little I loved the music. Davis, Armstrong, even Pat Methany. If it had a fancy rhythm and some blue notes, I loved it." Jazz closed her eyes and began to sway like she was hearing music in her head.

Danielle put her arm around her wife. "Wanted to be a musician didn't you, baby?"

Jazz nodded and then popped her eyes open. "Only problem is, I am completely and utterly tone deaf." She smiled.

"Oh no," I said. "That's sad."

"Nah," Jazz said. "Don't be sad for me. I found a new passion."

"Tea?" I asked.

"Tea," Jazz said, "and I married a woman who doesn't mind my off-key singing around the house. I'm good."

For the rest of the evening, my new friends and I swapped stories and laughed together. A bit belatedly, after my third cider, I realized I was tipsy, a fact that would normally make me anxious because I hated being out of control but that felt good tonight because, I realized even through my alcohol haze, I felt safe. It had been a long time since I felt that.

When Jazz dropped me off back at my aunt's house, Gray offered to walk me in. "No, I'm okay. You ride on back to town. I don't want you to have to walk back."

Gray smiled at me. "Where do you think I live?"

"I don't know. Somewhere in town," I said, suddenly feeling quite tired.

"Nell, I live in an apartment at the back of your house." Gray shook his head. "I should have told you. Sorry."

"Oh, really," I said, registering that this fact was probably important on several levels but unable to figure out exactly what those levels would be. "Well, that's good."

When Gray left me at my door and made me promise to take two aspirin and drink a big glass of water before I went to sleep, I thanked him, leaned against the wall as I went upstairs, and just managed to do as he directed before I fell into a peaceful, deep slumber.

Chapter Four

I WOKE the next morning hung over but probably not nearly as much as I would have been without Gray's admonitions, for which I said a mighty thanks as I stepped into the shower and began to plan my day.

I felt fairly confident about my strategy for the wedding the next day, and while I would review it a bit just to be sure, I hoped to spend the whole day laying out my own garden and starting to source seeds and tubers. For a brief moment, I thought of asking Gray to help, but then determined I was going to do this by myself. I needed to learn to be completely independent now.

As I stood in front of the fridge after my shower, I also made plans to go to the grocery store. I could not live on tea and toast, and I'd been stalling long enough. For now, I made do with a slathering portion of the fresh butter I'd found the day before on the counter in a butter bell. Four pieces of toast and a richly-steeped mug of Earl Gray at my side, I sat down again at the table, this time with my graph paper and pencils and all my enthusiasm about my very own cut flower garden.

I had gardened for years, both in containers when I'd lived in apartments and then in my own and my parents' backyards more recently. But while I'd certainly grown flowers, those had been mostly to help pollinate the vegetables that my mother most loved to have fresh – tomatoes, cucumbers, and the squash that the squash bugs didn't get to by mid-August.

Here, though, it was all about the flowers, and while I had my own favorites – poppies and cosmos among them – I had to focus on growing what was hearty enough to go into arrangements that had to last a couple of days at least. I began, therefore, with the dahlias. Somehow over the course of the night, I had come to decide, definitively, that the space next to the donkey paddock was going to be my dahlia and peony garden.

I sketched out four rows and then I alternated peonies, which I'd start from seed if necessary but hoped to get from buying live plants, and dahlias, figuring that by the time the dahlias were really going, the peonies would be done flowering and could be, sparingly, cut back a bit to give the dahlias more sun. When I finished this grid, I smiled down at the pink and orange cloud shapes I'd drawn, pink for peonies and orange for dahlias, although I certainly hoped to have both flowers in a variety of colors.

Now, I needed to figure out what else I was going to grow in the existing garden patch behind the house. From my tote bag that hung on the back of the chair, I pulled out the seed catalog I'd been perusing on the plane and flipped to the turned-down corners to see what had, at that moment, appealed to me.

I began with a list of all the flowers I loved – sunflowers, of course, and cosmos and poppies, but also sweet peas, alstroemeria, foxglove, oxalis, gladiola, cornflowers, baby's breath, and salvia. Then, I added the shrubs I'd need, in addition to the deciduous holly that Gray had suggested around the donkey paddock. I wanted hydrangea, both traditional and oakleaf, and I wondered if camellias and gardenias could make it in the Cotswold climate. I put a star by all the plants I needed to check the hardiness zone for.

Two things quickly became apparent — I was going to need more room, and I was going to need somewhere to plant the things that self-seeded. Quickly, I sketched the dimensions of the existing garden and divided one-third for "wildflowers" as I thought of them and two-thirds for annuals. Space would be tight, but that wasn't necessarily a bad thing. Close spacing meant fewer weeds, and while I did love to weed, I knew better than to think I'd have hours a day to give to that work come the height of the season.

My small plants relatively situated, at least in my mind, I wandered outside to take a closer look at the existing shrubs on the property and to see if there were any fitting places to add more if necessary. I had noted the boxwoods along the drive and was glad I wouldn't have to add those for winter sprays, and I quickly marked the placement of two hydrangea on either corner of the house, using my rough sketch of the grounds that I had brought out with me. I didn't, however, see any gardenia or camellia, and it was clear that the hydrangeas were the "ball" type, so I looked for areas big enough to warrant at least a couple of the oakleaf variety.

I was standing at the side of the house and staring at the sky with a hope of determining which direction was west when Gray stepped out from around the corner. "You know the stars only come out at night," he said with a smile.

"Not true," I responded. "They are there now. It's just that you mere mortals cannot see them during daylight." I returned his smile.

"Fair enough. So are you then, staring at the stars or are you, like most of us, merely a mortal?"

I laughed. "I'm actually trying to determine if this wall of the house faces west."

"It does indeed, my lady," Gray said as he took an exaggerated bow. "Thinking of planting warmth-loving things there?"

"Precisely," I said. "I'd like to add some oakleaf hydrangea and maybe some gardenias or camellias." I looked at him, noting his slightly disheveled light-brown hair and five o'clock shadow. "Do you know what the hardiness zones for those are by chance?"

He shook his head. "Not off-hand no, but we are in zone 7."

"Oh, well, that was my zone at home, I mean, back in the States, too. So gardenias maybe not, but camellias should be okay." I looked at the yellow stone wall. "Especially with the heat from the stones at night, right?"

"I'd think so," Gray said. "And maybe you could do a couple of gardenias in pots, bring them in during the cold nights?"

I smiled. "That's a great idea." I glanced at the hard rake in his hand. "Are you in the middle of something?"

"I'm mucking out the stable, but I'm always happy to take a break from that. I was actually on my way to check the orchard. Want to come?"

"Orchard?" I said. "We have an orchard."

"We do," Gray said. "This way." He pointed toward the west side of the house with his rake. "It's old, and as long as we spray, it's a pretty good producer." He stopped and looked at me. "Actually, you could use some of the apples in your arrangements in autumn, I'd imagine."

As we continued to walk, I thought about the colonial arrangements that adorned old Virginia homes around the holidays and wondered if I might be able to offer that kind of service during the season, too. I let out a long sigh. Things were coming into place.

The orchard was, indeed, old, and the trees were gnarly in only the way fruit trees can be, reminding me of old crones and witches in fairy tales with their twisty, bumpy branches. "Apples. What else?"

"A couple of peaches, although they struggle here, and a bunch of pears." He pointed to trees that looked somewhat like apples but were more spindly, so thin in fact that I wondered how in the world they held up their fruit. "Oh, I could use pears in arrangements too." I tapped my cheek. "You've got me thinking."

Gray grinned. "Excellent." He tilted his head. "Were you going to ask me about something before I rudely toted you off to your orchard?"

I blushed under the intensity of his focus and had to struggle to think of what I wanted to ask him. When I finally remembered, I found that a small smile had moved onto Gray's face as he continued to study me. "Oh yes," I said. "I'd like to put in some ornamental grasses and maybe some lavender. Do you have recommendations for locations?"

The two of them wandered around the entire property, and Gray suggested places that were dry enough for lavender and sunny enough for grasses as well as suggesting I could beef up the landscaping out by the road with salvia and some more grasses. "To double as landscaping and flowers," he said.

"I love that idea," I said with a smile. "I think this just might work."

"Oh, I know it's going to work. You'll make it work," he said with a strong nod. "I have no doubt."

"Well, thank you," I said tugging nervously on my sweater neck as if it was suit collar. "I appreciate the words of confidence." I studied the yard in front of the house again. Most of it was forest, beautiful forest with very little understory in fact. "These trees are interesting." I pointed toward the grove.

"Oh, that's our beech grove. See how the leaves hang on the smaller trees even now. It makes for a beautiful photo if we get a good snow."

I could picture it – the golden leaves against the white backdrop. "Beautiful." I stared a moment longer at the trees. "They look almost like they were planted, though." When I studied the trunks, I felt like I could almost see a pattern amongst them.

"Oh, they were. When I was a boy. My dad had the inclination to grow truffles, so he asked the misses if he could plant some beech trees. She loved the idea."

"Ooh, that does sound fun. How did the truffles do?"

Gray grew quiet. "He never got around to it." He shuffled his feet and then looked up at me. "Now if you don't need me any further, I better get that donkey shite cleaned up." He smiled, but it looked forced.

I nodded. "I'm good, and thanks for everything." As he turned and walked away, I studied him. Something had upset him.

By the time I had made a formal sketch of the grounds and drawn in, using my colored pencils, all the plants Gray and I had discussed, including the orchard, it was past 1, and I found myself in need of a nap again. I had just settled onto the couch when a car horn sounded outside.

I jumped up and went to the door, only to find Jazz and Danielle standing there. Jazz had a mischievous look in her eye that made me think of the Jack Sparrow in *Peter Pan*, a book I had just located that morning on my aunt's shelves and that I had intended to re-read that afternoon. I had loved the book as a kid and hated the movie, mostly because it made everyone, including Peter, seem so sickly nice. The Lost Boys were not that nice at all in the book, and I preferred that.

"Oh, Hi," I said as I gestured for my friends to come in.

"Nope, we can't. We actually came to get you," Jazz said.

"Get me to go where?" I asked.

"To Stanway. My brother said there was an empty room for tonight and offered it to us if we wanted to come early. It has two beds, and Dani here was able to get the weekend off after all. So we thought we might make a weekend of it." Jazz was bouncing on the balls of her feet with excitement.

"Um, well," I fumbled as I tried to think of what exactly might keep me from doing what my new friends suggested. Finally, though, I realized, with some degree of glee, that there was absolutely no reason I couldn't go. "Okay. But I need to pack first."

"We'll help," Danielle said as the two of them barreled by me and right up the stairs.

Within minutes, we had completely unpacked – by pouring it on the bed – my arrival suitcase, rifled through the pile of clothes and the few items that had made it to the closet or wardrobe, and repacked the suitcase with more than what I could possibly use over two nights. "There we go," Jazz said as she hefted the suitcase off the bed. "All set."

"Alright then. Let me grab my notes and laptop, and I'm good to go," I said as they caravanned back down the stairs. And within fifteen minutes of their arrival, the three of us were in Jazz's tiny car on our way to Stanway.

THE DRIVE TOOK LESS than thirty minutes, but I still managed to catch a power nap on the way. By the time we pulled up in front of the very impressive mansion, I was alert, more rested, and eager to explore. That thought, though, made me ask, "Are we allowed to look around?"

"My brother has rented the entire estate, so consider it your home for the next two days," Jazz said. "I'm knackered though. So I'm catching a nap. Some of us had to drive on the way over." She winked at me.

"And some of us had to stay awake to keep the driver awake. A nap sounds good," Danielle said.

"Great. I'll just take my suitcase up and then leave you two to rest," I said, eager to see the window that I'd read inspired Barrie to create Tinkerbell.

My things deposited and my phone in hand, I set off to explore the Stanway House and gardens. I was a bit surprised at how excited I was by the prospect of walking in the same hallways that J.M. Barrie had. I wasn't exactly a literary person. But maybe it was the full buzz of my new life or just that Barrie's work had helped me through some lonely days as a kid, but I was delighted at every doorway and turn of a hall.

Fortunately, I'd found a stack of pamphlets about the house in the foyer and had brought one with me, so I was able to follow the map through the various rooms even as I read about the centuries long history of the house and discovered, much to my surprise, that the home was still held in private hands. As I walked and looked at all the fancy sofas and elegant mantels in the various rooms, I wondered what it must be like to have people take over your home for their own weddings. I didn't know that I'd like that feeling, but then again, I didn't own several homes to which I could *retire* if I loaned one out. Maybe if I did, the idea wouldn't faze me at all.

Eventually, I wandered outside and made my way out to the road that sat in front of the house. There, I studied the yellow-gold house in the late afternoon light and saw, just on the furthest right-hand window of the ground floor a little shimmer of light and gasped. There she was, Tinkerbell herself, or at least the sort of reflection that had inspired Barrie to create her. I couldn't believe I'd been fortunate enough to see it.

My single touristy goal for the weekend accomplished, I wandered back inside, stopping briefly to see what lay behind Tinkerbell's window – a massive great room with three story windows, in fact – and then heading into the back courtyard where, I understood, the Tithe Barn stood.

The barn was almost as lovely as the house and made from the same stone, and when I wandered inside, the soaring ceiling with arched timbers and stone upper walls took my breath. It was a majestic space in every way, and suddenly, I realized I needed to massively expand my plans for the flower arrangements. They needed to be much taller to be in scale with this beautiful room. Fortunately, the original florist had ordered a large number of ornamental grass fronds, and until that moment, I hadn't understood why. Now, I got it. Clearly, the woman knew the space.

Before I lost the sense of scale from the barn, I hurried

back up to our room, hopeful that I wouldn't disturb Jazz and Danielle when I came in. Fortunately, the pair was up and scrolling their phones. I told them about my exploration and my need to adjust the plans for the flowers, and the three of us redid my sketches so that come noon tomorrow, we'd all be ready to begin with the assignments that I gave each of them.

"Thank you both," I said as we finished up and put away the plans for the next day. "I couldn't do this without you. Heck, I wouldn't even have this job without you."

"Are you serious?" Jazz said. "You are doing us a favor. Now we have a way to stay busy for the weekend. Otherwise, we would have probably been roped into tons of family stuff. No thank you."

I laughed but then paused. "I thought you moved here to be near your family?"

Danielle smiled. "She did, but *near* is not the same as *with* them at the most stressful event of their family history."

"Exactly," Jazz said. "My brother has some strange idea that we're all going to hang out and tell stories by the fire after dinner."

"Like in the *Haunting of Bly Manner*?" I asked.

Danielle clapped her hands. "That's precisely what I said. No thank you. This house has enough ghosts without us adding our own, thank you very much."

I looked out their bedroom window to the massive fountain that was, right on schedule, shooting over 300 feet into the air. It was beautiful, but I didn't quite understand the amount of space it was given in the pamphlet. I was far more interested in the house itself. The giant spray of water already boring me, I turned back to my friends. "So what now?"

"Now," Jazz said. "We explore."

I raised an eyebrow, about to say that I'd already done my own exploration, when Jazz held up a finger.

"We explore all the places most people don't get to go. Starting with the attic." Jazz's voice was bouncing with excitement.

"We're allowed to do that," I said.

"Yep, I explicitly asked because my wife here tends to get herself in trouble with things like this. But we are welcome to go anywhere on the property, including the attic," Danielle said.

As we made our way up another floor and then climbed carefully up a narrow staircase into the highest recesses of the house, I pictured us stumbling upon a skeleton or a magic book or maybe a fairy herself. But two hours later, after we'd combed every inch of the house, including the basement and the gatehouse, I found myself quite tired but also very relieved that the only things in any of those spaces had been run of the mill stuff like trunks and boxes. Nothing slightly spooky in the least, although I did wish I'd been able to look through the treasures that were gathering dust.

Just as we returned to our room to clean up from our adventures, Jazz's phone pinged. "We've been summoned to dinner," she said with a deep voice. "My brother says we are to gather."

"And gather we shall," Danielle responded in an equally sonorous voice. "Lady Nell, will you be joining us?"

I giggled and then curtsied. "If I may, I would be honored."

"But of course," Jazz said before breaking into laughter. "Just be prepared. My brother is a black guy from DC, but he acts like he is a true English blue blood."

"Accent and all," Danielle said. "Prepare yourself."

Despite their warning, I was not at all prepared for the fact that Antoine, Jazz's brother, was in full tails for dinner. His fiancée, Alex, was wearing what looked to be a vintage ball gown complete with beading and tulle, and Jazz's parents, while not quite as fancy, were dressed in beautiful suits, complete with a tiara for his mother. In comparison, I felt downright flabby in my flowered skirt and white blouse.

Fortunately, Jazz and Danielle had refused to dress up in the slightest and were, respectively, in jeans and yoga pants. So I at least felt like I'd hit the middle ground in attire, even if I didn't have anything sparkly on at all.

"It's nice to meet you," Antoine said when I shook his hand in the drawing room before dinner. His accent was, indeed, quite British but with the sort of soft end consonants of the American South. I was glad that Jazz had prepared me. I always felt a little awkward when I heard someone use a fake accent, but I had to admit that Antoine's was pretty authentic, Southern hints notwithstanding.

"Nice to meet you, too," I said. "Thank you for inviting me for tonight."

"You are most welcome, my dear," Mrs. Johnson said as she joined us. "Thank *you* for stepping in and saving the day at the last minute."

"It's absolutely my pleasure, and this place is amazing. That barn!" I exclaimed.

"It's is divine," Mrs. Johnson said. "A perfect place for the reception. And you know that the ceremony will be in the great hall?"

"I wondered about that. Is that the room with the floor to ceiling windows?"

"Yes, ma'am," a tall, thin man said as he joined them.

"Theodore Johnson. You must be Nigella. Nice to meet you."

I shook Jazz's father's hand. "Same to you. That room is magnificent. Am I right in thinking that's the window that inspired J.M. Barrie to create Tinkerbell?"

Antoine smiled. "No one is really sure which window it was. Some say that one, some a smaller one on the back wing of the house. But it's definitely true that Barrie spent significant time here." His face looked almost smug with that statement.

"That is so exciting," I said, wondering if I would soon run out of words of praise for the house and its grounds. I felt like maybe the Johnsons needed some level of social reassurance that the choice of their son's wedding venue was up to par. I, however, didn't think anything I said would really satisfy them. I was, after all, just the florist. But I still tried. "You have picked a gorgeous place for your wedding."

Both Antoine and his parents beamed. "Thank you, Nigella," his mother said. "And thank you for your part in making the day perfect."

A small warmth settled over me then. I was certainly in an odd position here as both help and friend of the groom's sister, and I had heard so many stories about the classism in English society. But the Johnsons seemed to transcend that, and I was grateful.

As the family drifted off to greet other guests, Jazz caught my eye and signaled for me to come over to where she was standing by one of the now-roaring fireplaces in the room. I made my way over and smiled when Jazz introduced me to Alex, the bride for the weekend.

"It's so nice to meet you," I said, putting out my hand.

Alex stared at my hand and then gave me a cursory smile. "Nice to meet you," she said in such a nasal way that

I wondered if I might have a cold. "It's so, er, unusual to have the help at events like this, but since you're a friend of Jazz's . . . ." She let her statement trail off as her gaze swept right past my face and on into the room. "If you'll excuse me," she said and moved off into the crowd without another word.

I stared after her for a long moment before turning back to my friends and smiling.

"Well that was just rude," Danielle said. "I'm sorry, Nell. We thought she might want to meet who was going to make her weekend beautiful, but apparently not."

"She is a royal b--, um, witch," Jazz corrected as an older man came within earshot. "Her family has had money since the dawn of time, and the only reason, as I understand it, that she is being allowed to marry my brother is because he is so successful at business."

"And because she had three fiancés, all of whom dumped her," Danielle said.

Jazz shot her a look of disapproval before laughing. "You said it. I didn't."

"Of course, I said it. She's not marrying my brother," Danielle quipped. "She is a piece of work, that one."

The three of us stood and remarked upon the outfits of the other guests, most of whom were dressed to the nines for the evening. "What is she going to wear to the rehearsal and then the wedding," I asked as a woman in a shimmering pink cocktail dress walked by, "if that's what she wears to the dinner two nights before?"

Danielle and Jazz shook their heads, but before they could say anything, a woman in a pencil skirt and a blouse with the widest collar I had ever seen came bustling over, took me by the arm, and began pulling me to the nearest door.

I looked helplessly at Jazz and Danielle, who started after me, only to wave them off. I could handle this, and Jazz needed to be at the dinner. "I'll see you in our room," I shouted before the woman tugged me through the door.

"My dear, apologies for whisking you away like that, but we cannot allow the help to dine with the family." She brushed an imaginary piece of lint off her skirt. "I'm not sure quite what you were thinking."

"I was thinking I was invited by the groom," I said, barely restraining my anger. I had already had quite enough of this stuffy snobbery. "Now, if you'll excuse me, you quite rudely pulled me away from my friends."

The woman stood up a bit straighter and said, "Do you know who I am?"

"No, I do not, and I'm quite fine with that," I said as my patience snapped.

"I am your boss," the woman said and then softened a bit as I extended my hand. "It appears we have gotten off on the wrong foot. I am Arabella Aris-Jones, the wedding coordinator for this event. It's nice to meet you."

I took a slow deep breath. "It's nice to meet you, Arabel—"

"Ms. Aris-Jones, if you please," Arabella interrupted.

"Ms. Aris-Jones," I said after clearing my throat and taking yet another deep breath. "As I was saying, it's nice to meet you, but I am here at the request of the Johnson family. So I answer only to them."

Arabella actually tsked. I wasn't sure I'd ever before heard a real tsk in my life, but I was quite sure I never wanted to hear it again. "That is not how things work, my dear. You answer to me." She straightened her skirt for the 15th time. "Now, I must see your plans for the flowers immediately."

For a very long minute, I just stared at this ostentatious woman, and then I said, quite simply, "No" and went back through the door to the party.

I heard the door slam open behind me, and the room grew a bit quieter as a voice, barely under control, said, "Ms. Hunt, I will speak with you this moment."

I pretended not to hear her and kept walking, even as my friends' eyes grew more wide the closer I got to them. I was just about to speak and tell them about my encounter when I was almost wrenched off my feet when Arabella grabbed me by the arm and, once again but with more force, tried to drag me from the room.

This time, though, I planted my feet and shook my arm free. "Excuse me," I said quietly and steadily. "Please do not put your hands on me without my permission."

Arabella stared at me for a long minute and then said, "I beg your pardon."

"Here in the 21st century," I said, "we abide by the rules of consent in all situations. You do *not* have my permission to touch me. Are we clear?"

For a long moment, the two of us regarded one another, and then, Arabella said, "I will be speaking to the bride's family about your insubordination. I expect you'll be leaving the premises shortly." With that, she turned on one heel and left the room.

I stared after her for a moment and then looked to find Jazz and Danielle right behind me. I tried to smile but found that I didn't really have it in me to do so.

"The nerve of that woman," Jazz said. "I'm going to go tell my parents about the situation, just in case."

"Okay," I said, unsure on what the proper thing to do when threatened by a wedding planner was. "Thanks."

"Let's find you a drink," Danielle said as her wife

headed across the room to her parents. "What's your poison?"

"I usually stick with wine or beer, but maybe something a little stronger," I said as the adrenaline from the encounter wore off.

"Hmm, sweet or dry?"

"Is salty a thing?" I said with a wry smile. "That's how I feel at the moment."

"I know just the thing," Danielle said and turned to the attendant behind the bar. "A dirty martini, please. Top shelf Vodka, light on the Vermouth." She turned back to me. "That should do it."

"You know your stuff, or at least I think you do. I don't know enough stuff to know if you really know your stuff, but it sounded like you did." I was rambling, and I knew it.

Danielle just smiled. "I was a bartender for a long time. I loved it, at least the people part of it. But the alcohol part, just not a wise thing for me."

The barkeep put the drink beside me, and I picked it up. "Would you prefer I not drink at all?" I said as I held the drink by the stem. "I don't mind."

"Not at all. There was a time when I needed to avoid it altogether, but now, I can be around it and be okay." She smiled. "Lots of good coping mechanisms in place these days."

With that word of assent, I took a small sip of the drink. It was sharp but also quite literally salty, and the flavor of the alcohol was very subdued. "This is very good, and it is just bitter enough to keep me from drinking it too quickly."

"Good. There are times, and those times may yet come this weekend, when you getting a little buzz might be necessary, but for now, it's probably best you kept your wits about you." She glanced over my shoulder. "Heads up."

I turned as Jazz and her father approached. "The situation has been dealt with, Ms. Hunt," Mr. Johnson said. "I am so sorry that you were treated so disrespectfully. You have my assurance that it will not happen again."

I smiled and thanked him, and then took another sip of my drink. Somehow, I doubted I had seen the last of Ms. Arabella Aris-Jones, no matter what this kind man might say.

Chapter Five

THE NEXT MORNING, I woke feeling rested and refreshed, despite the antics of the previous evening. Dinner had been delicious, and I had thoroughly enjoyed talking with Lord Underhill, the man seated next to me who, it turned out, was actually the Earl of Sandwich. He was charming and fascinating and full of, out of necessity I supposed, sandwich-related trivia, and he insisted I call him Jeremy, which made me feel cozy and warm toward him, even if he was a Lord of the Realm. Despite the earlier encounter with the wedding planner, I'd had an absolutely wonderful time and awoke feeling hopeful about the day.

Jazz and Danielle were just stirring as I stepped out of the shower, and while the two of them got ready for the day, I reviewed, once again, the plans for the flower arrangements. I'd made adjustments to incorporate the tall grasses in the center pieces, and I knew now that I wanted very simple swags at the end of the aisles for the ceremony. This place didn't need much ornamentation, so I adjusted my plans one last time and then closed the laptop. I was ready.

The three of us then went down to breakfast. Jazz had said it was provided, and I had formed some images of a hotel chain breakfast with waffle makers and boxes of cereal. Instead, I was greeted with a full banquet of every kind of breakfast food I could imagine including American-style bacon, slices of tomato, and toast set in these little letter-holder things and warming over a burner. I stared for a long time at the toast, wondering if I should take one slice or the whole array, and when a man smiled and stepped around me before picking up the entire holder with a pair of tongs, I gave him a grateful nod and followed suit.

"I love this thing," I said as I sat down with Jazz and Danielle. "Why don't we have these in the States?"

"Because we are terrified of carbs," Jazz said before shoving an entire half-piece of toast into her mouth.

I laughed and then spread jelly over the already buttered bread and took a bite. It tasted just like toast from home, but somehow that little holder made it feel special.

"So the flowers come at noon?" I asked after they had all gotten part of their breakfast into their systems.

"That's right," Jazz said. "Dad said we had a workspace to use out by the barn, so if you want, we can go check that out after we finish."

"Yeah, that would be good," I said. "Just need to be sure we can get water and have space for all the buckets as well as tables to work on."

Danielle looked at me. "I know nothing whatsoever about flowers, but if I can help, I'm happy to do so."

"Totally," I said. "We have all afternoon to put these together, and I'm happy to give you some pointers as we go along."

Danielle smiled. "Excellent."

I continued to enjoy my toast as I thought about how

great my first few days in England had been. My house and grounds were amazing, and I'd made new friends. I had my first job, and I'd met an actual Earl, the one who a core staple of American food was named. Not bad.

As I finished my meal, I stood up and began looking around for where to put my used plates, maybe a counter by the kitchen or a basin that the staff would carry back. But after taking a full tour of the dining room with my plate and mug in hand, I circled back to the table to find Jazz and Danielle grinning at me. "What?" I said.

"Were you trying to bus your own table?" Jazz said. "In an English manor house?"

"Well, yeah," I said. "I didn't want to be rude. Is that weird?"

"No, it's sweet actually. It's just that there's staff that do that here," Danielle added. "If we do it, they're out of a job."

"Oh, we have that same discussion about self-check-out in the US," I said with a nervous laugh. "Maybe that's a sort of quintessential difference between our countries. We put people out of work with machines. You insist they stay and work as servants."

Jazz nodded. "You may be on to something there."

"Hey," I said. "I've seen *Downton Abbey*."

Danielle rolled her eyes and then locked arms with the two of us. "Come on, you two Yanks. Let's go find that workroom."

With no firm schedule in mind, we decided to wander through the house on our way back toward the barn. We perused the books in the library and then made our way through what Jazz said must have been "the smoking parlor" and were heading toward the side doorway of the great room when my eyes caught on something behind the sofa near the fireplace.

I stopped and took a couple of steps back so I could take a clearer look, and when I did, I saw two feet sticking out from behind the settee. For a minute, I just peered at the legs in their black boots and gray stocking, trying to make sense of what I was seeing – a pair of sticks, some sort of tubes of wrapping paper. But then the reality that I was looking at a real person's legs hit me, and I rushed forward.

As soon as I rounded the furniture, I inhaled sharply. There, with a blood pool around her head, was Arabella Aris-Jones.

AFTER FIGURING out that I was suggesting they call an ambulance when I said call 911 instead of 999, Danielle had placed the call, and Jazz had gone to find someone to help. Meanwhile, I sat on a nearby chair to keep Arabella company. No one, not even anyone's body, should be left alone in a situation like this. So when first the groom and Jazz and then the bride and her family came rushing in, I was sitting there, looking distraught, with a dead body at my feet.

I realized too late that, given what had happened between me and the woman lying dead by the couch last night, I was probably the last person who should have been left alone with her body. The looks of everyone who came in passed from shock to confusion to a bit of disdain at my presence there. Clearly, I needed to distance myself from the room, but I didn't want to look like I was hiding. Plus, I assumed that when the police arrived, they would want to talk to me. So I simply moved across the room to another settee and sat down.

Shortly after the police arrived, Jazz and Danielle joined me, all three of us squished into the sofa built for two. I didn't mind, though. In fact, the physical closeness was rather comforting. "You, okay?" I finally asked Jazz, concerned that my friend would be distressed by this event at her brother's wedding.

Jazz nodded. "I mean aside from the horror of seeing someone dead, I'm fine. You?"

I looked over Danielle beside me, to Jazz. "I am, although I expect I'm going to be the prime suspect now."

Danielle sighed. "I expect so, sadly. Fortunately, we can vouch for your whereabouts all night and this morning. That should clear you."

"I hope so, but can you really say you know I was in the room all night?"

Jazz looked at me sharply. "Weren't you?"

"Yes, of course, I was," I said. "But I presume you were asleep at least for a few hours, right?"

"Of course, but I am certain I would have woken up if you'd left the room." Jazz held my gaze. "You've heard the banshee shriek the hinges let out when you open and close it, right?"

I hadn't thought of that, but Jazz was right. The door did squeak very loudly at even the slightest movement. "That's true," I said. "But I am the newcomer here, and I have motive."

Danielle scoffed. "Someone was rude with you at a party, and that means you murdered them? Who would do that?"

Jazz cleared her throat. "Unfortunately, I'm afraid some people might." She shook her head. "Or maybe I've just watched too many murder mysteries. Anyway, let's not borrow trouble."

I had always liked that expression, and I appreciated it especially now. "You're right. We might as well not jump to any worry without necessity." I looked around. "The flowers will be delivered soon, won't they?"

"Yep," Jazz said with a nod. "Antoine and Alex have decided they want to move forward with the wedding as planned."

"If the police give them permission?" Danielle asked.

"If the police give them permission," Jazz said.

I took a deep breath. "Alright, then perhaps they will allow us to go work on the flowers while we wait to be interviewed."

"I'll ask," Jazz said, popping up from the sofa. "Be right back." She jogged over to where her father was talking to a man in a blue uniform. After speaking to both men for a few minutes, she came back to the couch. "They say that's fine as long as we have a police officer escort us."

"And did they offer someone for that service?" Danielle asked.

"Indeed they did," a man said from behind them.

I turned to find our friend Ollie, all bedecked in his uniform, behind them. Jazz sprinted around the settee and hugged him before glancing around and pulling back, afraid that someone might see them.

"Hi Ollie," Danielle said. "I mean Constable West."

"Yeah, let's stick with that for today," Ollie said. "No need to raise any suspicions about the investigation by revealing our previous relationship."

I smiled because in addition to having a formal vocabulary now that he was at work, I was pretty sure Ollie's voice had dropped half an octave, too. "Sounds good," I said. "Constable West, do you mind escorting us to the workroom so we can begin work on the flowers?"

"Not at all, Ms. Hunt," he said. "After you." He bowed slightly and swung his arm toward the door.

The three of us women went ahead of the officer, careful to look stern and a bit sad as we paraded past the rest of the people in the room. Once we were surrounded by the flowers in the quiet workroom, though, the three of us began our work, and I found myself glad for the distraction.

We quickly sorted the boxes of flowers and got them into water. Then, I began showing Jazz, Danielle, and even Ollie how to create the center pieces, starting with six large fronds of the grasses to anchor the arrangements.

Whether from concentration or concern, it was hard to tell, but our quartet stayed mostly quiet as we worked. I, for my part, had some concerns about what would happen if the officers in charge found out we were friends with their police escort, so I figured it was better to talk less and work more lest Ollie be called upon to give account of what we said.

In this somber but focused fashion, the afternoon flew by, and before I knew it, we were carrying the arrangements to the tables in the barn and stowing away the boutonnieres, corsages, and aisle swags in water for the night. Then, with Ollie trailing behind, we made our way back to the great room where, thankfully, Arabella's body had been removed with the rug that had been beneath her.

The police, however, were still there, and so with Ollie's personal word that we had not discussed anything about Arabella or the murder in his presence, we were each taken to separate areas to give our statements.

Those statements recorded and our assurances given that we would be at Stanway House through tomorrow evening and could stay longer, if need be, the three of us went back to our room and prepared for what would surely be a subdued rehearsal and rehearsal dinner.

ON THE RIDE back to Stow the following night, we were all again quiet. We'd turned on our brightest selves for the actual wedding festivities since we didn't want the groom, especially, to have his wedding weekend ruined any more than it already had been. We'd danced and drunk at the reception, and Jazz had given a hilarious toast that had included the mention of Antoine's childhood nickname, "Snickers." The flowers had been well lauded.

But still, I couldn't help wonder if someday the couple would wish they had simply postponed the ceremony. I had, however, never been married, so maybe this was just one of those things I didn't quite get. Still, I was glad the flowers were to their liking, and I was grateful for the payment Antoine's father gave me after the bride and groom departed for their honeymoon.

Most of all, though, I was grateful when Jazz pulled her car into Aunt Jelly's courtyard and beeped as she drove away. I was an introvert at the best of times, and all the people – combined with the tension of a murder on site – had left me exhausted. All I wanted to do was brew some tea and get in bed with a gardening magazine and the extra piece of wedding cake Mrs. Johnson had insisted I take home.

My quiet night was disrupted, however, when I heard a noise that sounded halfway between an airhorn and a Godzilla's roar. It was awful, and if another person had been in sight to respond to it, I would have gone inside and called the police. The situation, however, sounded rather urgent, and I knew that, at best, the local police would take a few minutes to get there. So, remembering what I had vowed decades ago when I'd learned about Kitty Genovese's famous murder, about how the young woman had screamed and screamed and no one in the entire apartment building had responded, I told myself that I would be the person to respond as long as I wasn't putting myself in danger.

So I jogged around the house, leaving my suitcase in the middle of the courtyard, and headed toward the sound. The closer I got to the donkey paddock, the more sure I was the sound was coming from there. And as I sprinted the last few feet to the fence, I determined the sound was coming from a donkey, and when I stopped moving, I saw the screamer was Clover, who had cornered a rabbit and was holding the wild, dangerous animal at bay with her hooves.

For a long moment, I stood still and stared, unsure what to do. But then, sensing that Clover's patience for the terrified animal was wearing thin, I jumped the fence, scooped up the bunny, and tossed it before me through the rails before pulling myself over again and turning just as Clover lowered her head in what could only have been the intention to headbutt her new owner.

I was out of patience with all of life at that moment, and I stepped up on the lowest rail of the fence, raised my pointer finger, and shouted, "No!" as loudly as I could in Clover's face. The donkey, apparently stunned, took one step back and then brayed as loudly as she could.

Not to be dissuaded, I returned the shout with a shout of my own, and the two of us continued the interchange for several rounds until both of us were hoarse and red-faced. Then, Clover stood back, huffed, and then stepped slowly forward with her nose in the air.

I was not one to be taken in too quickly, so I watched

the animal warily for a few minutes, my hand resting now on the top of the fence. When the donkey eased closer and then nosed my fingers, I smiled and said, "Now, you'll respect me, right?"

As if to be sure I didn't get too cheeky, Clover nicked my fingers lightly with her buck teeth but then succumbed to a full-on nose and ear scratching from her new owner.

"Whoa," I heard Gray say behind me. "You, okay?" He stepped up beside me and joined me on the fence. "I saw your suitcase out front and was worried." He looked from me to the donkey. "Now, maybe I should be more worried. What evil schemes are you two planning?"

"Those are for Clover and me alone. We have reached an accord," I said as I continued to rub the donkey's rough ears with my fingers. "I saved her trapped rabbit, and we had to do a little sorting to get that settled. Now, though, we're good."

Gray continued to stare at my fingers in Clover's fur before he said, "I have never, ever seen her let someone pet her. The most even I can do is just a short scritch. This is a miracle."

I was too tired to care a great deal, but it felt good to pet my donkey. But a few minutes later, the bonding moment clearly over, Clover waddled off to join Bramble and Thistle who were waiting patiently at the gate.

"I don't know how you did that," Gray said, "but brava. Well done." He looked over at the donkeys. "I need to put them into the stable for the night."

I nodded. Suddenly, being alone didn't sound so great anymore; apparently, rage screaming made a woman more amenable to company. I needed to talk through things with someone, and Gray was definitely a someone. "Come in when you're done. I'll make us a cuppa."

Gray laughed. "Already adopted the English-isms, have we?"

I shrugged and headed toward the house. "Maybe," I said quietly.

WHEN GRAY CAME in a few minutes later, I had brewed us both cups of chamomile, put out a flowered creamer and sugar set I found in the cupboard, and cut the piece of wedding cake in half, being just selfish enough to give myself the portion with more icing. I was already sharing. I didn't have to be completely self-sacrificing.

"This is nice," Gray said as he pulled the chair out across from where I already sat sipping my tea. "Is this wedding cake?"

"It is. Jazz's mom sent me with an extra piece. It's good."

Gray took a big piece and said, "Oh, it is good. Is that hazelnut?"

"I think it's technically amaretto, but yes." I sighed. "Did you hear what happened there?"

"You mean besides Antoine marrying that, um, woman he's chosen?"

"Oh, we need to explore that statement in a minute, but yes, besides that."

"Nope. What happened?" Gray shoveled another big bite of cake into his mouth.

"No one called you?" I realized I was losing the point of the conversation, but I had questions.

"I don't have a cell phone."

"You don't have a cell phone."

"Yes, that's right. I hate the things." He sighed. "Land-line is good enough for me."

"Okay, let's put a pin in that point, too." I took a deep breath. "The wedding planner was killed. Murdered actually."

Gray almost choked on his cake. "What?" he finally sputtered.

"Yep, the day before the wedding." I let out a long, slow breath. "I was the one who found the body."

For a long minute, Gray looked at me, and then he put his hand over mine. "Are you okay?"

I swallowed back tears. Jazz and Danielle had been worried about me, but I'd done my best to put them at ease. It was Jazz's brother's wedding after all. The last thing she'd needed was to worry about me. "I am. I think," I finally said. "Thanks for asking."

"Of course," he said as he gave my fingers a final squeeze and moved his hand back across the table. "So do you want to talk about it?"

I smiled. "I think so. I didn't really get to process it, you know, while I was there. Didn't want to ruin the wedding."

"I'm fairly sure if anyone ruined the wedding it was the murderer. But you are a kind person. So tell me everything."

For the next thirty minutes, I ran through the events of the weekend, culminating my story with the discovery of Arabella's body. I felt like I should probably talk about the wedding, too, but I just couldn't bring myself to go there.

"Oh my," Gray said in what I thought might be one of the most British reactions to a murder I'd ever heard. An American would have sworn and asked a million questions, maybe jumped up if they were the exuberant sort. But Gray just sat there and said, "Oh my." Twice.

"I don't really know how to make sense of it all, you know?"

Gray nodded. "That is a lot. How are you feeling?"

I hadn't really taken the time to examine my emotions. I'd just been acting all of Friday and Saturday, and then I was simply exhausted. Now, though, I realized I was really, really scared and quite sad, too. I said so, and Gray nodded. "Of course you're sad. A person died. Any caring person would be sad." He started to reach for my hand again but pulled back. "I totally get the sad part, but why scared? Are you worried that the murderer might come after you?"

That thought hadn't even occurred to me, but now that he'd said it, I felt a tinge of anxiety at the thought. In those movies and books, the person who had seen something was always in danger. I didn't think I'd seen anything, but what if someone thought I had? What if I hadn't but the killer thought I did?

"You just went completely pale. Are you okay?"

I took a long deep breath and shook my head a little. "Yeah, yeah, I'm okay. No, I was more scared about the fact that they might think I killed her."

"Why would they think that?" Gray studied me carefully for another long minute. "I shouldn't ask this, and maybe you won't want to tell me if I do, but did you kill her?"

I jumped up, my chair falling to the floor behind me. "No, of course not. How could you--?" Then I saw the broad grin on Gray's face. "You're teasing."

"Of course, I'm teasing," he said. "If I thought there was any remote chance you were a murderer, I would not be sitting here having tea and leftover wedding cake with you." His voice was so sincere that I couldn't even stay mad.

I sat back down. "They questioned me, Danielle, and Jazz twice. They kept asking us how we'd felt about Arabella's treatment of me at the dinner the night before. Jazz and

Danielle said it was just the police being thorough, but I can't shake the feeling that they suspect me."

"I can't speak to what they think, of course, but if they were being harder on you, they probably did so because that woman was so awful to you and because every English person knows that Americans don't take well to being mistreated." He looked at me intently.

"How many movies have you seen about the American mafia?" Now I was the one teasing.

"So you don't put dead horses in people's beds when they defy you?"

I shuddered. "I can't even watch that scene, so no." But then I smiled. "I have been known to tail someone too closely when they cut me off, though."

"See, you're a loose cannon. The constable must have sensed it."

"Oh, well, that's interesting. Ollie was one of the officers who came to the scene." I had spent a lot of time the previous night trying to figure out what Ollie thought. I didn't want to disappoint my new friend, and I certainly didn't want to use him for his information. But I couldn't help thinking it would be really nice to know his perspective on things, I told Gray.

Gray's face broke into a smile. "Well, why didn't you say so? We'll have this all sorted by tomorrow."

"How do you mean?" I asked.

"Ollie is my best mate. He'll fill me in on everything if I ask." Gray picked up his mug and plate and carried them to the sink.

"I don't think so," I said. "He was pretty tight-lipped with us."

"Was his supervisor there?"

"Um, yeah."

Gray raised his hands in the universal gesture for "there you have it," palms up and arms level with his shoulders. "I'll let you know what he says."

I walked him to the front door and then; after washing up the dishes so I didn't have to see them in the morning, I grabbed my gardening magazine and headed up to bed. I was asleep before I made it through the first spread of photos.

Chapter Six

THE NEXT MORNING, I made my way, finally, down to the shops to get some groceries. I had hoped that maybe my aunt had left a car at the house, but the only thing I could find was a bicycle with a big, wooden box mounted over the front wheel. Inside, there was a net with hooks on the side, and when I pulled it out, I realized it was probably what my aunt had used to secure the things she was carrying in the box.

"We're not in Kansas anymore, Toto," I said as I wheeled the bicycle past the donkeys and out into the front courtyard. As I mounted the bike, I remembered when I'd first learned to ride, how terrified I'd been, how my parents had assured me that riding a bike was part of growing up. In that moment, I had briefly wished I would never be an adult if it meant doing something this scary. But as soon as I started to pedal and felt the wind on my face, I changed my mind. If I got to do things like this as a grown-up, I was in.

As I pedaled, I thought of Peter Pan and his Lost Boys, the children he had kidnapped. The popular cartoon had made it seem like the children had loved Neverland, had wanted to go where they could stay children forever, where they could fly and never have to make adult decisions.

Fortunately, despite the fact that I hadn't ridden a bicycle in years, my muscle memory had kicked in, and I'd found the ride pleasant, at least once I got the used to the weight of the wooden box. One close encounter with a mailbox had forced me to slow down while I adjusted my steering practices, and then I was back up to speed and in town in no time.

A quick Google search had told me there was a Tesco, and so I made my way there, eager to try the local shops at some point but also confident that a visit to a large grocery store would be enough cultural dissonance for one day. I was right. Nothing was in the typical order it would be in an American store, and it took me almost ten minutes to decide which kind of cereal I might like. My indecision was not sparked, however, by too many choices like it might have been at home but rather by the fact that I had no idea what Weetabix and Alpen were. By the time I'd picked up my staples for a few meals, I was exhausted, and I still had to make the ride home.

But first, I popped into a little corner market that advertised sandwiches on their window. I could do with a good sandwich, and when I saw that they did buttered bread with cheese, I couldn't resist the double-dairy option. After the young men behind the counter had finished making my fresh sandwich, I grabbed what looked like a thick granola bar and a Pepsi and found a nearby bench to eat my lunch.

The sun was out, and the town square was bustling with people on foot and in cars. Even a few bicycles like mine graced the road. And everyone waved as they passed me. I liked this town and found myself thinking about having my lunch this way more often, just so I had time to be with people without, well, actually being with them. I'd done the same thing back in the States at a coffee shop. I'd go sit and read in a chair in a corner while I people watched. The presence of people was sometimes really invigorating, as long as I didn't have to make small talk.

In this case, the rest restored some sense of equilibrium in myself, a sense that had been disrupted ever since I found Arabella's body. For the past two days, my mind had been leaping back to the image of the woman's legs sticking out from behind the settee and thinking about how Tinkerbell might have been flittering around in that very room. Somehow, that seemed appropriate given that the fairy in Barrie's original book wasn't the kind-hearted, overly-sweet Disney version of the character. In fact, Tinkerbell didn't seem to like adults very much at all, so I kept imagining a sneering fairy fluttering around and laughing. It was creepy.

Now, though, as the cool, spring sunshine shone down on me and the rich butter combined with the crumbly, strong cheddar, I found myself able to, once again, think about my flower farm. I was eager to get ordering my seeds, and as I opened up the granola-like thing, something called a *flapjack* the package said, I decided that was going to be how I spent the rest of my day – seed catalogs, my laptop, and lots of tea.

And also another flapjack. Those things were amazing. I slipped back inside and purchased one more, and as I came back out, I saw someone leaning over my bicycle a bit too closely. "Can I help you?" I said as I jogged over.

The person stood up, stepped back, and smiled at me. "Not unless you're inviting me over for dinner," he said.

I stared at him for a minute until I recalled why he seemed familiar. "Jay, oh, it's you. Sorry for shouting."

He grinned. "Was that shouting? I somehow thought an American might have more of a yell than that."

"Oh, you just haven't heard me during the Super Bowl yet. I can get really rowdy."

"You can?" Jay said. "I didn't take you for much of a sports fan."

"Oh sorry. Did I saw Super Bowl? I meant Puppy Bowl." My mouth fell open. "Wait, do you have the Puppy Bowl here?"

Jay laughed. "Never fear. We do. It's not as popular as it may be in the States, but we do have it." He smiled again. "I take it that means you're hosting a puppy bowl party next year."

"I am now," I said. "I just have to look up the day that other, lesser, sporting thing is happening, and I'll get the invites out to everyone."

"I look forward to it," Jay said before growing a bit more somber. "I hear it was a rough weekend. Sorry about that."

I sighed. "Yeah, but the wedding really was beautiful." I didn't know how much Ollie had told him, or if he had said anything at all. Maybe Jay had talked to Jazz or Danielle. "And Ollie did a great job."

"Did he?" Jay asked. "He was there then?"

"Oh, I'm sorry. I assumed he's the one who told you."

"Ah, no. It's in the paper today." He looked at me closely. "They even mention that you're the one who found the body."

"They do," I said as I looked around. "Where can I get a copy of the paper?"

"They'll have one inside," he said pointing to the shop that I had now been into twice. Then, he glanced at the flapjack in my hand. "Trust me when I say you're going to need another one of those."

"Oh this is my second one," I said as a little color rose to my cheeks.

"Still," Jay said. "They're addictive. Get another while you're in there."

I laughed and waved as Jay headed across the square. Then, I turned and went back into the shop for a paper and, yes, another flapjack, even though I was still a bit disconcerted at the way Jay had been studying my bicycle. What had he been looking at?

A FEW HOURS LATER, I was neck-deep in seed orders when a knock sounded at my door. I wasn't expecting anyone, but apparently, here in Stow, people came by without calling ahead. Somehow, I didn't mind that, even though I would have guessed I would if someone had given me a heads up about it.

When I peeked out the kitchen window, I saw both Gray and Ollie standing there, and suddenly, I was incredibly nervous, both about the fact that a police officer was at my door and that my friend might have told him that I was anxious about the investigation. I took a deep breath, reminded myself that being anxious about being anxious was part of the deal, and contemplated ducking upstairs and pretending I wasn't home. But by that time, Gray had seen me peeking through the kitchen window and waved.

"Shoot," I said to myself as I went to the door. Then, taking a minute to straighten my "I Wet My Plants" shirt and realizing it, too, was a little embarrassing, I pasted on a smile and opened the door.

Both men smiled when they saw me, and Ollie almost

spit on me when he read the words on my shirt. "That's perfect," he said before gathering himself and saying, "Hi Nell. Can we come in?"

I thought, for a brief minute, about saying something like, "That depends. What is this regarding?" like I saw the saucy women on TV do, but I was neither saucy nor on TV, so I said, "Sure, come in. Can I get you something to drink?"

"I wouldn't mind a cuppa," Gray said and winked at me.

"A cuppa," Ollie said. "Since when do you say, 'A cuppa.'" He stared at his friend.

"It's, well, it's a bit of . . . never mind," Gray said a blush coming to his neck. "I'd love some tea if you have it, Nell."

"Ollie?" I asked as I chose to ignore Gray's ribbing and also how much I liked it.

"Sure, I'll take a cuppa, too. Thanks, Nell." Gray and Ollie followed me into the kitchen, and Ollie looked at the assortment of magazines and lists I had spread across the table. "My gran used to do this every winter, too. Always said gardening began in January."

"She's not wrong," I said. "By this time in the States, a lot of the most popular seeds would already be sold out. Here, though, I'm finding everything easily. More supply."

"And less demand," Gray added. "We have about fifth the number of people you do over there."

"Really? Is it that much of a difference?" I asked as I poured the hot water out of the kettle.

"Yep, and we have about 2.8% of the space you do, so we're packed in here more tightly," Gray continued.

"Look at you and your statistics, mate," Ollie said.

"I may have been googling a bit last night," Gray said

and then refused to meet my eyes. "I got curious about how different it looks to garden here than it does there."

My cheeks warmed. "Well, from what I've seen in my brief time here, you all do not rely on lawns like we do. Most American houses have a lawn in front and back, and then they might put flowers and shrubs in at the edges." I set their mugs down between pages of seed catalogs. "Here, though, it looks like lawns are more rare, and people use more of their space for plants and shrubs. I have to say I prefer your way."

"Me, too," Gray nodded as he put a spoonful of sugar into his tea. "Lawns, if you want them to be really fine, take a ton of care and chemicals. I prefer intermittent pruning and planting to constant watering and fertilizing."

"Same," I said and was surprised to feel another flush spread to my cheeks as I smiled at Gray. "I'd really like to have an English cottage garden feel here."

Gray nodded. "Tell me what the idea of an English cottage garden sounds like to you."

"Casual, vivacious, full of color that changes as the seasons do." I paused and thought a second. "Just up the road on the way to town, there's a little thatched roof place where the entire front yard is full of beds and shrubs with a little bench amongst them for someone to sit on. I love that."

"Oh yeah, the Sumner place. Old Mrs. Sumner is a gardening guru," Ollie said. "You can totally do that here," he continued as he looked out the window.

Gray nodded. "That sounds lovely, but if it suits you, let's do that slowly. Put in a few things and then let you see how you live with them before we put in more. That way, you're cottage garden will grow kind of organically."

"Are you going to have a labyrinth?" Ollie asked after draining his hot cup of tea in one swallow.

I laughed. "Like the one in *The Shining*?"

Gray and Ollie looked at each other. "What's that?" Ollie said.

My eyes went wide. "Oh my, it's a classic American horror movie set at an old hotel that has a labyrinth." I grinned. "We'll have to do a viewing, and then you'll see why my answer is an adamant no to a labyrinth."

"That scary, huh?" Ollie said.

I nodded and then frowned as the mood in the room suddenly dropped. I sat down and sipped my tea as the three of us avoided eye contact. Eventually, though, I broke the silence because I couldn't take it anymore. "Ollie, can you tell me more about what happened at Stanway? To Ms. Aris-Jones?"

He smiled at me and nodded. "Of course. I can't tell you a few things just because I don't want to compromise the investigation, but some of what we know is totally fine to share."

"Especially if your boss isn't nearby," Gray added with a wink.

"Especially then," Ollie said. "Okay, so we know she was killed sometime between the hours of Midnight and 4am." He paused there, and I got the impression he was making a conscious choice not to give more detail there. If he had been inclined to say something like, "Given the lividity of her body," like they did on TV shows, I was grateful not to have that particular series of questions about what exactly that meant in my mind.

"As I'm sure you saw, she was bludgeoned. The blow was hard, quite hard," Ollie was watching me closely.

I nodded. "Okay, so did she suffer?" That had been the

recurring vision in my mind – that poor woman dying alone and in pain.

Ollie smiled just a little. "No, her death would have been almost instantaneous." He flipped a page in the small notebook he had in front of him. "Beyond that, we found a few hairs, and of course, there were fingerprints all over the room." He paused. "But none on the bookend that was the murder weapon."

The image of a person grabbing one of the large, wrought-iron owl bookends I had noticed in the room and striking Arabella with it sprung vividly to my mind, and I winced. Fortunately, the guys didn't notice.

"Do you have suspects?" Gray asked, and a wave of gratitude passed over me since I wanted to ask the same thing but didn't want to draw more attention to myself as a possibility.

Ollie nodded. "We do, but I'm not allowed to say much about that." He looked at me then. "You were, of course, under consideration, Ms. Hunt," Ollie said.

Reflexively, I corrected him. "Nell, please."

"Nell," he said. "Sorry. I'm in work mode." He smiled. "It's just standard to consider the person who found the victim as a suspect, but between the three of us, you're not under serious consideration. Still, I wouldn't do something like leave town or such."

I laughed just a little. "Oh, I'm not leaving." I gestured at the catalogs strewn about the table. "If anything, I'm putting down more roots."

Ollie threw back his head and laughed. "She's a good one, Gray," he said as his laugh died down, and I couldn't help but notice that a flash of red ran up Gray's neck and face, all the way to his hairline.

"Are you allowed to share who the other suspects are?" I

asked, hoping to divert the undercurrent of conversation away from me.

Ollie shook his head. "I'm afraid not. But I imagine that if you think about it a bit, you'll be able to determine that for yourself." He winked at me and then slapped both hands on the table. "I best be off. Thanks for the tea, Nell. See you later, Gray."

I walked him to the door and told him that I appreciated his visit and the information. "Truly, you've set me at ease a great deal," I said.

"Good, and if you get uneasy again, just let me know. I'll always share what I can with a friend." He tipped two fingers to his imaginary cap and headed across the courtyard.

When I walked back into the kitchen, I found Gray washing our tea mugs at the sink. "You don't have to do that," I said.

"I know, but I wanted to. I'm just a polite English boy, you know," he said as he intentionally deepened his accent. "Feel better?"

"Much," I said. "Have time to sit a bit more?"

He nodded. "Of course. Want to talk gardens?"

"Definitely," I said as I scooped up the catalogs and headed toward the comfier chairs in the living room. "But first, I want to talk suspects."

Gray smiled. "Ah, we're going to do some sleuthing. I like it," he said as he took a seat at one end of the sofa.

I set the magazines and notes down on the coffee table and put myself at the other end of the couch before picking up my notebook and turning to a blank page.

"Okay, so what do we know?"

Gray looked at me and shook his head. "I don't know anything. I wasn't there." He held out his hand to me.

I stared at him for a long minute, trying to figure out what he was doing and hoping he wasn't telling me I should curl up in his arms even as I kind of hoped he was.

"Give me the notebook," he said. "You talk it through, and I'll make notes."

"Oh," I whispered. "Good idea." I stood up and began to pace, not because I knew pacing to help my thinking but because all the great detectives, including Holmes himself, paced while they worked through a case. If it worked for them, maybe it would work for me.

I took a few strides and reached the other wall of the room before turning back. "Okay, so the victim was a pretty bossy person, and while it looked like she was really good at her job, I wonder if she treated other people the way she treated me."

"Oh, describe how she treated you?" Gray asked as he made some notes.

"Like I was the help, downstairs people," I said.

Gray nodded. "So the unfortunately common English classism, got it?"

I sighed. "I suppose so, although I don't know that it's common, I guess. But I was very adamant about my place and not shy about it." I recalled the way I had put her in her place, at least the place I had thought she should have.

"Did you see her treat anyone else this way?" Gray asked as he looked up at me when I strode by his end of the sofa for the third time.

I shook my head. "No, but I was with the guests most of the time, and I suspect she didn't think any of them were being inappropriate." I kept pacing. "Her staff seemed pretty serious, but I didn't hear anyone complaining."

"But then, they probably wouldn't have complained to you, would they?"

I stopped and looked at him. "You're right. But maybe they complained to each other?" I resumed my tour of the room. "So a member of the staff could be a suspect."

"Agreed," Gray said as he drew a slashing line across the middle of the page and wrote something. "Staff – suspect #1. Who else?"

I continued to do laps as I thought through the people I'd met. Jazz and Danielle were obviously not suspects since I knew they'd been in the room with me all night. No matter what the police might suspect about the possibility that one of us slept through someone leaving, I knew I absolutely could not do that. I was a light sleeper in any new place, and I'd been grateful to get a few hours of intermittent sleep. Nope, there was no way they had gotten past me.

Gray leaned back against the arm of the couch and popped off his shoes before stretching out and smiling at me. "Do you mind?"

I waved a hand and kept walking. "So there was Jazz's brother? He seemed very cool but also a bit controlled by his wife."

"What do you mean?" Gray asked.

"I don't know exactly. He seemed quite happy, but, and maybe this is just me projecting, but it didn't seem like he had a lot of say in what was happening at the wedding."

"And what does that tell you about the possibility of him killing someone?" Gray asked.

I shivered. "I don't know, and I hate to even consider him a suspect. But . . ." I couldn't pin down exactly why Antoine kept coming to mind, but he did. "I'll keep thinking."

Gray made a note. "Who else?"

"So the bride herself," I said. "Again, I might just be

judging her, but she struck me as someone very used to getting her own way."

"Alright, but does that make her a murderer?"

"Fair question." I walked a bit more.

"What if she and the wedding planner disagreed about something?" Gray asked. "Sounds like that would have been quite the conversation."

"Oh yes, fireworks completely." I nodded. "But then, if they had fought, wouldn't someone have heard them?"

Gray stared at the paper in front of him. "Maybe. But what if Alex couldn't get over something and just decided to eliminate the obstacle."

"I feel really icky thinking about Jazz's brother and sister-in-law like this." I wrapped my arms around myself.

"Yeah, me, too. Maybe we need to just stop," he said and put the notebook on the coffee table. "I need to get on out to the girls anyway."

The girls, I thought. And then I chuckled because I knew exactly who he was talking about. "Need any help?"

"Sure," he said. "You can feed Clover. She seems to like you best."

I grinned and grabbed an apple from the kitchen before following Gray to the paddock.

The three donkeys saw us coming and began to bray as if they were warning us of an impending asteroid. "Man, they are loud," I said.

"Oh, and they're just barely vocalizing now. Wait until the farrier comes. They love him."

"Even Clover?" I asked.

"Especially Clover. He's her favorite."

"Ah, I see," I said with a laugh. "My competition."

"Unless you plan on cutting Starburst candies into tiny

pieces and keeping them in your pockets, I don't think you can win this one," Gray said.

"Ooh, I'll definitely need to up my game then." I handed Clover the apple, which she happily took and swallowed after approximately two chews. "Does she ever choke?"

"Nope. I think she has a lead pipe for an esophagus." He opened the gate. "Want to lead them to the stable?"

I watched as the three animals walked through the gate and said, "Doesn't seem like I have much of a choice."

"Oh sure you do," Gray said. "You can either take them to the stable, or they'll follow you right into the house."

"Stable it is then," I said and began to make clicking sounds that I thought the donkeys might enjoy. But when I got to the stable and opened the gate, I turned around to find Gray laughing so hard, but silently, that tears were streaming down his face.

"What?!" I said as a wave of embarrassment spread through my whole body.

He laughed a bit more and then finally composed himself enough to say, "Were you imitating a clock because it's time for them to go to bed?"

I glared at him with mock fury. "That's how I used to call my dog when I was a kid."

"I see," Gray said as he stifled another laugh. "Well, whatever works."

"They followed me, didn't they?" I said.

Gray nodded and shut the gate. He was still chuckling when he waved goodnight at my front door.

I shut the door, a smile on my own face as well.

Chapter Seven

I DREAMT of donkeys in bridesmaid's gowns off and on all night, and when I finally peeled myself out of bed about 5am, still tired but unwilling to see the brightly colored hats perched over the donkeys' ears one more time, I realized just how fitfully I had slept.

When I got downstairs and remembered that I'd bought coffee for my French press when I was at the store, I took a little shimmy of joy and put the kettle on for water before sitting down to stare at my seed lists while the water boiled.

The notebook, however, was open to Gray's hand-writing and the list of possible suspects. Jazz and Danielle's names were there but marked through, as if Gray had been reading my thoughts since I had been careful not to say any of that out loud. I was the new friend in the group, and I didn't know if Gray felt enough loyalty to me yet to know that I was just musing, not actually considering our friends as suspects.

Below them, he had written "Wedding Staff" followed by Antoine and then Alex. Next to each name was a little sketch, a doodle that seemed to represent what I had told him about each of these people. Antoine's name was aligned with a couple of three-dimensional question marks, and Alex had a little devil in a wedding dress. The wedding staff line featured a chef's hat. They drawings were so cute and charming that I almost wanted to frame them.

Fortunately, I thought better of hanging a list of suspects for a murder investigation on the wall of my frequently-visited kitchen, but I did decide I was going to ask Gray to draw something for me soon.

The kettle clicked off, and I walked to the kitchen counter to pour water into the press. While it steeped, I paced again, wondering as I began if I might need to invest in one of those step-counting watches so that I could claim all this stewing was actually exercise.

Since the potential motives for the bride and the wedding staff seemed most obvious, I let my mind float to Antoine, as skeevy as it still made me feel to be considering that my new friend's brother might be a killer. Still, something about him kept snagging in my mind every time I considered the murder.

For some people, a systematic approach to considering him a suspect might have been useful, but I had an atypical brain – I'd lately considered I might be autistic actually – and so it was best for me just to talk and mull rather than frustrate myself with some sort of organized consideration.

So I did what I had done since I was a child: I talked to myself. "Alright, what do I know?" I said as I pressed the coffee and filled my mug. "He's successful and very polite. Handsome. Well-dressed. He loves his sister." I wandered out the front door and around the courtyard as I continued to talk this through.

"So what is bothering you, Nell? Why does he keep

coming up as a suspect for you?" I asked as I bent to pull a few weeds out of a small bed that ran alongside the brick wall by the roadway. "Something about the fact that he married Alex? They seem like a good couple in some ways, but he seemed so easy-going, and she definitely wasn't."

Carrying my coffee in one hand and the weeds in the other, I headed around the side of the house toward the back garden and chucked the weeds into the compost bin that Gray had just made out of pallets next to the plowed ground. "But you only talked with him for a few minutes. Maybe he isn't that likeable really."

"But Jazz loves him, and you do know Jazz a little better. I'd love my brother no matter what, of course, but she really went out of her way to make his wedding amazing, even though she obviously does not care for her sister-in-law. So no, it looks like your read on him is right." I was talking away as I came up to the donkey's paddock only to be snubbed by Clover because I had not brought her a treat. She turned her back to me, swirled her tail, and wandered off.

"Fine then," I said as I turned down beside their fence and wandered further into the grounds behind my house. "So maybe it's just the mismatch of he and his new wife that you're seeing?" I was covering the same ground again, but it felt like I was getting closer to something.

"Why would he marry someone so demanding? So prejudiced? He didn't seem like that kind of person. Maybe I was just nervous. Maybe she was normally really kind?"

I pondered that possibility as I entered a grove of trees that seemed to stretch off into the distance. "But that doesn't track. People are usually more their true selves under stress. Kind people can get snippy, but they don't get outright mean and ugly like Alex had been to me." I finished the last of my coffee and let the mug dangle from one finger. "No, she is definitely a snob, just like Arabella Aris-Jones."

I felt my mind snag on something then. "But Aris-Jones was working class. Her classism came out of self-loathing. Alex's comes out of a feeling of superiority." I laughed then. "What are you, Nell? A therapist now?" I turned and headed back to the house. I had gone too far into my own interpretations for this consideration to be useful anymore.

Instead, I turned my thoughts to the wedding itself. It had been a beautiful affair. Understated in only the way the most expensive things can be. The bride and groom each had two attendants, and the bride's dress had been a silk sheath with a row of soft feathers around the neck and the faintest line of beading at the hem. The entire audience had gasped when she'd stepped into the aisle, and I knew she must have looked stunning. But I was doing what I usually did at weddings – watching the almost-spouse stare at their beloved as they came toward them.

For me, this was the most powerful point in a wedding ceremony. When one partner saw the other and responded to their beauty and presence. But as I remembered now, Antoine had barely reacted. His smile hadn't gotten brighter. He hadn't cried. He hadn't even shifted his body position. In that moment, I think I interpreted that to surprise and nerves, but now, it seemed odd to me. I had never seen a partner not react in some way to their partner coming to marry them.

As I strolled through the knee-high grass that would soon become my flower garden, I tried to tell myself that it had been just nerves. After all, it was a really intense wedding, and someone had died the day before. *That had to be it,* I thought.

My next thought was, *Right?*

I couldn't let myself imagine Jazz's face if her brother was a murderer, so I moved on to other suspects. The bride herself was easy for me to picture wielding a heavy book-end. She just struck me as someone who kept only a thin tether on her anger. It felt like only the lightest blow could set her loose. I expected that was a result of unchecked privilege, the fact that she had rarely had to suffer the consequences for her actions or words.

Still, I had no evidence that it had been Alex, and I couldn't see anything awry with the wedding plans, at least as far as I knew them from Alex's wishes about the flowers. I couldn't cross her off the list, but she definitely wasn't at the top of it.

And since I couldn't fathom having Antoine as the prime suspect, even in my mind, I was left with the wedding staff. Given Arabella's ease in mistreating me, someone I had just met who was with the groom's family, it didn't seem a far stretch to imagine her outright abusing her staff.

I made my way back toward the house with a new focus – getting to know the wedding staff. How I was going to do that was something I'd sort with a little help from my friends. For now, though, it felt like I had a plan, and that felt so good that when Clover quite literally pooped at me as I walked by, I just smiled.

It was only after I got back to the house and texted Jazz, under the pretenses of wanting to network with the wedding company, that I realized I was pretty deep into sleuthing and didn't quite know why. I tidied the kitchen and pondered my interest. Ollie had said I wasn't really a suspect, and at the time, that had eased my worries. Now, though, the fact that I was a suspect in a murder on any level felt really heavy.

Plus, I decided as I loaded up my bag and headed out to get the bike from the garage, someone had done this awful thing at my friend's brother's wedding. That felt significant, and I wanted to do something about it.

Still, I knew there was something more to my interest than self-preservation and friendship, and when I was really honest with myself, I realized I was looking for a thrill, a little stimulation, a bit of some intrigue to fuel me.

I got distracted, though, as I approached my bike. Something was different. I looked at it carefully, and realized that instead of the large wooden box that had been mounted to the front, two saddle bags of considerable size were now hanging from below the seat. A note was taped to the handlebars. "Didn't want you hitting anymore mailboxes," it read and was signed, "Jay."

I grinned. That had been why he was looking at my bike. What a kind gift. I had to make a point to thank him.

I mounted my bike and headed into town, appreciating how much lighter and more balanced the bike was now. I was hoping to find a bike path or quiet street where I could just ride and think before stopping to get another flapjack. I eventually made my way to a neighborhood of cottages and streets that wound between and around them, and as I pedaled past the beautiful gardens and walled yards, I realized that while I was falling in love with the Cotswolds, I was also, in fact, missing a bit of the zing of my busy life back in the States.

There, I'd had my parents' affairs to handle and my customer-facing job. Even my neighborhood had been full of people walking dogs and exercising, so I got human contact just by going into my own yard. Here, though, life was quieter. Sure, people were out and about, and everyone waved. But there wasn't the sort of social familiarity that many Americans had, and I was surprised to find I missed it. Back home, I had hated small talk. Now, I found myself craving it.

The ride around the village let me work through some of my uneasiness, and by the time I pulled up in front of my favorite little shop for my flapjack – clearly, this was going to be a highlight of my trips into town – I decided that for once, I was just going to do what I wanted just because I wanted to. So with flapjack in hand, I headed to the store-front that I'd looked up online and opened the door to Cotswold Ceremonies and Parties.

Of course, the shop was quaint and charming, tucked into an old building as it was. The ceilings were beamed and a little lower than felt quite normal, but the wide windows at the front gave the entire space a warm, welcoming glow. "May I help you?" a petite woman with curly red hair and the most gorgeous peacock feather earrings said with a smile.

"Actually, yes. My name is Nigella Hunt, and I'm starting a flower farm out—"

The woman didn't let me finish. "You're out at Auntie Jelly's place!" She stood up and came around the desk with my arms wide. "I've been wanting to come and meet you," she said into my shoulder as I hugged me. When I stepped back, her smile was broad and open. "I'm Scarlett Wren, and your aunt was one of my favorite people in the world."

I stared at her because, apparently, my aunt was the favorite of everyone in town, and for a moment, the pang of loss at not knowing this woman better was piercing. I recovered, though, and said, "Well, it's nice to meet you, Scarlett."

She smiled and gestured toward the chair in front of my desk. "Please, take a seat. Can I get you any tea?"

If I drank as much tea as was on offer here, I would definitely float away, but still, I didn't refuse because it only felt mannerly to take a drink on offer. When Scarlett returned from the back room with a tray holding a beautiful rough-thrown teapot and two matching mugs, I added milk and sugar to my cup and smiled.

"What can I do for you, Nigella?" she asked after sipping her own tea.

"Please, call me Nell. Actually, I was hoping to get added to your list of flower-providers for events, if that's possible." I was eager to be on anyone and everyone's list, truly, so I didn't feel too guilty about my ulterior motives.

"Oh, of course, you're actually already on there. The bride and groom from this weekend told our staff that you were wonderful to work with and created the most beautiful arrangements." She smiled at me again. "We'll definitely be calling on you for future events."

My heart skipped a little at that because, of course, I was eager to get my business up and running but also because I now had the perfect opening for my queries. I was, however, surprised that given Alex's exacting standards, I had warranted a recommendation to anyone. Still, I pressed forward. "Actually, I was going to ask you about the staff. They were all so professional, even in light of what happened, but I realized when I left, I didn't get anyone's names." I tucked my head in a bit of performative shyness. "I'd hate to run into them around town and not be able to greet them. Do you think you could help me out?"

Scarlett immediately stood and got a binder from a shelf behind her. "Of course. Let's see." She flipped a few pages. "Yes, of course. Bindy was there as was Joseph. And then there was Francoise." She looked up at me. "Actually, would you just like me print out this list for you? It might be easier than writing everything down."

I had taken a notebook and pen out of my bag, but I was having trouble keeping up with just the staff's first names. Plus, I couldn't imagine how to ask for last names. "That would be amazing, and maybe you have photos on your website so I can match names to faces?"

She frowned at me for a moment. "We do, actually." I paused. "You could just look there to find the people you recognize, couldn't you?"

A wave of panic zinged through my chest. I had mis-stepped. "Oh yes, I did do that already, but – and this is kind of embarrassing," I said, "given the circumstances of the weekend, I found that I could only recognize a couple people. Bindy for sure, and maybe a—" I swam around in my head for an English name that would sound probably – "Seamus? Is that right?"

Scarlett's shoulders relaxed just a fraction. "Oh yes, I'm not surprised you remember Seamus. He 'cuts a fine figure' as our dear Jane might say."

It took me a split second to realize she was talking about Jane Austen, and I nodded quickly. "That he does." I didn't actually remember any particularly attractive men on the staff, but given that most of them were a couple decades younger than me, that wasn't surprising. "Anyway, I'd be so grateful for that list so I can memorize it for future reference."

For a long moment, Scarlett studied my face, but then she smiled again and popped open the binder to remove the page. "Just one moment." She made my way over to a copier in the corner and ran the page through before giving me the copy.

I glanced down and smiled. "This is perfect. Not only

can you help me with knowing your staff, but I'll be able to know more about Stow, too, presuming that some of these folks live here."

I knew I was pushing my luck a bit, but I sighed quietly in relief when Scarlett smiled and said, "Oh yes, most of us call Stow home." I put the page back in the binder and returned it to the shelf. "Actually, a bunch of us are getting together tonight at the pub if you want to join us. Give you a chance to chat with folks a bit."

"That sounds great," I said. "What time?" And then I added quickly, "and which pub? There are so many."

Scarlett laughed. "Like bars back in the States huh?"

"Kind of, but pubs are cozier and have less neon."

"I'll take your word for that. We usually meet up about 7 at The Rambling Rose. Do you know it?"

I shook my head. "Can I find it on GPS?"

This time her laugh was lighter and more teasing. "Of course, but I can also just walk outside and point to it if you'd like."

"Well, that seems easier," I said. "Please."

After Scarlett had shown me the faded wooden sign with the roses on it and thanked me for coming by, I climbed back onto my bike, stopped for another flapjack, and made my way home. It was time to start preparing the fields for planting if I was going to have any flowers at all this summer.

APPARENTLY, Gray had the same idea because when I rolled across the gravel to put my bike back in the garage, I saw him back in the garden with a tiller at hand. "Great minds," I said. "I was just coming back to begin getting the soil ready." I smiled at the tiller. "I was going to do it by hand, but this seems easier."

He laughed. "Yes, in the future, we can do this the weedless way and not have to till. That's better for the biome and mitochondria of the soil, but for this fresh start, I think we need to take it all the way back. You okay with that?"

I nodded. I was definitely a fan of weedless gardening because, as Gray said, it was healthier, but I was also a fan of being able to afford food and so needed to get this garden going. "That sounds perfect," I said. "I can take it from here."

"And cut me out of playing in the dirt? I don't think so. Which do you prefer, the tiller or the hoe?"

I chuckled. "You may think I'm crazy, but none of the men I've ever worked with or for have let me use the tiller. They're afraid it will mess up my lady parts or something with the shaking."

Gray looked at me askance. "Is that a real thing?"

I shook my head. "I doubt it. I believed it when I was younger and working on grounds' crews. But now I think it's probably a bunch of malarky. We women are tough stuff. I expect the men meant well but that this was a part of the patriarchy."

"Well yeah. You all push humans out of your bodies. I think you can handle a little tilling." Gray said with a wink. "Want to give it a go?"

"I do, but I have no idea what I'm doing," I said. "Can you give me a demo?"

He grinned. "Yep, it's super simple."

Gray wasn't wrong, and within ten minutes, I was tilling away, and within the hour, the entire garden patch was tilled and raked level. It looked amazing.

"Holy cow," I said. "This looks," I took a deep breath, "and smells incredible. I love the scent of dirt."

"Me, too," Gray said. "Petrichor tops my list, but newly-tilled soil is a close second."

"If I say I also love the smell of fertilizer, will you think I'm weird?" I added.

"Not at all, but I do need a clarification – manure or manufactured?"

I chuckled. "Both actually, but the manure only from afar."

"That's a fair stipulation," he said with a laugh. "Alright, want to start marking rows?"

I smiled. "Ah, so you're one of those people who uses stakes and twine, aren't you?"

"You're not?" he said with what I thought appeared to be honest surprise.

"Nope, I am for straight, but I'm usually too impatient to plan things out. You wouldn't believe the number of half-charted garden plans I have."

"Well, I'm a master planner, so why don't you tell me what you've decided to plant, and then I'll sketch it out so we can run the rows?"

"Deal," I said. "And some tea and flapjacks while we, do it?"

"Oh no, you have discovered flapjacks?"

"I am on a quest to taste every variety." As we walked into the house, I listed the types of flapjacks I had already tried and heard Gray's opinion about each.

"You know, though, that Americans get addicted to those things?" Gray said as I made us tea and set my latest flapjack flavor – Raspberry – on a plate for us to share.

"Is that so?" I said. "Is that something Brits are warned

about when Americans come over, that they need to help them curb their flapjack addiction?"

"Oh no," he said with a smile. "It's just the opposite. We know our economy is going to hit a boon because of your addictions, so we encourage them."

"Ah, I see. This is revenge for the Boston Harbor Tea thing. We took that revenue, so you try to get us back with oats and butter."

"Seems fair," he said as he lifted his half of the buttery goodness to his mouth.

"Agreed," I said as I followed suit.

BY THE TIME the afternoon was over, we had a plan for this part of the garden and had actually put in rows and grids for the plants. It was going to be a gorgeous, close-grown garden with lots of flowers and, hopefully, very few weeds.

"Thanks so much, Gray. This is going to be amazing," I said as I admired the network of twine tied to small green posts pathway.

"I think so, too, and tomorrow, I'll stake out our plan for the field, if that suits."

I nodded. "I should be around, so just come get me when you start, and I'll run the tiller again."

He laughed. "Oh, we're not going to use the tiller on the field. I have a better tool for that."

I raised my eyebrows. "Oh yeah? What tool is that?"

"You'll just have to wait and see," he said. He grew still then. "Um, I was wondering. Do you fancy getting some dinner with me tonight?"

I looked at my watch. Almost 5:30. As if cueing me to the answer I preferred, my stomach growled, but something in my brain was arguing against it. So I just stood there, staring at Gray.

He shook his head. "Never mind. You're probably tired."

"Actually, that sounds great," I said. "I just have to be at the Rambling Rose by 7, but you can come with me if you want."

"The Rambling Rose, eh?" he said. "Meeting some rugby players, are you?"

"What?! No," I said. "People from the wedding staff."

Gray threw back his head. "You've found where they hang out and are going to do some sleuthing. aren't you?"

"I can neither confirm nor deny," I said in my most serious tone. "But should I be, every sleuth needs a sidekick, don't they?"

"And I'm to be the sidekick then, eh?" Gray was smiling.

"Only if you're willing. I do not believe in coercive techniques," I said with a smile.

"Well, then I agree. Let's go get some bangers and mash, though. I'm starved." He rubbed his belly heartily.

The part of me that really liked clarity and definitiveness was inclined to ask, not-so-subtly, if this was a date, but I decided that I could live without a definition for the night. So I ran in, changed out of my dirty shirt and jeans into a peasant blouse with a cardigan and, well, more jeans and met up with Gray at the end of the driveway.

He was looking all English lumberjack in plaid flannel and denim with one of those beanie hats that hipsters wore for irony, and he wore, I assumed, for actual warmth. He looked completely huggable.

I was a little giddy and tired after the gardening, which is why I didn't think twice before I slipped my arm through his as we headed up the lane toward town. It was the perfect night for a walk. Cool and clear but warm enough that it was pleasant when we walked. The scent of spring hung in the air – floral and sweet, and dusk was almost golden in the lengthening days. We walked along in companionable silence, and I let myself feel, more deeply than I had before, that this was home.

When we reached The Rambling Rose, which Gray assured me did bangers and mash very well, we took a seat near the back and made our orders. I decided I might need to take a bit of the edge off my nerves and ordered a cider and black, and Gray got a Guinness. "I don't know how you can drink that," I said. "It's so bitter."

"Oh, it's definitely an acquired taste, but I'm telling you, once you acquire it, everything else will be too sweet and too thin. Then, you'll need to try oatmeal stout," he grinned at me.

"Danielle said the same thing. I take it that oatmeal stout is intense?"

"Like drinking an alcoholic milkshake, without the sugar," Gray said with a laugh. "But we need your tolerance and your tastebuds to be acclimatised before we even try such a thing."

The server brought our plates, and I was delighted to see the two plump sausages and a massive heaping of mashed potatoes. It all looked delicious except for the pitiful pile of what I thought might be carrots on the side.

Gray watched me push the orange lumps around the plate and said, "If you're looking for fresh veg, pubs are not your best choice. But we do have a good farmer's market once the fresh veg starts coming in."

I nodded and tasted the carrots. They were remarkably sweet and salted perfectly. I imagine they had been saved from the previous season's garden, and I vowed to carve out a small vegetable bed of my own so I could have carrots for the winter.

I was just about to make that suggestion to Gray and ask his thoughts about where to put it when I saw Scarlett Wren come in and nudged Gray with my foot under the table. "She's here," I said without lifting my eyes from my plate.

"The lady from the wedding place," he asked just loudly enough that I flinched.

"Yep," I said as I looked up at him and saw Scarlett see me over his shoulder and wave. "She's waving. And now, she's coming over."

Gray met my gaze and looked at me with the same expression a child might have if it was caught stealing ice cream from the freezer. Something about that face made me start to laugh, and when I began giggling, he did too. So by the time Scarlett had walked the twenty or so feet to our table, we were both almost crying with laughter. "Hi Scarlett," I managed to wheeze out.

"Oh my goodness. You two are having a time of it. Long day?"

I nodded. "So long. We got the garden laid out and planned. This is sort of a celebration of sorts, I suppose."

She grinned. "Well, when you're ready, come on over, and we'll join the celebration." She pointed toward where a young man and a young woman had sat at my table. "That's Bindy, remember?"

I nodded because the woman did, indeed, look familiar.

"And that's Jake. He was in the kitchen, so I don't know if you'd have seen him," I said.

"Yeah, he doesn't look familiar. But I look forward to meeting him. We'll be over in just a bit," I said. She waved as she turned back to her table.

Gray smiled up at her and then looked back to me

before we both started laughing again. "Why are we laughing?" I asked as our hysterics died down.

"I have no idea," Gray said. "I think I just felt like we'd been caught by the kids having a date."

I swallowed hard. "Oh, so this is a date," I said.

Gray looked startled. "Or maybe not." He was blushing.

"No, no," I fumbled. "I'm really good with it being a date. I just wasn't sure what you were thinking."

Gray started laughing again. "We are bad at this."

"What? Dating?" I said as I giggled more. "Yes, yes we are." I grinned at him and realized that I was even more relieved to hear that he was considering this a date than I had thought I'd be. I really liked him.

But even as I thought that I reminded myself to slow down, to take my time, to not feel I had to settle into a relationship with Gray – or anyone – quickly. I could take my time. That was a lesson I had been trying to learn my entire life, but now, it felt like maybe it was sinking in.

We talked about vegetable locations while we finished up our dinner, and after we each paid for our meals but kept our tabs open for our drinks, we carried our glasses to the table where Scarlett, Bindy, Jake, and now three other people were sitting.

A quick round of introductions told me that the other man who had joined them was Davy and the two women, Constance and Leaf. After all the hands had been shaken and drinks refilled, the table filled with chatter. Apparently, Jake was in the midst of refurbishing an old motorbike, which when I asked, Gray explained was a motorcycle. "The parts are almost impossible to find here in the UK," Jake said. "But I bet you have them everywhere in the States." He looked at me with interest.

"Um, maybe?" I said. "I don't know much about motorcycles, but if I can help by posting parts requests to friends on Facebook or something, let me know."

Jake brightened. "That would be pretty amazing. Thanks. I'll get your email from Gray here and send you a list of parts, if you really don't mind."

I smiled. "Don't mind at all. Maybe I'll learn something."

"And when I get it running, I'll give you a ride if you'd like," Jake added with a quick glance at Gray.

Gray smiled. "Don't ride with this fiend," he said. "He'll break your neck."

I laughed again. "So noted. Leaf, your name is so interesting," I said a moment later when the silence at the table became heavy.

Everyone at the table looked at Leaf, and I noticed my friends were holding back smiles. When she nodded at me and said, "Yeah, my mother is a gardener, and all of us kids are named something plant-related."

I nodded, trying to imagine what her sibling's names were.

Apparently, Leaf commonly answered that question as well because she immediately said, "Blossom, Berry, and Petal."

I took a deep breath and tried to hold back my smile, but Leaf was onto me. "It's okay. You can laugh. It's so Englishy and adorable that I'm sure I'll love it when I'm 90."

"I'm sure you will," I said and then took the leap into the conversation I had hoped would give me some answers about the murder. "I don't know if I saw you at the wedding last week." I paused to let the change of subject settle and to give what felt like a little respect to the loss of their colleague a little space. "What's your job in the company?"

Leaf sighed. "Yeah, you wouldn't have seen me, proba-bly. I do sound set-up, so I'm usually in and out early and then come back late."

I nodded. "Do you do the sound during the ceremony and reception themselves?"

This question prompted an exchange of looks between the colleagues, and then Leaf said, "No, Ms. Aris-Jones preferred to have another staff member to do that work."

"Oh," I said, knowing that I was roaming right into nosiness here but not caring. "That seems weird to me. Since you do the set-up, aren't you the most qualified to run the systems at those crucial moments?"

Leaf sighed and said something I couldn't quite hear but that sounded like, "You'd think."

Scarlett cleared her throat. "Ms. Aris-Jones had a seasoned team that she always worked with in the front of house. She was, one might say, quite particular."

"You mean she was a snob who only wanted pristine people who met her visual standards to be seen by the clients," Davy said with a sneer. "None of us qualified."

I glanced at the people around the table and couldn't see anything that might lead them to be less than appro-priate in appearance for any event. Everyone was groomed and bathed, and as far as I could tell, their manners were impeccable. Still, it felt like one step too far to ask for clari-fication.

Fortunately, the conversation had apparently hit a nerve because Leaf said, "Did I tell you what she said about my new piercing?"

I studied Leaf's face and saw a tiny gold hoop in her nose and several more in her ears. I wasn't sure what kind of piercing would qualify as inappropriate, but surely not these.

"She didn't like you getting another earring?" Constance asked. "Unbelievable."

I must have looked shocked because Constance turned to me and said, "This was her problem with me." She turned over her arm and showed a simple line of words tattooed into the underside of her forearm. "She wanted me to either cover it up with a sleeve or make-up for any event when I was on the floor."

"Wow," Gray said. "She was particular."

"About everything," Scarlett said quietly. "I don't want to speak ill of the dead, but things might be a bit smoother now that she is gone."

I stayed silent, unsure about what I had to contribute that wouldn't feel prying or inappropriate.

Gray apparently thought faster on his feet than I did because he said, "Yeah, didn't she give you a bit of trouble, Nell?"

I looked over at him and saw his slight nod that told me to go forward. "She did, but I figured she was just stressed out by the wedding."

Davy scoffed. "She was always like that, even at the office." He looked at me and shrugged. "Sorry she went at you, too, though."

I nodded. "Why did you all stay if she was so hard to work with then?"

Everyone but Gray and I looked toward Scarlett, and then Leaf said, "Scarlett is the other wedding coordinator, and she's awesome." All her colleagues nodded.

"Yep, the chance to work with Scarlett more than makes up for Arabella's nonsense," Constance added.

"High praise," I said to my new friend. "Will you be picking up the other weddings, the ones that Ms. Aris-Jones was coordinating?"

Scarlett nodded. "At least until we can hire another coordinator." I smiled. "It's going to be a busy season."

"Sounds like it," Gray said.

From there the conversation wove back to what everyone was planning to do for the weekend and where I could get the best fish and chips in town. It seemed like no one was suspicious at all of my line of inquiry, and I was grateful.

I really enjoyed the evening and felt like I had made new friends, as long as one of them wasn't the murderer, but after my second pint, I knew it was time for me to go home. The combination of the hard work in the garden and a bit of alcohol had made me quite light-headed.

When I stood to go, Gray rose with me. "Good night, everyone," I said. "It was nice to visit."

The group waved goodbye, and Gray tucked his arm around me to steady me a bit as we headed out the door.

I wasn't drunk, not even tipsy really. Just very, very tired, so the walk home felt like it was going to take a long time, a fact that I didn't mind since I liked the feel of Gray's arm around my waist.

"So it sounds like all of them could have motive," Gray said, "if being mistreated and discriminated against was a reason to kill someone."

I nodded. I'd been thinking the same thing. "But really, is that a strong enough motive? I mean, she didn't fire any of them, just made them work in the background." I stared up at the starry sky and said, "In fact, I would have probably preferred not to work with the clients myself."

"Same here," Gray said. We walked in silence for a few feet, and then he continued, "But Scarlett, maybe she had more motive. Surely, she'll get paid more for running twice as many weddings."

"That's a good point," I said as I looked over at him. "And her tips would probably go up sizably, too. As I understand it, money is often a good motive for murder."

"'As you understand it,' in your vast experience with murder investigations?" Gray teased.

"Hey, I had Brit Box. *Grantchester* and *Midsomer Murders* taught me a great deal."

At this Gray chuckled and pulled me a little closer. I didn't pull away. "Let me guess. You, like every straight woman I know, had a crush on Sidney."

I leaned against him gently. "I can neither confirm nor deny."

"What, are you a spy now?" he said as he leaned toward me. But before I could answer, he kissed me.

Chapter Eight

I WOKE up the next morning with a flittering giddiness in my chest that it took me a moment to put to a source. But then I remembered Gray's kiss and the way he had quietly walked me home before kissing my cheek and heading around the corner to his own house. Just the memory made my heart beat a bit faster. That had been a good kiss.

Something about me, though, always pushed me to think past the happy thing to what could go wrong, and often those thoughts were related to events ahead of me. So I immediately let my mind leap into the to-go list I had as I prepared myself to feel the drudgery of life suck most of the delight out of my spirit.

Surprisingly, though, as I thought about my day, I realized that everything I had on my mental to-do list was exciting to me. I was going to get dahlias in the ground after Gray and I prepared that new planting area, and then, I thought I'd start seeding some other annuals from the supply of seed packets that had begun to arrive.

I was in the middle of reading a book I loved – *The Long*

Way to A Small, Angry Planet – so I wasn't dreading downtime, and Jazz, Danielle, and I were going out to dinner later, so I even had a social event to look forward to.

As I sat up on the side of my bed and stretched, I realized that for the first time in a very long time, I was looking forward to everything about my day and wasn't having to stay myself against the things I didn't want to do. I wanted to do everything I had on my schedule, and that felt incredible.

"First, though, Nell," I said out loud to myself. "Coffee." I'd long called coffee "the elixir of life," and even though I was now in the land of tea-drinkers, I didn't see that changing. I did enjoy tea, but there was nothing like the earthy, roasted scent of brewing coffee. I wrapped my warm robe around myself and slipped on my wool slippers before padding downstairs to the kitchen.

There, I saw a note in the middle of the kitchen table. "Brought you a little something for your morning brew. – G" I smiled at the sweet tenderness of Gray's note and then looked around. I didn't see anything new in my kitchen, and while puzzled, I decided he must have meant he had something for me later.

I turned on the kettle and measured out the coffee for the French press before pulling a mug off the rack above the sink and opened the fridge. There, a tiny white ceramic pitcher sat in the middle of the top shelf with another note with a smiley face attached to the front. I picked it up and peered inside. Creamy, thick liquid shifted inside, and I grinned. "Cream," I said to no one in particular.

I poured some of the delicious dairy into my chosen mug and slipped the pitcher back into the fridge before adding water to my coffee, spooning two teaspoons of sugar into the mug, and then pouring a cup of deliciousness that filled the room with delight. But if the smell was good, the taste was miraculous. "Holy moly," I said out loud again, "this is best coffee I've ever had."

Just then, I heard a faint scratch outside the door and sprinted over to it with a delight that led me to fling it open in anticipation of thanking Gray for his kindness. But instead of a handsome man, I found a very large, very shaggy dog curled up in the door frame.

"Well, hello," I said, reaching back to put my mug on the hall table. "Who are you?"

The massive gray pup turned and looked up at me. He seemed a bit shy, but I knew dogs well enough to know that if he hadn't sprinted when the door opened, he probably wasn't scared. And scared dogs are the ones who can hurt you.

I knelt slowly down and when he didn't stand or pull his head back, I lowered my fingers, nails forward, toward his nose. Without hesitation, he stretched up and sniffed me, and then I heard one of the best sounds in the world – a rhythmic thump. I looked over, and sure enough, his tail was wagging.

With permission granted, I reached over and scratched his neck and then ran my hand down his long, curled flank. "You are a beautiful boy," I said. "But no collar? I wonder who belongs to you."

His tail thumped harder, and when I stood up to give my knees a break, the dog stood and walked past me into the house, where he quickly found his way to the rug in the kitchen and immediately curled up again, falling asleep faster than any creature I'd ever seen. Within ten seconds, he was snoring.

"Well, please, make yourself at home," I said to the snoring pooch. "Don't mind me." I wanted to be annoyed, or rather, I thought I should probably be annoyed by such presumption, particularly from someone who obviously had not bathed in quite a while. But I couldn't be. He looked so peaceful and content that I knew I couldn't throw him out.

So I settled on confirming two things that I had noted as he walked in. Gently, I put my fingers to his neck again. Nope, no collar. Then, cautiously, I lifted one of his rear legs. "Yep, definitely a boy."

I chuckled. "Guess I'll be asking around about you today, huh?"

His response was a long, teeth chattering snore.

I sat down beside my temporary companion and sipped my coffee. "Mind if I tell you about my day?" I said, happy to not be talking just to myself this time, even though the pup was so asleep that I didn't think he could even hear me.

For the next half-hour or so, I prattled on about my plans and sorted through my seed packets while he slept, and when it was time for me to meet Gray as we'd planned the night before, he was still sound asleep. So I quietly closed the door to the kitchen and asked my phone to remind me to come back in an hour to let him out. He'd be rested by then, and maybe he'd find his way home.

Somehow, that thought made me a tinge sad. I liked him already, but I knew that his owners must certainly be missing him terribly.

When I got out to the field beside the donkey pen, Gray was already well into work. He'd tilled up about half the area we'd discussed and was now wielding a hard rake like a mattock as he chopped up the bigger clumps of dirt. "Good morning," I shouted as I stopped beside the donkey fence and gave all three of the cuties apples and then slipped Clover a mouthful of spinach, too. I was no dummy. That girl needed special attention to keep my favor.

"Good morning," Gray said as he slammed the rake down into the dirt so that it stood at an angle. "Get good sleep?"

I nodded as I picked my way through the dirt toward him. "You?"

"Well, I had thoughts of pleasant things to dream of, so yeah." He leaned forward and kissed my cheek before he blushed slightly. "What do you think?" he said by way of diversion from the slight awkwardness now between us.

"It looks amazing," I said. "You must have been up early."

"Well, I wanted to get a head start, but this didn't take long." He looked at me like he was going to say something else but stopped himself. "What's your pleasure?" He gestured toward the rake and then the tiller, which was parked beside him. "Or if you wanted you could use her?"

I followed his hand to where a bright orange tractor stood. "What?" I said. "I have a tractor."

"You have a tractor." Gray smiled. "She's all fueled up for you," before he picked up his rake and returned to pounding clods into soil.

I stared at the tractor for a long minute, and then shook my head. "I think I'll perfect my tiller skills today."

He grinned but didn't say anything, even though I saw him watching me out of the corner of his eye as I leaned down to pull the starting cord. I appreciated that he didn't presume I couldn't do it. Then, with one try, I tugged lightly, felt the resistance of whatever in the engine actually started the thing, and then pulled up quickly and steadily. The little girl started right up.

For the next hour, Gray and I traded off tasks as we got the field ready for planting, and when we were done, we had a flat, fragrant field ready for flowers. "Yes!" I said as I fist-pumped. "Ready for dahlias!"

Gray grinned. "That she is. Do you mind, though, if we take a bit of a break first?"

"Oh you thought I was going to plant tubers immediately." I smiled. "Oh no, sir, I need more coffee and something to eat. Join me?"

Without hesitation, he fell in step behind me, and we made our way back to my house. As soon as I opened the door, I remembered that a certain someone was sound asleep in my kitchen, or at least he had been, and I felt a splash of worry that my kitchen might be totaled. But when I opened the door quietly, the fluffy mass was in exactly the same position that I'd left him in.

"Shh," I said as Gray came in behind me. "This guy was at my door this morning. He's been sleeping this whole time."

Gray studied the charcoal gray dog. "Looks like a wolfhound, maybe a full breed." He lowered himself to the floor and gently spoke to the pup. "Hey mate, you okay?"

The dog opened his eyes slightly, and I heard the already familiar thump of his tail on the stone floor. I poured Gray and I each a mug of coffee, and then joined the two guys on the floor. As soon as I sat, the dog lifted his head and wagged his tail more fervently.

"Looks like you already have a friend?" Gray said as he took the coffee from me. "He must belong to someone. Wolfhounds are expensive."

"I was thinking the same thing because he's well-fed and looks healthy enough, but he doesn't have a collar." I rubbed the dog's head. "I guess you guys probably microchip pets here, right?"

"Indeed we do. Let's take him down to the vet's office

and have him scanned. Maybe we can get him home today." Gray stood and then helped me to my feet. "Do you have a piece of rope or something we could use for a leash?

"Let me go see," I said and headed for the back hall closet where I'd seen a variety of household tools and such. The dog stood and then trotted along behind me. When I had found a ball of twine, I carried it back to the kitchen, and my new shadow followed right behind.

"He certainly fancies you," Gray said and then more quietly, "Can't say I blame him."

The blush spread through my whole body, but I just smiled at Gray. "Thank you." I looked at the ball of string in my hand. "Maybe we don't need this?"

"Doesn't look like it," Gray said. "We'll take my Rover. More room for the big guy."

I nodded, and the three of us made our way around the house to Gray's parking spot, where an ancient Land Rover sat. The dog and the vehicle matched, and when Gray opened the back, our new friend leapt right in with the grace of the white-tailed deer I knew from home. "Wow, clearly, he knows what to do," I said.

Gray nodded and then went around to the right side of the Rover. I followed, thinking he was going to open my car door for me. Only when I glimpsed the steering wheel inside did I realize that I was on the wrong side of the car.

"Oh, did you want to drive?" Gray said with a wink.

"You're mean," I said and laughed as I made my way to the passenger door.

The drive to the veterinary *surgery*, as Gray called it and then had to explain that it was just a doctor's office for animals, not a place where the dog would automatically get surgery, was quite short, and when we arrived, our friend hopped down and followed me right inside. There, I checked us in, and then, when we sat to wait for the doctor, the dog sat next to me, his haunch resting against the side of my foot.

"He looks like one of those statues you see outside the front doors of mansions," I said quietly.

"He is very regal," Gray replied.

"He should be," a woman in green scrubs said as I stepped into the waiting room. "That's a full-blooded wolfhound."

"You were right," I said to Gray as the three of us stood, and then I turned toward the vet, "Do you know him?"

She looked carefully at the dog. "No, I don't think so. But he looks healthy. He's not yours?"

I shook my head. "Just showed up at my door this morning."

"Nell is Aunt Jelly's niece and is living in her house now," Gray added.

"Well, it's very nice to meet you. I'm Preetamda Newhouse." She turned back toward the door. "Let's get this guy checked out then."

We followed behind her, the dog bringing up the rear, and the four of us crammed into a tiny room with a large metal scale and a small counter.

"You are a big boy," Dr. Newhouse said to the dog. "Can you step on the scale?"

The dog did just as he was told and climbed up on the scale. Then, while Dr. Newhouse kept a protective hand on his neck, she pressed a lever and raised him to waist height. "Since he's not yours, I expect you'd like to start with a microchip scan?"

"Yes, please," I said. "He's so sweet, and I'm sure someone is missing him."

The doctor smiled at me and took out a wand that

resembled the ones I'd used at self-check-out back home. She waved it over the dog like she was a fairy godmother getting him ready for the ball, but when she stopped, she was frowning. "No chip."

"Oh, no," I said. "He didn't have a collar either." I turned to Gray. "I think we're going to need to put up flyers."

"That's a good idea," the vet said, "and we'll take a picture of him to hang on our lost pets board, too."

I nodded. "Thank you." I looked at the dog, who was sitting as royally as ever on the scale. "Do you mind giving him a once-over, be sure he's healthy?"

"Absolutely," she said and began her examination. The dog was in perfect health. "Good weight. Good teeth. Doesn't seem to have arthritis, not that I'd expect that in a dog this young."

"How old do you think he is?"

I smiled. "Well, he's not fully-grown yet, and he has a couple of puppy teeth still to lose, so I wouldn't put him at more than six months old."

I stared at her for a long moment. "He's still a puppy." The scale had weighed him at 5 stone, which I quickly googled to see was about 70 pounds. "How much bigger will he get?"

The vet laughed. "Most wolfhound males get to be about 3 feet tall at their shoulders and weigh over 11 stone." She noticed the shock on my face when my phone gave me the calculation of 150 pounds. "But this boy," I continued as I rubbed his shoulder, "he's on the big side. I'd say he'll be 12 or 13 stone."

I couldn't believe my eyes when my phone screen said that meant he could be 180-200 pounds. "He'll weigh as much as I do," I said.

"Probably," I said. "He's going to be big." She scruffed his ears. "But the good news is that the breed is pretty docile and super loving, and he's already had some training. He's a good boy." Her voice slipped into the universal sing-song of dog lovers everywhere.

The dog wagged his tail in response and then looked at me as if he had a question.

"Yes, you can stay with me until we find your owner." His tail thumped faster, almost as if he understood what I was saying. "I expect I can get him what he needs here?"

Twenty minutes later, we loaded the dog, a crate, a dog bed, a bowl, some treats, two balls, a collar and a leash, a long lead line, and a massive bag of dogfood into the Rover. Then, because the back was full, the dog took the back seat, sprawling himself out over the width of the vehicle and falling immediately to sleep.

"He seems exhausted," I said as I looked back at the pup. "I wonder if he travelled a long way."

Gray shrugged. "Could be," he said. "But he's safe now, and we'll get him home." He glanced over at me. "Unless you want to keep him."

My heart twisted a little. "I do like him, but he would be better with his family."

"Are you sure?" he said, keeping his eyes firmly on the road as if giving me time to answer.

I nodded slowly, but inside, I wasn't sure at all.

WHEN WE GOT BACK to my house and unloaded, the dog seemed quite rejuvenated and eager to be outside. So I took the lead line I'd bought as well as the new collar, and installed him on a ground peg – also a new purchase – near where Gray and I would be working. The line was 150 feet long, so he'd have room to move but also wouldn't be able to slip away.

It was already mid-afternoon, and I really did want to get the dahlias in the ground, so Gray began hoeing a row for me at one end of the field, and I walked behind him placing tubers and then using my foot to cover them gently with soil. While we worked, we returned to our conversation from the night before about the murder. "So did you get any more sense of who might be guilty?" I asked as I removed a tuber from the tote bag on my shoulder and pressed it into the soil before tapping earth over it.

"Of the people we saw last night, you mean?" he asked as he turned and looked at me.

"Yeah, I hate to say it, but Scarlett seems to be the most likely," I said as I stood again.

"That was my thought. I really liked her, but she did seem to have the most motive." He turned and continued hoeing. "But then we also have Jazz's family to keep in consideration, right?"

I sighed. "I suppose so." I placed a couple more tubers while I let my thoughts coalesce. "I don't know that her brother and sister-in-law have a clear motive, though, do they?" I couldn't be sure if I was biased so much because of how much I enjoyed Jazz or if I was actually right. But then, Gray probably was more biased than I was in this regard.

"Yeah, I think you're right. Unless, of course, there was something that happened with the planner that gave them motive." He glanced over his shoulder at me.

As I continued down the row in silence, I had to agree that he was right. We still hadn't heard about anything that might have disgruntled the couple. The protective part of me wanted to say that this was because there was nothing to hear, but from what I understood, the British sentiment was a stiff upper lip and more privacy than was usual for American sensibilities. So I guess we'd have to explore a bit more. "Know any quintessential town gossips who might know more? That's what happens on all the Brit box shows."

Gray turned to me with a twinkle in his eye. "Actually yes. How do you feel about going to church tomorrow?"

I stared at him for a very, very long minute. "Must I?" I said. I didn't have any problem with Christian religion; it just wasn't something I believed. And my experience of church services had almost always been stuffy rooms with complicated physical maneuvers that I was almost always a beat behind on.

"If you want to be unobtrusive when we talk to the most informed woman in Stow, then yes," Gray said. "There will be coffee and cookies," he added.

"Good coffee?"

"Actually, yes. They bring it in from Jazz's shop in town." He reached the end of the row and looked back at me. "In?"

I sighed as I placed the last of the tubers in the row. "I suppose, but if the cookies are stale, you owe me lunch."

"Deal," he said and then kissed me gently on the lips before pulling back and whispering, "I was going to buy you lunch anyway."

BY THE TIME we had finished the other two rows of dahlia tubers, we were both tuckered out, and it appeared that our dog friend had worn himself out playfully chasing the songbirds who had flitted near him. I'd noticed, though, that he never really tried to get them. It was like a game of tiny bird-giant dog tag. Now, though, he was sprawled in a sunbeam snoring again.

When I went over and unclasped the lead from his collar, he glanced up at me and then pried himself up to standing. His legs were almost as long as mine, and he looked a bit like a baby giraffe trying to stand for the first time. But he got there, shook himself out, and followed us back into the house.

"I'll get my computer," I said. "Do you mind putting on the kettle?"

Gray smiled and headed toward the counter while the pup looked at me, saw I was heading toward the stairs, and laid down by the kitchen table instead. Smart dog.

A half-hour later, we had mocked up a flyer with a photo of the pup, included my phone number and asked people to text if they knew the dog. Then, Gray offered to take them into town and hang them up. "You've got dinner soon, right?"

I glanced at the oven clock. "Shoot. I had totally forgotten." I stood up and then looked back down at him. "You sure you don't mind."

"Don't mind at all," he said. "Want me to keep Dante here with me?"

"Dante?" I said with my eyebrows near my hairline.

"He seems like a Dante, and we have to call him something in the meantime."

I studied the dog a long moment, and then nodded. "Dante fits. And yes, if you don't mind watching him until I get back, I'd appreciate it."

"No trouble at all." He headed toward the door. "Come on, boy. Let's get ourselves some dinner."

Something about the pair together made my stomach a little swoony. "See you for church then?" I said as they reached the door, my voice about as flat as I could make it. "What time?"

"Be ready at 9:45? We'll drive over." He smiled at me and then led Dante out the door and into the golden slant of late afternoon.

I MET Jazz and Danielle at The Fox And The Compass, and found them at the same table we'd used the last time. They had pints in front of them, and as soon as I sat down, the bartender caught my eye, and when I nodded, he poured me a cider and black. "Wow," I said as I joined my friends. "Already feel like I'm a regular."

"You are a regular," Jazz said. "Hungry?"

"You have no idea," I said and told my friends about the work Gray and I had done on the flower garden. "But the best part of the day was that I found a dog."

"You *found* a dog?" Danielle asked.

"Yep, he was at my door when I went out this morning."

"Oh, so he found you," Jazz said with a smirk.

I rolled my eyes and nodded. "I suppose so. Thing is, he's not microchipped, and he didn't have on a collar." I pulled the folded copy of the flyer out of my pocket. "Have you seen him before?"

Both of my friends studied the flyer but then shook their heads. "Is he big?"

I put my hand just at the bottom of my rib cage and nodded. "And he's only six months old."

Jazz whistled. "Whoa. That's a horse, not a dog."

"Come to think of it," I said, "he's already bigger than the miniature donkeys."

"Do the donkeys like him?" Danielle asked.

"They didn't really seem to notice him, and he didn't bother them, so it was okay." I sighed as I tried to push back an image of the big dog playing with the little donkeys sometime in the future. "Gray is out hanging fliers right now so that we can find his owner."

Jazz and Danielle exchanged a glance. "You and Gray are spending a lot of time together, Ms. America," Jazz said.

I glared at her. "If I'm Ms. America, you're the Potato Princess."

Danielle snarfed her seltzer water up her nose, and when she finally could breathe again, she asked, "Is that really a thing?"

Jazz and I both said, in unison, "Probably." We then went on a long ramble about all the types of princesses and queens that get crowned in the States. I was very proud to say that I was Facebook friends with someone who had once been the Corn Princess, and that sent Danielle into another fit of laughter.

I could have spent the night in this kind of goofy conversation, conversation that carefully avoided the Gray question, but I felt the pull of Arabella's unsolved murder and, when we all stopped giggling, tried to sound super casual when I said, "How are the newlyweds?"

Jazz sighed. "Good, I think. Alex is just one of those people who has a critique for everything, so the resort for the honeymoon didn't have soft towels and the pool was too chlorinated."

"Didn't they go to Bali and stay in a hut overlooking the ocean?" Danielle asked.

"Yep," Jazz added. "But I haven't heard anything about that, just the towels."

"Ugh," I said. "Was your brother happy with the wedding at least?" I hoped I sounded casual, and when Jazz just nodded, I figured I had.

"Alex wasn't, though, right?" Danielle prompted.

"Oh no, of course not," Jazz said.

"Well, to be fair, her wedding planner was murdered the night before the wedding," I said.

"True, but she was not really upset about that. She thought the food was bland, and she noticed a few of the windows at Stanway were a bit spotted. She filed a formal complaint." Jazz took a long drink of her pint. "Unfortunately, my brother listens, and he's thinking of filing a lawsuit against the location, both for the murder and the less-than-optimal site conditions."

I was flabbergasted and couldn't speak for a long minute. "A lawsuit because someone else was murdered?"

Jazz shook her head. "Because of pain and suffering caused by the murder that the location didn't prevent. It's her idea, I'm sure, but she can convince my brother to do anything."

I took a deep breath and tried to form a response that was both understanding and not too critical of my friend's family. "Well, I'm sure it did cause them some distress." It sounded weak even to me.

"Not as much distress as it caused the wedding planner," Danielle said with a harsh laugh. "And I expect Stanway took a blow, too."

Jazz nodded. "Probably. But the truth is they were already unsatisfied with everything before the weekend even started."

"Yeah?" I said before I took a long sip of my cider and black.

"Oh yeah," Danielle said and opened her mouth to answer before catching the look her wife was throwing her and shutting it again.

"Sorry, I didn't mean to pry," I said.

"You didn't," Jazz said. "It's just embarrassing. Alex or Antoine acting for Alex had complained about every single aspect of the wedding from the seating chart to the choice of venue – which was theirs originally, I might add – to the flowers." She looked at me meaningfully.

"That's why the first florist backed out," I said with a nod. Now it made sense.

"I'm sorry that I didn't tell you. I wasn't sure you'd do it if I did." She looked at me with wide eyes as she waited for my response.

"I would have done the same thing if I had a brother who was getting married. No worries. In the future though, maybe you can tell me what I'm walking into just so I can be prepared." I smiled at her and put my hand over hers. "We're good."

Jazz smiled. "The truth is that the way Antoine described how Arabella was handing the event, I was kind of pissed at her too. They talked about her like she was ignoring everything they said and just doing what she wanted."

"Was she?" I asked.

Danielle shrugged. "We don't know. As you saw, she, er, had a strong personality, so that's a possibility. But then, we're talking about Double AA here so who knows?"

It was my turn to choke on my cider. "Double AA?"

"Antoine and Alex – they never do seem to wind down," Jazz said with a sly smile. "Better than the Energizer Bunny, don't you think?"

"Slightly," I said. For the rest of the evening, we ate and talked and goofed around like friends should, and I had a lovely time. But when I walked out the door and got on my bike to go home, I couldn't help but think that a lot of people in Jazz's family seemed to have trouble with the wedding coordinator, including Jazz herself. I didn't like that feeling.

When I got home that night, I found both Gray and Dante asleep in the living room. Gray was stretched out in a club chair with an ottoman under his feet, and Dante was sprawled the full length of the sofa, his back legs hanging just off the edge. I went to the dog first. "I see who's in charge here. You got the sofa, huh?"

Dante pushed his head a little harder into my hand before dropping it back to the cushion and immediately snoring again. *This guy clearly had a deviated septum,* I thought. *Did dogs have septums?*

I walked over and gently shook Gray's calf to wake him. "I'm home," I said. "Thank you for watching him."

Gray rubbed his eyes and for a split second I felt like I could see toddler Gray in the softness of his cheeks. "No problem," he said. "All the flyers are up, and I told the shop-keepers to let us know if anyone comes looking."

I put out my hand and helped him stand. "Thank you," I said. "I so appreciate it."

He didn't let go of my hand as we walked to the door of my house. "My pleasure." He gave me a soft kiss before going out the door.

Chapter Nine

I COULDN'T SAY I had ever been excited to go to church before, but then, I'd never been escorted to church by a handsome Englishman. I smiled as I looked into my closet, pulled out a pink flowered dress I'd bought for a networking event, and pulled on my red Ruth Janes. It was the kind of outfit I loved — beautiful yet comfortable. The dress even had pockets.

After applying a scant bit of make-up, including a light pink gloss that tasted like bubble gum and immediately cast me back to junior high, Dante and I went downstairs for breakfast. Once again, he managed to eat his food in less time than it took me to fill the kettle, so as my coffee brewed, I took him out for his morning constitutional. We hadn't had any leads at all about his owner. No one had called Gray or me, and Pree hadn't heard anything at her surgery, she'd told me via text that morning.

I had to admit I wasn't disappointed by that fact. But still, I was careful to hold myself back just a bit because I didn't want to be devastated if he went to his real home.

Still, I realized that his companionship was something I really did enjoy and made myself a commitment to always have a dog, even if it wasn't Dante.

But man, I hoped it was Dante.

His business done and deposited in the lidded trashcan Gray has procured for just such a purpose, the two of us headed back inside, where he bathed the kitchen floor in water, and I sipped my coffee and ate a piece of peanut butter bread.

Then, at 9:40, Gray knocked on the door, and when I walked out to meet him, I stopped short. He was in a charcoal gray suit with the jacket open and a light-blue shirt with no tie beneath. His tooled leather shoes were just funky enough to make the suit less formal, and his hair was styled in a messy way that seemed genuine but also church-ready. In short, he looked amazing, gussied up but still very much himself.

"You look beautiful," he said as he leaned over to kiss my cheek before slipping my arm through his and leading me to his Rover, which he'd parked out front.

"And you, sir, are very handsome," I said, this time smiling when he walked me to the passenger side of the car and opened the door. "Thank you."

The drive to the stone church was very brief, less than five minutes, but I was glad we had driven because it had rained overnight and the number of puddles we encountered was probably more than my dress could have handled and stayed pristine.

When we reached the church, Gray parked, and while I could clearly see that most people were entering through a door off the cemetery, he led me around the other side and told me to brace myself. I wasn't sure why I needed to brace myself to see a church, but then, we rounded a corner, and there, as if from a fairy tale, were two trees framing a doorway. Tears sprouted in my eyes at the beauty, and I found that I was walking toward the trees with my hands out to touch them.

I stopped just before my fingertips reached the splintery bark and looked at Gray. When he nodded, I put my hand flat against the tree and closed my eyes. These were yew trees, old yew trees, and they felt both magnificent and humble in their stead as guardians of the door. "I can't believe this," I whispered.

"The story is that Tolkien himself used these doors to inspire—"

"The doors of Durin," I almost shouted. "Yes, I can see that completely." Tolkien's books were some of my favorites, and the idea that the man himself had stood here, in this place where I stood, left me almost breathless.

A large bell rang in the majestic tower overhead, and Gray took my hand before saying, "We can come back anytime."

I nodded and followed him around to the main entrance to the building.

As expected, the church was filled with wooden pews set in long rows across its width, and an altar and a pulpit with what I assumed was the choir loft were on a raised dais at the front. The building itself was spectacular with vaulted arches and stained glass made of prime colors that lit the whole space with a kaleidoscope of light. It was gorgeous, and I had so many questions about the architecture.

Gray led us to a pew toward the center of the sanctuary, and while I had hoped to sit near the back so we could make a quick getaway, I soon changed my mind as a choir began to sing. The sound was breath-taking, and when Gray leaned over and said, "The building was designed for music," I didn't doubt him.

For a full ten minutes before the service started, the choir sang what sounded like hymns but more angelic, and the organist, apparently seated with the choir behind us in the balcony, was masterful. By the time the priest began the procession down the aisle, I was more than glad we'd come. I was feeling downright worshipful.

I lost a bit of the heightened feeling when the standing, kneeling, and sitting got a little confusing, but Gray never let me fall behind. And when the choir sang John Rutter's composition of "All Things Bright And Beautiful," I let myself cry in delight. My mother had always loved Rutter, and I had grown up singing his cantatas and songs in a community chorus. And so the beautiful setting and the glorious music brought a wave of joy and grief that was so bittersweet that I could only sit, listen, and cry.

Gray silently handed me a handkerchief before slipping his arm around me, a position he held through the rest of the service. Fortunately, the sermon was quite brief and quite good, all about the way the natural world shows God's deep love for us, and the chance to hear the choir and then the organist one last time made me more than willing to sit right until the last notes were played.

"Wow," I whispered as the final chord rang in the air.

Gray smiled. "I thought you might like it."

"It's been so long since I heard choral music like that. Are they professionals?"

Gray shook his head. "No, but people do travel a fair ways to sing with our choir. Want to meet the director?"

I nodded and followed him up the stairs at the front of the church to where a beautiful woman in her 60s with short, blond-gray hair stood talking to two of the choir members. We waited for her to finish, and meanwhile, I gaped at the pipes of the organ and the mind-boggling view of the church from the balcony.

"This is truly amazing," I said.

"It's one of those beautiful things most people don't know they're missing," the woman we'd been waiting for said as she walked over.

I stared at her for a long moment as I realized she had two strikingly different-colored eyes — one sky blue and one golden brown. Fortunately, Gray moved right into the introduction, so my fascination was unnoticed, I hoped.

"It's nice to meet you, Nell," the woman said, and I realized that I had totally missed her name.

I put out my hand to shake hers, and said, "You, too, er."

"Ruth," she said. "Ruth Anne, if you're my mother." She tapped her temple. "I get these from her, too."

I blushed. "I'm sorry. Your eyes, they're just so striking."

Ruth flipped the hair that didn't hang down to her shoulder and laughed. "Why thank you."

I laughed and said, "That music was amazing. I haven't heard Rutter in a long time."

"Oh, you recognized the composer? Wow, now that's striking. Are you a musician?" she asked, and I felt Gray turn his eyes to me.

"No, not really. My mother was, and I sang when I was younger. We did the *Requiem* in our community chorus when I was in high school."

Ruth grinned. "Well, then I hope you'll join us sometime. If not for every Sunday, maybe when we do our holiday concert."

Surprisingly, the idea appealed to me. "I'd like that," I said. "Thank you."

Gray smiled and then said, "Actually, Ruth, we do have a question for you. Do you have a few minutes?"

"Of course, but can I be so presumptuous to ask if our few minutes can be over lunch? I'm famished," Ruth said with a rub on her belly.

A flush of relief when she agreed. After all, not everyone might enjoy the fact that they were known as the town busybody. Ruth, however, didn't seem to let it bother her.

"Great idea," Gray said. "Any place in particular?"

Ruth turned, draped her robe over the back of a chair by the organ, and started walking toward the stairs. "It's lovely out. Fancy a sandwich in the park."

"That sounds perfect," I said. I jabbed Gray in the side with my elbow, "And you'll get off easy."

Ruth turned back and looked at me over my shoulder. "Should I have picked someplace fancier? Make him really pay for the privilege of our company?"

I cackled. "Next time," I said. "Definitely."

AFTER WE HAD GONE to Baker Brothers, my favorite shop, and gotten our sandwiches of choice – I was pretty sure I'd never eat anything but sharp cheddar and butter on bread from there ever again – Ruth suggested we eat in the cemetery. "It's beautiful and quite peaceful."

I nodded. Cemeteries were one of my favorite places, oddly enough, and when Gray didn't object, we headed back toward the church, where Ruth led us to a secluded corner and jumped up onto the wall, her legs dangling. "This, okay?" she asked.

"This is perfect," I said, setting my sandwich and soda on the wall and levering myself up beside Ruth with far less grace than she had displayed. "How old is the church?"

I heard Gray chuckle beside me, and then Ruth began an intricate history of the church, starting back with the Saxon church that was on the site first. My historical lesson continued for about 15 minutes, and I thoroughly enjoyed it, although I really needed to read a basic book of English history. I had no idea when the Normans had been there, much less when the English Civil War was. Still, I was fascinated, and when Ruth finished, I smiled. "There you have it," she said and took the first bite of her sandwich. She chewed and then said, "Your turn. You probably didn't ask to talk to me about church history, I imagine."

"Well, no," I said. "But that really was amazing. Thank you." I cleared my throat. "We were actually wondering if you knew anything about the murder of Arabella Aris-Jones at Stanway a couple weeks back." I felt incredibly awkward asking this question, especially of a church woman since I thought I remembered the Bible said something about not gossiping.

She, however, seemed completely unfazed and nodded. "Oh yes, terrible thing that. Ollie was just telling me they found something new." I glanced at me. "But he'll have to tell you that himself. You can ask, right?" she looked at Gray.

"I can," he said. "Mostly, I thought you might have some impressions, some intuition about things."

She nodded. "You're worried about Jazz and her family?"

"Aye," Gray said. "And for a bit, even Nell here was a suspect."

"Still are, aren't you?" Ruth said but not unkindly. "New girl always is."

I hadn't thought much about the fact that I was still technically on the police's suspect list, but Ruth's reminder sent shivers up my back. "I am," I said simply.

Ruth finished her sandwich, carefully folded up the wrapper, and tucked it in her pocket. "Truth be told, that Arabella was something. Don't like to speak ill of the dead, mind you, but I don't know anyone who didn't find her a 'tough personality.'" She made air quotes as she spoke. "Near as I can tell, she rubbed everyone the wrong way, even me from time to time." She winked at me.

I really liked this woman. "Think of anyone she rubbed wrong enough that they'd want to kill her?"

"Well, human nature being what it is," she said, "who knows? I can say, though, that I doubt Jazz, or her wife could have done any such thing. The two of them are so wonderful and so self-aware, that I imagine they'd have curbed any anger with healthy means before they got to murder."

"They do practice yoga and meditation," Gray said. "Is that what you mean?"

"In part, but also that they are so devoted to one another and the people they care about, that I can't imagine either of them doing something to ruin Antoine's wedding day, no matter how mad they might have been." Ruth stared off past the old gravestones just in front of us. "That's not the same for every member of Jazz's family, I'm afraid."

I perked up at this news. As glad as I was that Ruth thought so well of my friends, I really wanted a direction in which to look. "Yeah?" I said.

"Yeah," Ruth repeated in a terrible American accent and then smiled at me. "Jazz's parents can be, shall we say, a bit too invested in the British class system, at least for my taste. I prefer a much more open society, in all ways." She winked at me again, and I was fairly certain there was some level of innuendo in her statement.

"What about her brother? Or his wife?" I asked, foregoing any sense of stealthiness in light of Ruth's forthcoming comments.

Ruth met my gaze and then looked out at the cemetery once again. "Antoine is a curious chap, for sure, and perhaps I will refrain from making comment on his bride, Alexandra." The sour expression on her face, however, told me that she felt much the same way about the bride as I did.

We let that perspective sit in the air for a moment, and then Gray said, "What about Arabella's staff? Anyone there strike you as capable?"

"Hmm," Ruth said as she tilted her head. "I hadn't taken my musings that way yet." She sat still and quiet for a long moment before saying, "I have to say that I don't know those young people very well yet, but I did see that Scarlett has purchased a brand new Mini."

She made no further inference from that observation, and I had to admit I appreciated the way her forthrightness stayed on the side of respectable. She wasn't so much a gossip as an observer, and given what she said next, one who cared a great deal about the people she observed.

"I should hope, however, that nothing you or I believe would cause us to say or do anything that might cause harm to someone's reputation. Evidence is most paramount when such grave occasions are at hand." Ruth turned then and smiled at us. "Thank you for a lovely lunch, and Nell, please if you'd like to sing with us anytime, you are most welcome."

I watched her as she walked across the grass, stopping from time to time to put her fingers on the top of a tombstone as if greeting the person settled below it. "She's love-ly," I finally said.

"She is," Gray said. "What do you make of what she said?"

"I'm still pondering, but you know what?" I stood up. "I could definitely ponder better by the Tolkien door."

He laughed and took my hand. "Then let's go gather his wisdom from the yew."

UNFORTUNATELY, Ruth's insight, even powered by the lingering energy of Tolkien's spirit, didn't get us much further than we'd been before. We still had the same suspects, but we did know now that Scarlett had bought a new car.

"I don't know that the car tells us much, though," I said when I had petted the yews again and finally taken a seat in a sunny patch of grass near them. "After all, she could have been saving for that for a long time."

"Or she could have gotten an inheritance or some-thing," Gray added. "I agree. It's far from conclusive. But I will say Ruth wouldn't have mentioned it if she didn't think it important."

"You know her well, huh?" I asked as I lay down in the grass and relished the sun shining on my face.

"Since I was born. She used to be my nanny."

I pushed myself up onto one arm. "You didn't tell me that."

"Yes, I did. Just now. My mom worked a lot of hours, so Ruth was the person I stayed with most afternoons after school. She's still my mom's best friend."

"Oh, that's sweet," I said, thinking of a little Gray and

that charming woman playing together. "Did you ever sing with her?"

"Every day," Gray said with a slight blush. "I still do the Christmas cantata every year because she asks me to."

"Whoa, so you really sing?" I somehow hadn't thought of the rustic, earth-loving man as a performer. "Tenor? No, baritone."

"Tenor," he said. "What about you?"

"Alto, sometimes second alto or tenor, when needed." I laughed. "My singing voice is rather deep."

"And mine is rather high," he said and smiled. "We'll have to sing together sometime."

"Oh, I don't know about that. I like choirs because I can blend in." I looked at him and then leaned forward and kissed him. "But you never know."

Eventually, we said goodbye to Tolkien's door and headed back to my house. My shoulders and back were aching from the work the day before, and since we'd already been to church, I declared the day "a day of rest" and asked Gray if he felt like reading with me.

"Like the same book?" he said as the corners of his eyes wrinkled.

"Of course not, unless you want to read aloud to me. I'd love that." I led him to the kitchen and turned on the kettle. "I just like the idea of reading with someone, maybe opening a window and sharing a couch."

"That sounds perfect. Let me run home and change. Be right back." He literally jogged to the front door, prompting Dante to jog after him. "I'll bring him back," Gray called.

As the kettle warmed, I went upstairs and changed, too. Each day, I'd been choosing clothes from my wardrobe that felt the most flattering to me. As much as I really believed that bodies were all good, I still had a good dose of body shame, especially now that middle age had come with a larger number on the scale.

Today, though, I was determined to be completely comfortable and completely myself. So I pulled out a pair of yoga pants that were ultra cozy but also losing their elasticity, a giant American Cancer Society t-shirt that I'd received for doing some fundraising for them, and my Bombas slippers. I tugged an elastic into the tiny portion of my hair that I could pull back and then slipped a headband to hold back the strays. There was nothing more frustrating than trying to read through my own hair.

By the time I got back downstairs, Gray was already back and was standing at my counter in a pair of super soft-looking sweatpants and a hunter green t-shirt that was slightly torn at the collar. Apparently, we'd had the same idea about attire for the day.

When he turned and saw me, he grinned. "You look so snuggly," he said.

"Well, isn't that the point?" I added. "You look perfectly snuggable, too."

He headed toward me with our mugs and then led the way into the living room, where I saw he had placed a copy of Percival Everett's *James* on the side table. "Are you a fan of Twain?" I asked.

"I do like him, but I especially like books that tell the stories of characters from their own perspective." He set his mug on a coaster next to the book. "And I love Everett's writing."

I smiled. "I think the only one of his that I've read was *Erasure*."

"That's a good one," he said and slid onto the couch. "What's your reading choice for the day?"

I held up my paperback. "Nothing quite as heady as yours, but it is British. Do you know Matt Brolly?"

He shook his head.

"He writes these great thrillers set over on the coast, I think. Weston-Super-Mare. Such a strange name for a town."

"Oh yeah, I know of it. Cool."

For the rest of the afternoon, we read our books, legs wrapped together gently, and took naps as the mood struck us. Dante snored the whole time, and the sparkle of joy in my heart had me glowing.

Chapter Ten

THE NEXT MORNING, I woke up slightly fuzzy-headed from my three pints and completely tight-chested from anxiety. All night, I'd dreamed about various members of Jazz's family doing strangely violent things – breaking windows, punching each other, etc. – until I had finally put a meditation podcast on and let the voice of the coach lull me into deeper sleep. Now, though, all the worry that had haunted my dreams was in my body.

I took a long, very hot shower to try and calm my nervous system, and when that only did a bit of the work, I laid out my yoga mat on the floor in the living room and did a somatic series of asanas. They helped a great deal, but the best stress-reliever of the moment was Dante, who tried, at least it seemed like he tried, to do every posture I did. He was particularly good at downward dog, not surprisingly.

Feeling much more relieved and very tender toward my temporary canine companion, I went into the kitchen and put on the kettle for coffee. Then, I fed Dante, who ate his food in two bites, I swear, and then put him on a leash and took him for a short walk in the front of the house to do his business.

The dog was very strong, and I found I had to brace myself to keep him from pulling me off my feet. "We'll need to get some leash-training for you," I said before I remembered that I wasn't keeping him and didn't need to train someone else's dog. That realization brought back some of the tightness in my chest.

Back inside, I drank my coffee as I sorted the seed packets again, determined to actually get some of the annuals in the ground today. I didn't expect Gray would be joining me. He needed some time off from this place, and while I would miss him, I also kind of relished the idea of solo work for the morning.

With some toast in my belly and coffee in my bloodstream, Dante and I headed out to the former vegetable garden to start planting. The donkeys peered at us over the pasture fence, or at least Blossom and Thistle did. Clover was trying to play nonchalant and had her side to us. I laughed. She was quite the character.

For about an hour, Dante casually chased birds, and I dug rows and planted poppies, calendula, and cosmos. It was a bit chilly until the sun came out, but as soon as it did, I hung my light sweater on a fence post and kept going even as I reminded myself to buy sunscreen. I didn't need a burn, or worse, skin cancer to slow me down now.

I was just taking a water break when I heard the sound of voices from the front of the house. "I'm back here," I shouted to let whoever it was know they wouldn't find me inside.

A moment later, Gray came around the corner with Jazz, Danielle, Ollie, Jay, and even Dr. Newhouse. "What is happening?" I said.

"We thought we could volunteer our time this morning to get the rest of your garden in, and then we could maybe convince you to go to Avebury with us," Jazz said with a grin as she watched Gray kiss me on the cheek.

"Avebury? What's there?"

"Oh, you'll see," said Ollie. "It's one of the best places in England."

"But a surprise," Dr. Newhouse said. "How can we help?"

"Dr. Newhouse, I didn't know you hung around with this ragtag bunch," I said.

"Please, call me Pree," she said with a laugh. "Well, when I called Gray to check on our friend over there," she looked at Dante, who was on his back with all four legs in the air as a sunbeam warmed his belly, "Gray mentioned what was happening. I don't know much about gardening, but who wouldn't want to be outside on this gorgeous day? So I invited myself along."

"Well, thank you," I said to her and then turned to everyone. "Thank you all." For a moment, I just stared at these people, these new friends, who had come just to help me push my dream forward, all because they wanted to take me somewhere. It felt amazing.

Gray watched me for a moment, and then, apparently sensing my stupefaction, suggested that we work in pairs. "Pree," he said, "Maybe you could keep Ollie and Jay in line." That took care of the odd number of people easily, and everyone seemed happy. "Now, Nell, what do we need to do?"

I pulled the seed packets that I had intended to finish today out of my back pocket. "Well, Jazz and Danielle, you could put these in," I said as I handed them zinnia, daisy, cornflower, and strawflower seeds. "Gray can show you where they go." I trusted he remembered our layout.

"The five of you can start digging rows just as I've done here," I pointed to the string line and the white pickets with the kind of flower in each row that I had just finished. "And I'll be back with your seeds in a moment."

I practically ran to the house to get the rest of my seeds and came back with my arms full of packets. I had grabbed all of them, even though I'd been thinking I'd wait on a few simply to see if I had room since I wasn't sure how they'd do in this climate. But with this kind of crew, I was game to see if we could reasonably place them all, and I'd chalk anything that didn't make it up to a learning experience.

I distributed seeds according to my sketch, and then Gray and I headed with the sunflowers, delphinium, and snapdragons to the new field. We'd be staking dahlias here shortly, so it made sense to plant the other tall, potentially topply varieties in the same field. "I'm going to need a lot of stakes," I said to Gray as we followed yesterday's pattern with the sunflowers.

"True, but can you imagine how gorgeous this is going to be?" he replied.

"I cannot wait," and it was true. I knew most of these would not bloom until late summer, but I was hopeful that the small peony plants that Jazz and Danielle were placing at the other end of the field would bloom, at least a little, this spring. "I'll be ready for weddings by August," I said.

Gray turned and smiled. "You're going to be amazing." He blushed and as he turned back to his hoe I was pretty sure I heard him say, "as if you aren't already."

Within two hours, we had planted everything I'd bought, and in the smaller plat, we still had some space for a few vegetables, which Ollie told me we would pick up seeds or starts for on our way back from our afternoon expedition. "We'll get those in when we get back," he said.

Tears pricked my eyes as I watched my friends stream into my house, Dante in their midst, and take turns washing up in the bathroom and changing clothes upstairs if needed. I had never had friends like this, people just willing to come and help without being asked. It was miraculous.

And when we loaded up in two cars, Pree leading the way in her Delorian, just like Marty McFly drove, I couldn't help but laugh out loud. She took Ollie and Jay with her while Jazz and Danielle came with us.

"What?" Gray asked after he caught me staring at him.

"I'm just so happy. I don't know how I got this life, but I'm so glad I did."

Jazz and Danielle chuckled quietly in the back seat when he reached over and took my hand. "Me, too."

From the back hatch, a low woof echoed through the car, the first I'd heard from Dante. "Apparently, your dog agrees," Jazz said.

"He's not my dog," I said quietly.

But he woofed again.

"I think he disagrees," Danielle said.

"He's definitely your dog for now," Gray said and squeezed my fingers. "Now, you just enjoy the scenery. It's about an hour's drive."

I heard the sound of a giant puppy collapsing with all his 80-feet of legs onto the floor and decided to follow suit, in the seat, though. The floor was a little snug for me.

I leaned back against the headrest as I watched cottages and gardens give way to fields and fields lined with stonewalls. It was absolutely beautiful.

According to the genetic tests that my dad had done a few years back, we didn't really have much English heritage.

A bit, yes, but oddly enough, given our very fair skin, our most predominant genetic markers were from Eastern Africa and Brazil, a fact which sent my father on a two-year genealogical spurt that ended up with identifying our first ancestor on American soil as a man from Eastern Africa. Our Brazilian roots traced again to international trade in enslaved people. So while we looked white, our genetics told another story, a story we were all proud to carry.

And yet, while I wanted to go to Angola and the other regions of Eastern Africa that my ancestors had come from, it was the English countryside that I was drawn to the most. It felt most like home. I supposed that spoke something of Eurocentrism and white normativity, but I expected it also came from my mother's heritage and the way, at least from the readings I'd done on epigenetics and heritage, a place can live long in your DNA, even if you haven't lived in the place.

I also couldn't discount the fact that my reading education, through school and general access – again eurocentrism at its "best," -- had given me a certain anglophile sensibility. I'd loved Sherlock Holmes when I was a pre-teen, and then I'd moved onto Emily Bronte in high school. I hadn't ever visited the Moors of the Hound or the Heights, but there was something about that sort of moody, weather-bound location that really appealed to me.

And given that I, like most kids, had been fascinated with Stonehenge when I was a kid, I had a deep desire to understand this part of England. Throw in the number of great books that had been inspired in the Cotswolds itself, and I was primed to become as English as an American-born woman could be.

The four of us spent the drive in companionable silence, and when we pulled off the highway and then approached a small valley with the most quaint village I'd ever seen spread across it, I gasped. "What is this place?" I asked.

"Ah, this is Avebury," Gray said with a smile. "But you haven't noticed the best part yet."

"Something is better than this?" I said with incredulity and heard Dante whine behind me. "You don't believe it either do you, Big Boy?"

But then, just a few moments later, as we wound our way down the hill toward the town, I noticed something odd. "What's the big circle at the edge of the town? A giant race track."

At this Gray laughed so loudly that it made Dante bark. "Oh, now you see it. Just wait."

A few moments later, we parked next to Pree and then walked just a few feet toward something large and grey. My friends were lagging behind me, but I couldn't wait. Something felt like it was pulling me closer.

A few steps later, I realized it was a monumental boulder, standing on its short end. "What?!" I said as I stepped up and put my hand on the stone and then looked to my right, where another similar rock stood on end. "Is this Stonehenge?" I asked, confused because it didn't look at all like the pictures. The only similarity was big rocks.

"Ah, no dear," Danielle said. "Welcome to the Avebury Stone Circle. It's older than Stonehenge and far more magical."

I walked slowly from stone to stone, asking each time if I could touch them and being assured that I could by each of my friends in turn. "Who built this?" I finally asked after we had done a full circuit of the massive ring.

"No one is really sure about who or why," Ollie answered. "It's old, Bronze Age, I think." He looked to Jay.

Jay shrugged. "It's been a while since I was in school, mate, but yeah, that sounds right."

"And we can just walk around in it?" I said as I stepped through the stones, half-expecting to travel in time like Claire in *Outlander*.

"Yep, it's part of the town," Gray glanced toward the few buildings that spread into the circle. "It's protected for sure, but since not as many people know about it as they do Stonehenge, it's still pretty open."

I walked further into the circle toward what looked like another circle of slightly smaller stones. "This is amazing," I whispered, feeling reverent and quiet.

Jazz joined me as I strolled. "I felt the same way when I first came here. Anything this old in the States was destroyed or plowed over by colonialism and Manifest Destiny. We think we have old places, but we don't."

"Not like this, no," I said. "I want to say it's creepy, but that's not it. I'm not scared."

"Magical is the best word I've been able to come up with," Jazz said. "It just feels like anything is possible here."

The two of us made our way from stone to stone. Somehow, the spell wasn't even broken when we reached a road that cut straight through the center of the circles. "This is incredible," I said. "I want to live here."

"You could," Jay said as he joined us. "But it's a bit of a commute to your garden."

I laughed. "For you Brits, it is," I said. "But us Americans, we drive two hours each way for work. This would be nothing."

"And we wonder why the earth is getting warmer," Danielle said as she bumped my shoulder. "Fancy a pint?"

"There's a pub in here?" I asked.

"The Red Lion. Great Shepherd's pie," Gray said and

lead us toward an old white building with a cobblestone parking lot. "After you," he said to me as he opened the door.

A sparkle of light caught my eye from one of the windows on the door, and I thought of Tinkerbell again. What if, I mused, all the sparkles on all the windows were fairies? That thought gave me a shiver because, well, fairies, but also because according to Barrie, fairies weren't the nicest of sorts.

My magical musings shifted, though, once we got inside. I stared at the bare stone walls and the lion sculptures dotted throughout the space, but then my eye was immediately drawn to a sign that read, "The Red Lion, the most haunted pub in the U.K." I loved ghost stories, and in this place, with all the ambience of centuries, I could not wait to learn more.

Dante, who had been strolling calmly with Ollie this whole time, was apparently not afraid of ghosts at all because he pulled his handler into the pub and headed toward a large table at the back, where we could see the circle of stones out the window.

It was still taking me some time to get used to the fact that dogs were fixtures in pubs here, but just because I wasn't used to it didn't mean I didn't like it. I loved it, and when Dante settled himself against my ankles under the table, I loved it all the more.

We ordered our meals – I went with a dish that Jazz said was bacon and mashed potatoes but was called "pork belly and mash" while several of us ordered steaks and Jazz got "The Garden Plot," an array of vegetables that looked amazing when it arrived.

It was all wonderful, and I was truly coming to love the atmosphere of a pub, where you could get great food, but the expectation was that you were going to linger, even after you ate. That just wasn't how American restaurants operated.

After our server gave us the best ghost story of the place, a tale of Florrie who cheated on her husband while he was away and was killed by him for it. Apparently, her body was thrown down the well, which the server insisted I see. When I walked over, I was able to peer down a long tunnel into the ground and was very, very grateful for the thick cover on it. I didn't want to join Florrie.

"So did you see her?" Jay asked when I returned to the table.

"No, alas, she must be resting up to really get her haunt on later," I said. "But the story is disconcerting and very tragic."

"You sound like you don't believe in ghosts, Nell," Ollie asked. "You've never seen anything you can't explain?"

I paused, struck by the fact that it was the police officer who had asked this question. I had a hard time imagining most police back home even entertaining the thought of the supernatural.

"I don't know really," I said. "I've seen things and wondered, but I guess I just can't decide what I think about the afterlife."

Danielle nodded. "I kind of think it makes sense that the energy of a person could hang around, but then wouldn't it dissipate over time." She glanced toward the well. "I mean, Florrie wouldn't still be hanging out here, would she?"

"Do you believe, Ollie?" I asked.

He shrugged. "Same as you, I guess." He lowered his voice, making me think he might not be as comfortable as

I'd originally thought with this idea of ghosts. "Sometimes, I've felt things, or thought I had."

"Like cold spots?" Jay asked with one eyebrow raised.

"Yeah, but also just like someone was passing by me or watching me."

Pree had been very quiet during this conversation, but now she spoke up. "I believe. Completely. I've seen enough animal spirits to build my own zoo."

"A ghost cat and dog zoo," Jazz said. "That sounds amazing."

"Don't forget the iguanas and the monkey," Pree said with a smile.

"Remind me to ask you about the monkey," I said. "But really, even as a doctor, you believe in ghosts."

Pree nodded. "I believe that there are many things science hasn't figured out yet. I'm willing to hold space for mystery until we do."

I tilted my head. I couldn't disagree with her, and when I looked over at Gray, he was nodding, too. "So you're a believer, too?" I asked, a little bit surprised but unsure why.

"Oh yes." He waggled his eyebrows playfully. "I even saw a ghost at Stanway once."

"What?" Jazz squeaked. "I have to know this story."

Gray lowered his voice and launched into a tale about a woman in a green dress that he had seen walking up the stairway out of the dining room. "She didn't walk, though," he said with dramatic effect. "She floated."

We all laughed, a little nervously, and then Ollie leaned in toward the middle of the table and said, "Maybe she killed the wedding coordinator."

For a long moment, the table grew entirely silent, and I forced myself not to look at Jazz. Then, Pree said, "What are you talking about?"

The tension eased a bit, and Jazz explained that the person who had managed her brother's wedding had been murdered the night before.

"What?! That's terrible," Pree said. "Do they know who did it?"

All eyes except Pree's turned to Ollie.

He shook his head slowly. "Not yet, but we did discover something interesting."

I leaned forward until my chest was pressing uncomfortably into the table. "What did you find?" I realized I might seem a bit too interested in this situation, but when I glanced around, everyone else was looking expectant, too.

"A feather," Ollie said. "A white feather."

Dante shifted against my legs. "A feather?" I asked. "What kind of feather?" I glanced over at Jazz, and she looked terrified.

"We're still trying to figure it out. It's not synthetic, that much we know, but believe it or not, it's pretty hard to find someone who can identify bird feathers," Ollie continued.

"Do you want me to take a look? I don't know them all by sight, but I might be able to help. Or I can point you to an ornithologist in Cheltenham who will definitely be able to ID it?" Pree asked.

"That would be amazing." He pulled his phone out of his pocket. "I know a photo might not be enough, but I do have an image." He tapped his phone and then handed it to Pree.

She stared at the screen for a long moment and then shook her head. "I can't tell enough from the image, but the bird must have been small. If it was larger, the pin would have been longer."

"Can I see?" Jay asked, and when Ollie nodded, Pree

passed the phone to Jay who looked and then sent it around the table.

When it got to me, I glanced at the image and saw a basic white feather. Nothing striking about it to me at all.

I handed the phone to Jazz, and she looked at the screen and quickly passed it to Danielle, who didn't even look when she gave it back to Ollie.

"Nothing?" he said.

Everyone shook their heads. "Well, if you think of something," he looked at me, Jazz, and Danielle, "let me know?"

I nodded. "Can I ask where you found it?"

"Sure. Stuck to the bottom of the sofa next to the victim's body," he said as he put his phone face down on the table.

For the rest of the night, we were more subdued, as I assume is appropriate after a discussion of murder. We each drank another pint, except Danielle, and then headed to our cars to drive home.

The companionable quiet of the drive down had been replaced by a sort of nervous energy that I couldn't find a source to. The day had been lovely. The food delicious. The conversation lively, even despite our talk about Arabella's death.

Now, though, something thrummed in the air around the four us as we drove back, and when I glanced at Gray, I saw the tightness in his jaw. He felt it too.

When we stopped at a little garden center at the edge of Stow to pick up the vegetable plants and seeds, Jazz and Danielle asked if I needed them for planting, and when I said I could handle it, they waved and walked toward home.

I almost jogged after them to ask if they were okay, but I didn't think we were at the place where I could be pushy with my concern yet. So I let them be and decided I'd call them the next day to check in.

A HALF-HOUR LATER, Pree, Ollie, Jay, Gray, and I were wrist deep in the garden again, this time tucking cabbage, broccoli, and cauliflower plants into the ground. Back home, it would be too late to plant these, but all my consultations of the online gardening guides for this part of the UK assured me I could plant until late May and sometimes even into the summer.

The starts in the ground, we prepared a row and put peas in, and then while I still had help, we constructed a string trellis for the peas to grow up. Finally, we planted a square of spinach by scattering the seeds across the ground and then lightly raking over them.

As the five of us surveyed our work, I felt a swell of deep pleasure. The first round of garden was in, and I wasn't even completely exhausted. Plus, I'd had the pleasure of a great day with friends and still had room for more veggies as the days got a bit warmer and longer.

"Thank you all so much," I said. "I can offer you tea if you'd like."

"No, thank you," Ollie said. "I'm ready for some telly and a lay down. See you soon, though."

Jay waved, and Pree thanked me before catching up to Ollie and telling him he could bring the feather by her surgery on the next day if he'd like.

Gray took my dirty hand and walked with me over to the donkey paddock, where the three girls stared at us expectantly. "I didn't bring any apples," I said and swore I saw Clover sneer at me with her wide lips.

"Ah, but we always have a secret stash of goodies, don't

we, ladies?" Gray said as he reached into a box that I had thought was a birdhouse and pulled out a handful of animal crackers.

"They eat animal crackers?" I said with a laugh.

"They like the elephants best, but they'll tolerate the others." He dropped a handful into my palm. "Here you go."

For a few moments, I felt the gentle, slightly gooey nuzzle of donkey muzzle on my hands, and then Gray and I unhooked Dante and headed inside for a cuppa.

Chapter Eleven

I SPENT the rest of that evening finishing up my thriller. I'd been tempted to invite Gray over to read again, but I knew better than to get my time too enthralled with someone too soon. It create a sense of connection and commonplace connection that could really make actually getting to know someone hard. So instead, I'd told him I'd see him in the morning and taken Dante up to an early bedtime.

Whether it was the scary descriptions in Brolly's books or the fact that I'd been spending an inordinate amount of time thinking about a murder, I couldn't say. But all night, I dreamed of dead bodies and feathers and a bright green Mini Cooper. I knew the car was spurred by Ruth's mention the day before, but I was pretty sure Matt Damon's appearance was some sort of unprocessed experience with *Ocean's 11* that might warrant some exploration in therapy when I found my new therapist here.

Still, the sleep had been hard, and I woke up feeling rested if a little achy from all the digging the day before. I knew, though, that the best way to work through muscle stiffness was to work those muscles, so as soon as I'd had my coffee and toast, Dante and I headed back out to the garden to get ahead of the weeds.

I had no idea how tiny plants could push themselves out of a seed and up through the soil in a matter of hours, but they always did. Already, the rows of dahlias had little tiny spots of green weeds coming up between them. I knew better than to let these babies get ahead of me, so I walked up and down the rows, hoeing the tiny plants under and chucking the larger ones that the tiller had missed into the grass.

That chore finished, I decided to poke around in the sheds and garages that I hadn't explored yet. Mostly, I was looking for a lawn mower because it seemed like the grass could use a trim, but I had to admit I was also just curious about what hid in there. Back home, barns were the sources of some of the best treasures, at least if those antique salvage shows were to be believed.

I started with the chicken coop, sure that I'd heard of priceless things being tucked into such spaces. Quickly, however, I abandoned that search because the laying birds weren't too happy at my intrusion, and I didn't realize how much dust chickens could kick up. I also didn't want to spend too much time thinking about what was in that dust.

For the same reason, I ignored the loft space over the coop and instead moved to what looked to be a small, attached shed. I opened the door and studied the almost empty space inside. Nothing old in here except. . . I leaned forward and noticed the long board with two round holes cut in it. "Oh my word," I shouted. "It's an outhouse." I loved it instantly and decided that when funds allowed, I would fix the space up, not to be used but to just be lovely.

I was still staring into the outhouse when Gray spoke from just behind me, "Something amiss with the plumbing."

When I turned around, he was grinning. "You found the privy then?"

"I did," I said, "and it's amazing."

"That it is. A two-seater even." He winked at me.

"That brings up an interesting point, doesn't it? I am not exactly inclined to share the facilities with anyone. I assume you are the same." It felt a little premature in, uh, whatever this was between us to discuss bathroom habits, but since the subject came up.

"I'm definitely of the same mind," he said. "But if you were a mom with a wee one, it might come in handy, huh?"

I nodded. "Good point," I said as I closed the door and headed toward the shed across the way. "I'm just exploring," I told Gray as he trotted along beside me.

"Looking for anything in particular?"

"Well, a lawnmower, but mostly I'm snooping."

"I don't think it counts as snooping if it's your own property," he said with a smile. "Would you like me to tell you where the mower is or are you preferring the scavenger hunt?"

"Oh, please don't tell me. The hunt is so much more fun that way."

"Fair enough," he said. "Want company, or is this a solo venture?"

I smiled. "I'd love the company, but no spoilers."

He raised both hands in front of him, after setting the leaf rake he'd had propped over his shoulder against one of the buildings. "No spoilers."

The next building we checked out was the garage, and while Gray assured me that all the bits and pieces of things on the shelves and in the corners were important to repair the farm machinery, I was most interested in the bright orange tractor we found in there. "You'll teach me how to drive this, right?"

Gray looked a little dubious but nodded. "She's a good ole gal," he said as he patted her back tire. "A little finicky about her gears, but a good girl nonetheless."

"Does she have a name?" I asked.

"A name?" He looked at me like I had grown a third arm. "No."

"Well, then, I will call her," I paused for dramatic effect, "Pumpkin."

"Pumpkin?" Gray cleared his throat. "Okay, then Pumpkin it is." He stared at me as I climbed up in the seat and looked at the various levers. "Do you want your lesson now?"

"Oh no, thank you," I said. "I'm just getting to know her and letting her get to know me."

"Um, okay," he said.

I glanced down at him. "You're the one that said she was finicky. I'm just taking our relationship slow."

Now, Gray was laughing, but he didn't say anything further while I abided with Pumpkin for a bit. When I finally felt we'd connected—or at least that I'd waited long enough to amuse Gray and give him a story for his friends later – I climbed down and said, "Now where?"

He led me out of the garage and then fastened the doors shut with an eye and hook. "I'm not precisely sure what exactly you're seeking. I know you said a mower, but this feels like more than that." He looked at me until I nodded. "In that case, the real dragon's hoard is in that building." He pointed to a small stone shed just past the donkey paddock.

I started after him and then stopped and spun him toward me by the shoulder. "Wait, are you saying we have a dragon?"

This time, he rolled his eyes. "The closest thing we have to a dragon is Pumpkin."

I sighed. "Pumpkin isn't really a very dragonish name. If I had known she was a dragon . . . " I mocked exasperation.

"Come on, you," Gray said and pulled me by the hand toward the shed. When we reached the old wooden door, he pointed to the hook and said, "You have the honors."

I lifted the hook and let the door swing open, and then I stood, mouth open, in the doorway for a good minute before I could say anything. "Gray, this is amazing!"

"According to your aunt, everyone in your family has kept their important but not currently useful things in this building." He pointed toward a phonograph in the corner. "That was your great-aunt's father's phonograph."

I stepped around several trunks and what looked to be a small metal bumper car and ran my fingers over the horn of the machine. "There's not even any dust?!"

"Aye, that's part of my duties. I clean in here every fortnight."

I looked at him. "You clean up old stuff every two weeks?"

"Just part of the job, and I kind of love it." He grinned at me then. "You and Pumpkin have your thing. These bits and I have ours."

I laughed and then made my way across the small room. "What is this?" I said pointing to a low trunk with brass hinges.

"Ah, yes," he walked toward me. "That's your great-uncle something's steamer trunk from when he traveled to India, I believe. Go ahead and open it."

I flipped the latch, and there inside were fabrics of the brightest colors I'd ever seen, a stack of letters, and a leather-bound book that looked to be ancient but sturdy. "Are these saris?" I asked as I picked up a hot pink piece of material that was embroidered with the most beautiful silver flowers.

"I don't know much about Indian women's attire, but yes, I think so. I have them cleaned every six months," he said as he turned toward another trunk.

"Wait, you have antique saris cleaned twice a year and they just stay in this trunk?"

"Don't worry, the cleaner is a specialist," he said with a look of concern.

"No, I can see that. They're perfect, but why are they in this trunk?" I couldn't fathom caring for something so well only to store it away.

"Ah, that I don't have an answer for. Your aunt had her ways, and I just did as I was asked."

I stared at him a long moment, "Well, we need to take these inside. I want to hang them up, use them as décor." When he frowned, I said, "Is that not allowed?"

"No, everything here is now yours." He smiled at me. "I'm just trying to figure out how you will use strips of fabric as decorations."

I winked at him. "You'll just have to wait and see."

As I made my way back toward the front of the shed, Gray picked up Great Uncle Whoever's trunk and moved it to the small stone stoop in front of the building.

"I'm going to savor this and go through the things in here slowly, if that's okay with you." I looked over at him then. "Do you mind continuing to take care of them while

I do? If you do, I can go through all of them immediately."

"Not at all," he said. "When I clean in here, I put on a
podcast, and I enjoy the work. It's perfect for a rainy day."
He glanced out one of the small four-paned windows in the
wall. "Speaking of which."

I looked out and saw the clouds gathering. "Oh right.
Okay, I just want to look at this hat box. I love old hats."

The box itself was cream and silver, and once again,
impeccable. Even the label, from a haberdashery in
Niagara-On-The-Lake, Ontario was perfect. Inside, I found
an eggplant-colored cloche made of wool felt. It was
banded with an off-white ribbon, and into that ribbon were
placed three light-pink feathers that had small rhinestones
attached to them. It was absolutely amazing.

"Let's take this inside, too," I said as I put back the hat
and picked up the box. "Looks like we better hurry."

Gray led me out the door, and I pulled it to and hooked
is behind us. Then he lifted the trunk and headed toward
the house. We had just made it to the back door, when the
sky opened up, and we hustled in with our finds.

It was only when I heard the barking from the backyard
that I realized I had left Dante tethered by the garden, and
when I ran out, the donkeys had gotten as close to him as
they could. I couldn't tell if that was because they were
trying to comfort him, to remind him, as my granny had
said, that he wasn't made of sugar and wouldn't melt in the
rain, or to warn him to be quiet. Either way, as soon as I
unhooked him, he jogged right into the house, and the
donkeys headed toward the run-in shed, clearly glad they
didn't have to manage the loud dog anymore.

As soon as I entered the house, I smelled the somewhat
nostalgic and completely horrible scent of wet dog and

decided, on the spot, that it was time for Dante to have a bath. When I posited the idea to Gray, he nodded vehemently. "Yes, please. I'll help."

But it turned out that Dante didn't require much from us at all. As soon as I said, "Bath," he trotted up the stairs, went into the bathroom, and climbed gracefully into the claw-foot tub. Then, for the next 20 minutes while I sudsed him up with strawberry-scented shampoo and then rinsed him, he just sat there, completely content to be pampered. When we were done, I told him so, and he stepped out and waited – without shaking, a fact that felt like a miracle – until I wrapped him in an old towel and said, "Okay."

Then, with the towel managing to contain only a small portion of the water in his wiry coat, he shook from head to toe and then headed downstairs. When I followed him and Gray down, after wiping up the water in the bathroom and rinsing the tub as best I could of hair and a gray film of dirt, the dog was sound asleep in front of a roaring fire. "That looks so cozy," I said.

"I made you some tea, and I found some shortbread in the cupboard." He pointed to a small tray sitting on the coffee table. "Maybe we could look through the things from the shed?" He glanced out the window again. "Not much we can do in the rain, and I just cleaned everything a week ago."

I laughed. "That sounds perfect. Then, if it's still raining, maybe we can read again?" I had noticed that Gray had left his copy of Everett's novel on the side table, a sign I had taken that we'd have more reading afternoons together.

"Excellent," he said as he sat down cross-legged on the floor. "Where do you want to start?

"The saris, of course," I said as I flipped open the trunk

and pulled out a deep orange piece with gold embroidery. "Want to see how I'm going to use these?"

"You're going to hang them over lamps like we're in a harem?" Gray asked and then scowled. "Sorry, that might have been a little culturally insensitive."

"No, nothing like that," I said with a smile as I gently turned the fabric into long twists and then slipped a safety pin into the bottom and top. Then, from the same sewing stand where I'd gotten the safety pins, I took out a small ball of bright green yarn, made a loop in the sari fabric, and threaded the end of the yarn through the loop. "Next one, please," I said and held out my hand for Gray to give me another sari.

Within minutes, I had created a beautiful curtain of brightly-colored saris that I then enlisted Gray to help me hang, via the yarn, from the door way at the back of the living room. "A way to keep the more public spaces separate from the private," I said.

Gray chuckled and hammered small nails from the toolkit in the back closet into the plaster. "I have to admit, that looks very cool," he said when we were done. "But we still have a bunch more saris."

"Oh, don't you worry. I have plans." So for the next hour, we folded, twisted, pinned, and strung fabric to make two more curtains, one for the back hallway just beyond the bathroom, and one for the stairwell. "This way," I told Gray as we finished, "if flower customers come, they have access to the living room, kitchen, and bathroom, but not to the private areas."

"Smart," Gray said. "Also, here, we call them *toilets*. If you say *bathroom*, some people might think you are telling them about a room where they actually bathe."

"Noted," I said. "Ready for more tea?"

"Yes, indeed. Looks like the rain hasn't let up." He smiled at me.

"Oh darn," I said. "We'll just have to stay in and relax."

Unsurprisingly, Dante had not moved since his bath, and I found myself very eager to curl up with him. When I leaned back against him, the hatbox in my lap, he stirred very slightly, as if shoring up his position, and then went back to snoring. "That looks comfy," Gray said as he slid down to the floor next to me.

"You know, it's not physically, but emotionally, it's amazing," I said. "I really think I want to wear this," I said as I pulled the hat from the box. Think I can pull it off?"

"No question," Gray said as I put the hat on my head. "Now, you just need a beaded dress."

"And somewhere to wear it," I added. "Take my picture?"

"Sure," he pulled his phone from his pocket and snapped my pic before showing it to me. "You look cute."

"Ah, thanks," I said as I looked at the picture. Something about it struck me, and it wasn't just that I needed to think more seriously about lipstick. I took the hat off my head and held it in front of me. "Do these remind you of anything?" I said as I pointed toward the feathers.

"Actually, yes, I was going to say something but didn't know if it would put you off the hat."

"They're a lot like the feather that Ollie showed us a picture of, right?" I said as I studied them.

"They are. I think these are little bigger, and obviously, they're not the same color, but yeah, they're pretty much the same." He ran his pointer finger over the almost fluffy, spidery feathers. "What are you thinking?"

I glanced over at him and squinted. "How do you know I'm thinking anything?"

"Seriously, I haven't known you long, but I know you're always thinking. So what is it?"

I smiled. "I'm wondering if the feather Ollie had come off of someone's clothing, if maybe it was a decorative feather like this one."

"Yep, I was wondering that. Do lots of clothes have feathers on them?" he asked.

"Not these days, I don't think, at least not real ones. But something vintage like this, maybe?"

"Was anyone wearing vintage clothes at the wedding?" He asked.

I closed my eyes and tried to remember what people were wearing. Given that I wasn't much interested in fashion myself, I normally didn't pay much attention. Still, I had been in florist mode that weekend, so I maybe at least noted something, something that would complement or clash with my flowers.

For a few silent moments, I sat and remembered what I could of the wedding weekend, but besides the wedding party's clothes, I couldn't remember much at all. But then, suddenly, a flash of Alex coming down the aisle to meet Antoine came to me, and my eyes flew open. "Yes, someone was wearing feathers: the bride."

FOR A VERY LONG TIME, Gray sat quietly, Dante's snore the only sound in the room. I wasn't sure what he was thinking, but I imagined it to be along the lines of "Holy crap. How do we tell Jazz," but in a more British way like maybe with the word *blimey* or something. I didn't know. I was just kind of freaked out.

Finally, he said, "We have to tell her. Better to come from us than from the police."

"The police. Poor Ollie. Yes, far better for us to tell her than for him to have to." I took a deep breath. "But maybe we need to confirm first. Maybe I'm wrong."

"Do you have your laptop?"

"Yeah why?"

"Aren't there wedding photos on Facebook?" he asked.

"You're a genius," I said and climbed up to get the laptop from the kitchen. Quickly, I navigated to Jazz's profile and pulled up her photos. Sure enough, there was Alex in her form-fitting dress with a feather border around the bodice.

"You were right," Gray said as I closed the laptop. "Now what?"

I shook my head. "I still think we have to be sure." I thought for a second. "Pree is going to look at the feather, right? Maybe she's already done that and can tell us something."

"Good thinking," Gray said and picked up his phone. "Hi, Pree?"

I stood by and listened while he told her about what we were wondering and asked if she could share anything about what I'd seen on the feather.

Then, Gray put the phone on speaker and let Pree know I was listening.

"I couldn't tell what kind of feather it was, specifically," she said. "But it wasn't a pin feather. Too light and airy for that. Maybe some sort of down or something."

"Alright," I said. "Thanks."

She continued. "I did tell Ollie about my friend who's an ornithologist, so maybe that will give him some more information." Pree sounded hopeful. "What about the feather has gotten you so interested?"

I told her about the hat we'd found and how it had

made us wonder if the feather could have been from some article of clothing. I stopped short, though, of pointing out that the bride had worn feathers. I didn't want to taint anyone's reputation without cause.

"You are true sleuths," Pree said with a laugh. "Hope to see you soon." I hung up, and Gray and I sat back, this time with Dante under my knees instead of at my back. He made an excellent bolster, especially since he still hadn't moved.

I pulled up the picture of Alex's dress again and zoomed in. "Sure looks sort of airy to me." I passed the laptop to Gray.

"Yeah, it does." He set the laptop on the couch behind us. "Think it's probably time to call Ollie."

I studied Gray a minute. "I expect he already has this is hand, don't you?"

"Probably," he said, "but I don't like to think of holding things back, even if he may already know it."

"But we haven't told him anything so far," I said, puzzled at my own reluctance to share our information. It wasn't like I didn't want this murder to be solved.

"You don't want to tell him?" Gray said as he sat forward and looked at me.

"No, I do," I said and then sat quietly as I checked in with myself about what I was feeling. I realized I was feeling a little possessive of what Gray and I had learned together, and I was also concerned about how all this information might affect Jazz. Still, it was going to come out eventually anyway, and my friends' sadness over the situation didn't even compare to the importance of making sure someone dangerous was held accountable. "No, we should tell him. I'm just hesitating because I know we've been nosing around, and I don't want Ollie to think less of me. And I don't want to hurt Jazz." I decided talking about how I wanted to keep things that Gray and I share private was a little premature in whatever kind of relationship this was.

Gray smiled and sat back. "Believe me, Ollie will appreciate the help. He's not got an ounce of ego in him, and he's always happy to hear my ideas for his cases, and those are a lot more hare-brained than this one."

I felt a little better because of what Gray said, but I also wasn't going to let something as superficial as appearances stop me from helping to locate a murderer. "Okay," I said. "Let's call him."

When he called Ollie, Gray had explained very clearly that we wanted to talk to him about Arabella's murder, and when I'd asked why, he'd said, "Ollie has to account for his time, and every bit of investigating he does helps him climb the ranks a bit. He'd like to be a DI one day."

"DI? Detective Inspector?" I asked, drawing on my British crime show knowledge once again.

"That's it," Gray said. "So this gives him a chance to bring new information to the table, if it is new information, and gives him a little shine."

"Well then I'm doubly glad he's coming."

And with that, there was a knock on the door, and there stood Ollie in his freshly-pressed uniform, a stern but kind look on his face. "Thank you for calling," he said as I led him to the kitchen.

He gave Gray a crisp nod, and I couldn't help having the impression that it felt a bit like he was playing cop. I knew, though, that he was just making the situation clear so we could keep our roles in this conversation straight. "May I?" he said as he pointed at the kitchen table.

"Yes, please," I said. "Fancy a cuppa?" I said in a terrible English accent.

A smile tugged at Ollie's lips. "Thank you, Nell." He sat down and put his notebook in front of him. After I set the mug down, he looked from me to Gray. "So what have you got for me?" he said.

Gray took a deep breath. Very efficiently and clearly, Gray explained our thoughts about the feather, about what Pree had said, which Ollie noted but obviously already knew, and about our memory of Alex's dress. "So you see," Gray finished, "we thought you'd probably already made this connection but wanted to be sure."

Suddenly, I felt a little foolish. The bride had been wearing feathers. They had found a feather at the crime scene. Surely the police had already made this connection. "Ollie, I fear we've brought you out for no reason. You must already have thought of this?"

He smiled at me. "We had, yes, but not quite in this way."

I couldn't tell if my new friend was just being kind or really meant that, but Gray knew him better and said, "Can you tell us more?"

For a split second, Ollie was quiet but then he nodded. "Yes, I believe I can because I may just need your assistance."

I resisted the urge to clap my hands with delight at the prospect that I might get to assist in an actually British murder mystery. Quickly, though, I sobered. This wasn't a TV show. Someone had really died, and I forced myself to remember Arabella's body on the floor. That did the trick at pulling me back into reality. "How can we help?"

Ollie sat back and folding his hands on his belly. His stomach was rather flat, so the gesture didn't quite have the charming, jovial affect I imagined Ollie thought it did. "Well, we have determined, from studying photographs, that the feather found at the scene and the feather in Mrs. Johnson's dress *appear* similar." He leaned heavily into the word *appear*.

"Ah, but you don't have a sample from the actual dress to compare it to?" I blurted. "And you need me to see if I can get access and pull a sample for you?"

Both Gray and Ollie looked at me blinking for a long second, and then Ollie slowly nodded. "Yes, exactly."

"Okay," I shrugged. "I can do that. I'll get to it." I started to stand, but Ollie put a hand on my arm.

"Slow down, Nell. We need to talk through this a bit," he said, his voice and eyes much more serious now. "If Alex Johnson killed her wedding planner, then she is dangerous. You can't just march in there and ask for a feather."

I rolled my eyes. "Of course not." Both men were staring at me with worried expressions. "You two think I'm that stupid? I mean, we don't know each other well, but seriously, guys." I was a little annoyed.

"No, that's not it," Ollie said. "You're just so keen." His brow furrowed more deeply as he looked at me.

I took a deep breath. Ah, there it is was, my impulsivity leaping to the fore and scaring people again. It had happened all my life. My brain worked very, very fast, and often, I didn't consider the consequences, or if I did, I didn't remember to communicate that I had considered the consequences.

"Right," I said. "Might we work out a plan then?"

I felt the relief slip off of the men as I looked from one to the other. "Yes, please," Gray said quietly. "And I can help."

I nodded, remembering again how so many of my friends had told me they would help if I'd let them know I could use some support. "Okay," I said and forced myself to settle into my chair and take a sip of my own tea.

"What are you thinking?" Ollie asked, and I smiled. He was assuming I wasn't rash, and I appreciated that.

"I was actually going to take the hat," I said as I pointed to the hat box now sitting at the other end of the table, "and ask Jazz if the feathers resembled her sister-in-law's gown. Tell her I wanted to replace the two that had fallen off and thought Alex might have a recommendation."

Gray sat back and crossed his arms over his chest. "Well, that's pretty good," he said quietly.

Inwardly, I beamed, but I kept my face stern. "Do the Johnsons know you found a feather at the scene?" I knew my answer as soon as I spoke. Ollie had told all of us about the feather when we'd been at Avebury. "Never mind. So I have to be particularly cagey since Jazz might get suspicious?" I looked at Ollie.

"Yes," he said simply. "I think you might send up some flares if you go about this directly. Could be that even bringing up the dress would put her on guard."

I sighed. He was right. Jazz would know something was up the moment I asked. She didn't know me well, but she knew me enough to know I'd be on high alert. How could I not be? "Right," I said.

"We need something less obvious, less direct maybe," Ollie said and then looked at Gray. "Does that sneaky mind of yours have any ideas?" Ollie smiled at his friend.

"I'll choose not to be insulted by the idea that you think I'm *sneaky*," Gray said with a smile of his own. Then, he sat quietly and stared out the window.

When neither men spoke for a couple solid minutes, I found myself getting fidgety, so I stood, took everyone's mugs, and made another round of tea for us all. Then, I dug into the cabinet, found a long roll of crackers, and put them out with a plate of ham slices and cheese sticks I'd picked up at the store.

I carried the very mediocre charcuterie tray to the table and set it down between the men, who took one look at it and immediately started laughing.

"Oh come on, now," I said. "I know it's not fancy, but it's snacks. It can't be that funny." I was a little hurt honestly.

Gray took a deep breath, steadied himself and said, "You know these are biscuits, right?"

I stared at the cracker in his hand and then at him. "No, they're not. They're crackers. Biscuits are fluffy and light. These are crackers."

"No, love," Gray said as he handed me the cracker. "Take a bite."

I screwed up my face and looked at him before reaching for some ham and cheese to add to the cracker.

"No," Ollie said. "Try it by itself." His face was wiggling with contained laughter.

I sighed and jerked the cracker from Gray's hand before shoving the whole thing into my mouth and biting down. . . into a cookie. I let my head drop back as I chewed. Of course, these were *biscuits*, English biscuits, as in cookies. I felt like a dolt, but within a minute, I was laughing so hard that cookie crumbs were flying out of my mouth.

The guys were now doubled over and laughing, which of course caused me to spit out more crumbs and then, nearly choke. Then, when I tried to clear my throat with tea, it was too hot, and I ended up spluttering it all over the table in front of me.

By the time I could speak, the three of us were in tears, the charcuterie was covered in crumbs and tea droplets, and

I was feeling every bit the American in a foreign land. I wondered if E.M. Forster had been able to laugh at his snafus when he was in India. I suspected not, but at least I was like E.M. Forster in one way, I decided.

"Alright, so would someone like to show me what actual crackers look like?" I said as we settled.

Gray stood, opened the small cabinet, and pulled out what looked to be exactly what I had served, but the word *crackers* was clearly on the label.

I stared as he set the roll in front of me. "Are you serious?"

He nodded. "Sometimes they come in a box with a bag inside. You don't have these in the States?"

I shook my head. "No, we have exactly these in the States. That's what I thought I was putting out. Why would you ever put cookies in a tube?"

The two men started laughing again, but finally Ollie said. "Okay, so you know this, I think, but just to lay it all out, here, cookies, as you call them, are *biscuits*. We don't have what you call *biscuits*, I don't think. Crackers are these things." He pointed to the roll on the table, "but they are also loud popping toys we use at Christmas to celebrate."

I stared at him for a long moment. "Oh, firecrackers. Got it." I sighed. "Lord, this is confusing."

Gray nodded. "Yep, welcome to the English language."

"Harty har har," I said. "Your English is a mess."

Ollie scoffed. "You do realize you stole our language just like you stole our land." He was smiling now.

"Your land?" I snapped. "What about all the indigenous people your colonies kicked off the land?" I wanted to continue this mock fight, but I could feel a little bit of real ire rising up in me. Colonization was a fraught topic, and one I'd thought a lot about from an American perspective. I wasn't ready to delve this deep with these two, not yet. "Okay, so seriously, do you want another snack?" I said with a giggle.

"Actually no," Gray said as he picked up a slice of cheese and a, er, biscuit. "These go well together. It's the ham that's throwing it off."

"You don't eat ham with crackers?" I said.

"No, we do," Ollie quipped. "Just not usually with biscuits."

This sent us all into another wave of laughter, but eventually, we settled and picked up our snacks, without ham, and Gray said, "I have an idea."

Ollie and I both turned to him. "Yes," I said around a mouthful of cracker and cheese. I had basically spit food all over these men, so talking with my mouth full was the least of my worries.

"What if we did a 'Teach Nell English night'?" Gray said before putting a biscuit with cheese into his own mouth and looking at me as if he was making a completely innocent suggestion instead of poking fun at me again.

"What do you mean?" I said suspiciously, a smile playing on my lips.

"Well," Gray slid the hatbox across the table to me. "What do you call this type of hat?"

I looked at him then down at the box. "A cloche," I said pulling the style out of some repository of vocabulary that I didn't even know I had.

The men chuckled, and Gray nodded. "Yep, here a *cloche* is a cover that you'd put over a plant, like an orchid, to protect it."

"Oh yeah, we use it that way, too, but not as often," I replied as a tingle of recognition started to hit. "So you're suggesting we host folks so they can tell me what the English terms of things are?"

"Precisely," Gray said, "And we use it as a chance to get all those things you want out of the shed."

Ollie was grinning. "I have no idea what else is in that shed, but this sounds like a perfect way to bring out the hat *and* poke some fun at Nell here."

I sighed. "Excellent, let's use my foreigner status to solve a murder." I spoke like I was terribly put off by the idea, but actually, it did sound like a lot of fun.

Chapter Twelve

WE PLANNED THE "TEACH NELL ENGLISH" Night – the name stuck – for two days later, on Thursday evening. We had plenty of time to get things set up, so I made the decision to make a routine for myself, a rhythm to keep me focused and on top of the various activities I needed to complete.

Each morning, after coffee, Dante and I went to the garden to weed for a bit. Then, we traipsed back inside to work on our new website for The Statice Symbol for a while. Every mid-morning when I opened the Dashboard, I read the company name and felt it lacked something. I couldn't quite pin down what that was. I still loved the name, but for some reason, now, here in my life as it would be, it felt incomplete, unsettled somehow.

But each day, I failed to figure out what was missing and immersed myself, instead, in finding the most beautiful stock photos I could afford to accent the descriptions of flowers I crafted with exquisite care. Gray had sent me a variety of photos of my house during various seasons of the year, and so throughout the site, I incorporated those in such a way that I hoped my visitors would feel part of the experience of growing the flowers.

And of course I hoped that if the visitors felt that way, they'd soon become customers. I was still fine financially, thanks to Aunt Jelly, but I wanted to be more than fine. I had big dreams for this landscape and this business, and big dreams require, most times, big budgets.

Still, I could see that the number of hits on my site was growing each day, and soon it would include a calendar, a link to schedule a consultation with me, and one day, a huge portfolio to show off my work. Today, though, it was time to build the dahlia page.

I had just slid in the final photo of a brilliant swath of Boogie Woogie dahlias that, I prayed, mine would emulate come late summer when Gray came in, a trolley at his back packed with more things from the shed.

Over the past two days, we had taken over my living room and some of the hallway too with items from the shed. For a small building, it could hold a lot of stuff including the most gorgeous pieces of antique luggage I had ever seen. Besides the old steamer trunk I'd seen before, it had hard-sided suitcases, smaller trunks, and even a hatbox that looked like it was sturdy enough to carry the Crown Jewels on a dumptruck without letting them get damaged.

As we'd sorted the items for the "English Nell Night" as Gray had taken to calling it, we also made a mental list of what I wanted to sell and what I wanted to keep. The luggage was definitely staying because I could already imagine filling pieces of it with flowers for photo shoots or even as props for quirky weddings. I also had an entire table full of vases that I would use daily.

Most of those things, though, we tucked away in a

bedroom upstairs since we knew that I was keeping them and what they were called. Turns out that the English call *luggage*, well, *luggage*. But the shed had yielded a variety of gifts for me to learn from as well as for us to sell. The phonograph, as charming as it was, was going to go, and the beautiful old Martha Washington sewing stand, which Gray assured me was not, here in the UK, titled after the wife of the first President of the United States, was also going to be sold.

By the time we arrived at Thursday afternoon, the house was full of gorgeous old things, things that I could understand why my aunt hadn't wanted to part with but also things that I could not, as much as they were beautiful, afford to keep, especially since I'd decided the old shed would be The Statice Symbol office. Sure, I had garages and out buildings galore, but it just felt a shame to keep these things stored away when someone else would really enjoy them. Even so, it was a little sad to let them go.

"I'm going to miss you," I said late Thursday afternoon as I stroked my fingers over the top of a barrister bookcase that had wavy, curved glass fronts for each shelf.

"You can keep it, you know?" Gray said as he adjusted things one more time. "None of this has to be sold."

I nodded. "I know, and I would keep it, but I just don't have the space." I looked around the now very crowded living room and sighed.

"You also don't have to keep anything of your aunt's that you don't want, even if it's in the house, Nell," Gray said.

I looked up at him sharply. "But this is Aunt Jelly's house, I—"

He interrupted me. "No, Nell, this is your house. You

need to do what you want with the space." He glanced around. "What don't you love in here?

I smiled and said, "Besides the array of garden geese in tiny doll clothes, you mean?"

"Yes, besides that," he said with a laugh as he patted one little fellow in a sailor suit. "What house furnishings do you not like? We can sell them or take them to the tip if they're not sellable."

I looked at him carefully and said, "To the dump?"

He squinted. "Is that what you call *the tip*?"

"Is that what *you* call *the dump*?" I asked back with a grin.

"Yes, we can throw them away." He looked at me closely. "But you're stalling. There's something in here you don't like. Tell me."

I glared at him both pleased and annoyed that he already knew me so well, and then I gave in. "I hate that sofa," I said and pointed to the faded red, floral thing sitting by the window. "It's comfortable, but I just don't like the pattern."

Gray moved swiftly to put a green piece of tape on it. "Fair enough. We'll have a garage sale on Saturday then." He said GAH-rage with the emphasis on the first syllable, and I grinned. Same word. Totally different feel.

"Okay," I said, and then, as if I had been let loose, I went around the room and immediately marked a few more things to put out there, including the old rocking chair in the corner that I swore rocked on its own from time to time. "There," I said. "Now, that bookcase can go in that corner." I pointed to the shadowy corner to the right of the door from the kitchen. "It'll be out of direct sun but also beautiful with an old lamp on it."

Gray smirked but didn't say a word, just moved to slap more green tape on the "to go" things before shifting the rocker out of the way and enlisting my assistance to carry the four parts of the barrister bookcase over to the corner. Once it was in place, I immediately placed a red-glass lamp on the top and smiled.

"That looks amazing," Gray said. "How do you do that? Are you picturing the room like you want it?"

I shook my head. "Nope. I don't have much of a visual imagination. It's more about the feeling. I want things to create a mood, set a tone. Same with my flowers. I understand color theory and all that, but it's much more intuitive for me."

Gray was studying me then. "You are fascinating," he said.

I mock curtsied and said, "Why thank you. But we better get to cooking or we'll have no chili to serve our guests."

Gray had assured me that English people did, indeed, eat chili and often preferred it spicy. I had suggested we could do a curry instead, but he insisted that I make my chili just as I did at home. "It's only fair that we get a bit of the States, you know."

So now, we were in the kitchen opening cans – "tins," Gray kept correcting me – of beans and tomatoes and adding them to the spiced ground beef that I had browned a bit earlier. Then, we poured in beef broth, some more chili powder and cumin, and left the mix to boil on the stove. It smelled heavenly, and when the corn bread started baking in the oven below, the whole kitchen filled with delicious aromas.

I couldn't imagine a better meal for tonight when the stereotypical English drizzle had come in with a cold front that made the fireplace with bowls of something hot sound absolutely perfect. And when our friends started to arrive, each of them took a whiff of the scent as they came in and did their own patented groan of delight. I thought, for a moment, of recording them for some strange Instagram reel, but thought better of the plan.

Gray and I had decided we'd try to bring as many people as we could reasonably invite to this event, a chance for us – and for Ollie, the actual policeman – to see what people said when we gently steered the conversation toward the murder. So Jazz and Danielle were coming, of course, as were Jay and Pree, but then we invited Scarlett and the other crew from Arabella's wedding company. It was going to be a cozy night, but the three of us hoped it would lead us somewhere.

As soon as everyone had stuffed themselves with chili and cornbread, I did a quick round of clean-up while Gray pulled the things we'd tucked away from potential chili spills out into the open. One of these things was the hatbox, from which he removed the hat and set it on the closed lid before pulling out a collection of photos that he had told me had more than enough objects to keep the game going for quite a while.

Then, the game began. It had two stages, as Ollie had designed it. The first was for all the Brits to choose an item that had, they believed, a particularly British name, and then sit down until all the Brits were sitting. Because the game was designed for me to learn the particular brand that was British English, Jazz would assist but had to let me take a few good guesses first.

Normally, a game intended to show what I didn't know would stress me out to no end. I had just enough of a perfectionist in me to not like making mistakes, especially in front of other people. But somehow, with these particular people, I wasn't anxious. I knew it was all in good fun, and even better, with the hope of solving a murder.

The first person to volunteer was, by his own design, Ollie. He'd found an old stick in the mix of things that Gray, and I had pulled out. I had suggested we practice my fumbles, but he had pointed out that acting was probably not my strong suit and maybe we should go for authenticity.

So now, here I sat cross-legged beside the fireplace while Ollie paced back and forth in front of me with a large stick. "A cricket bat," I said with obvious silliness.

Ollie rolled his eyes. "No," he said. "Try again."

"A Billy club," I said this time, having wracked my brain to come up with that phrase after Ollie had shown the stick to me.

"Correct," he said with a smile. "In the U.S. this would be called a Nine Millimeter." He grinned at me, and I rolled my eyes.

"But now," Jay added, "you don't carry that do you, Ollie? You carry a baton."

"Right-o," Ollie said and reached behind the sofa cushion where he'd been sitting. "Like this?" He flicked his wrist and from the magic wand-sized stick in his hand extended into a long rod.

"You hit people with that?" I said, a little surprised.

"Better than shooting them, right?" Jazz said with a serious expression, and I couldn't disagree.

"Much better," I said.

"My turn," Pree shouted as she wheeled a stroller out from behind the sofa. The only time I had seen anything like it was in *Mary Poppins*, and I knew there was an English word for it. "Starts with a P," I think.

Pree nodded, but when I couldn't come up with the rest of word, I said, "What do you call it in the States?"

"Well, a modern one of those would be a stroller," Jazz said.

I looked over at her. "But an older one, would we call it a buggy?" Then, like lightning, the p-word came to me. "Pram. It's a pram."

The whole room clapped. "Very good," said Gray.

"Thank God for Julie Andrews," I said, and the room erupted in laughter, a warming reaction to my slanted Poppins reference.

We played on, and surprisingly, I knew most of the terms although I did get completely stumped on the *driveway*, *parkway*, *pavement*, *sidewalk* quiz that Scarlett arranged from the box of photographs. I was fairly certain I would never keep that straight.

After a few rounds, what we had hoped would happen happened – Danielle picked up the hat and slid it onto her head, doing a model's walk up and down the center of the room for a few fun minutes before saying, "Okay, Nell, what's this?"

Jazz was sitting right next to me, so I asked Danielle if I could hold the hat in the hopes that Jazz would take a good look at it, too. "I suppose *hat* is too obvious, right?"

"A round of applause for our genius American," Ollie said with a laugh.

"Alright, alright. Well," I glanced over at Jazz, "isn't this called a cloche? You know, those hats from the Flapper era."

The room was giggling now as the two Americans talked about a hat as if it was a plant cover. Jazz nodded as she took the hat from me. "Yes, I think so, but here, a cloche covers a rare flower or something like that." She looked up at Danielle for confirmation, and her wife nodded.

But then, Ollie broke the script and leaned forward. "Wait a minute. Those feathers look a lot like the one we found at Arabella's murder scene." He put out his hand. "Can I see that?"

Jazz nodded and handed him the hat while studying him. He put one large index finger on the soft feather and nodded. "Yes, they were almost like this, just white instead of pink."

At the mention of the color, Jazz and Danielle's eyes snapped to the other's. They knew.

For a brief moment, I thought they were going to keep what they knew to themselves. It was Jazz's sister-in-law, after all, who would come under suspicion now. But the silence only lasted a split second before Jazz said, "My brother's wife had feathers like that on her gown." She didn't elaborate, but she didn't waver either.

Ollie nodded. "Okay, then." He paused a minute and put his hand on Jazz's before standing. "I'm afraid I have to go," he said.

Jazz nodded and stood, too. "Me, too, everyone." She hugged me. "Thank you for a good night." And without a further word, she and Danielle followed Ollie to the front door, donned their coats, and headed out into the evening.

The rest of us sat quietly for a long few minutes, not quite making eye contact with each other, until Scarlett said, "How can I help with tidying?"

That simple request broke the quiet spell of dread that had settled over us, and everyone began to move. Gray, thankfully, took the lead, and soon, he had everyone moving items into their designated areas for giveaway or sell. Then, Pree asked if she could buy the sofa because she was looking for a place to try out her new upholstery skills, and a few of Scarlett's crew asked if they could purchase a few more of the other things we'd designated for sale.

Before I knew it, we had a greatly reduced sell pile, and

everything I had wanted to keep from the shed was now in its place in the house. The guys had very willingly hauled a low wooden trunk and a hat stand up to my room, where I was going to store blankets and hang up my "not yet dirty enough to wash" clothes.

Then, as if they hadn't been helpful enough already, each of them took a couple of flyers about the yard sale we were going to have on Saturday, promising to hang them as well as bring their own tables and items to sell. "The more stuff, the more customers," Scarlett said as she filed out after everyone else but Gray.

I smiled. "At least something is the same in the States as it is here." Scarlett leaned over and hugged me.

Gray and I tidied up the last of the things and did the dishes, and then we sank down onto what was now Pree's sofa. Dante had, perhaps because there were so many people in the house, spent the evening upstairs, a small gift that I very much appreciated because I'd had fleeting visions of his face in chili bowls. Now, though, he came and sprawled himself across Gray's and my feet and, immediately, went to sleep.

"I wish I could do that," Gray said as he shifted his foot under the dog. "It's a true talent."

I nodded, and then I turned to him, "This is awful."

"Yeah, it is," he said. "But it's not awful we created, Nell. Whoever killed Arabella brought this on." He took my hand in his. "Don't carry this as your responsibility. It's not."

Tears welled in my eyes, both because I was sad about the situation but also because I didn't know how Gray did it, how he knew just what I needed to hear. "Thank you," I said and put my head on his shoulder.

After a few minutes of letting my feelings settle, I looked

around my living room and smiled. "Seriously, anytime I need major work done at the house, I'm just going to throw a party." I spun around slowly. "It's amazing." I stopped and looked at the windows and then turned to Gray.

"What are you thinking?" he said with a small smile.

"When was the last time you pulled an all-nighter?"

He furrowed his brow. "That must be an American term that I'm not familiar with."

I picked up a sofa cushion and threw it at him.

THE NEXT MORNING when I woke up on the couch, a blanket over me and a snoozing dog beside me, I realized I hadn't quite made it all night. But we had made good progress in making the room truly mine. We'd taken down the floral curtains and put up some almost transparent scrims I'd found in the hall closet. Then, we'd rearranged all the furniture, pushing the sofa toward the hallway so Pree could pick it up when she was ready. Finally, I'd gone through the house and filled the bookshelf in the corner, being sure, however, to leave at least a book or two in every room since it felt important to me that anyone who was anywhere in my home should have something to read on hand.

Sometime well after midnight, I had taken a short break on the sofa and then, moments later, found myself staring into a fully sunny day outside. I felt that familiar flush of panic that I'd overslept and starting to leap up and check the time. But then, I remembered I was my own boss and didn't have to be anywhere at any specific time. So while Dante continued to snore, I scrolled through my phone, sent my friends back home some silly memes, and eventually made my way into the kitchen for coffee.

It was just before 9am, so not late at all by most people's standard, and yet just seeing the time flipped up a spark of anxiety in me. "I have so much to do," I said out loud before correcting the Always Busy part of myself by saying, "No, you don't. You have things to do yes, but remember, we don't have to rush." Somewhere inside the lower part of my chest, something eased, and I smiled. All my work in therapy was finally paying off.

I had slowly been letting Dante explore a bit without a leash. We'd walked the perimeter of the property several times, and from what I'd read, a lot of dogs would begin to understand that those boundaries were their territory and not go past them. I wasn't quite ready to let Dante go completely free, but this morning when we walked out, I didn't hook him to his lead but instead kept a close eye on him as we walked around the house toward the garden.

The loping pup trailed along beside, behind, and ahead of me, but he, too, kept glancing over, just to be sure I was close. "This might just work," I said as I reached the donkey stall.

"What might work?" Gray responded from inside the chicken coop, causing me to nearly toss my coffee down my front.

"You have to stop scaring me," I said and took a deep breath. "This," I said as Dante sniffed his way over to Gray and started wagging his tail.

"Look at you, big fellow. You're wild and free."

"Shh, don't give him ideas. He's free-ish," I said with a smile.

"Noted," Gray said. "What are the two of you up to this fine morning?"

I stared at him. "Currently, I'm trying to come to full consciousness. How are you so chipper already?"

He shrugged. "What's there not to be chipper about?" He looked around. "The sky is clear. The animals are healthy. There's a beautiful woman I get to spend time with, and a goofy dog who is going to make himself ill eating chicken poo."

"Well, when you put it that way, I guess you're right." I looked closely at Dante, who was indeed, eating chicken poop like it was a delicacy. "Come on, Dante. Let's go terrorize Clover."

As if I had spoken some magical incantation, Dante left his snack and trotted over to stand beside me. "Will you look at that?" I said.

"He's clearly bonded to you," Gray said as I raked the last of the dirty litter out of the coop. "Maybe it's time you realize you're keeping him."

I sighed. "Let's get through the weekend," I said, unwillingly to let the last wall of detachment I had from the dog fall away just yet. "Maybe someone will recognize him at the yard sale."

"Alright then." He followed behind us as we walked over to where the three big-eared loves were waiting. Clover flicked an ear directly at Gray and turned to me as if to say, "Hello dear friend, who is this ruffian you have brought with you?"

I laughed and pulled an apple out of my sweater pocket while Gray fed the other two some orange slices he'd had in his own pocket. "Clover, I have an idea." Both her ears turned toward me. "What do you think about Dante hanging with you guys for a bit? I think he'd like to explore your pasture."

I glanced over at Gray, who didn't seem the least bit concerned about the idea, and then walked over to the gate and let the excited wolfhound in.

I'm not sure I've ever seen a friendship more instantaneous. The dog was the same size or larger than the donkeys, but despite his size, they must have taken my permission for him to join as permission for them to play because in just a few moments, the four of them were romping and jumping in the pasture like children. It was beautiful.

"Well, now you can be sure he won't leave. He's got three more girlfriends," Gray said.

The rest of us – and the flock of chickens now roaming the yard – spent the lovely spring morning outside. Gray and I weeded, the donkeys and dog romped, and the chickens chuckled in a way that I was truly coming to love. In every way I could think of, it was a perfect morning, except for the small pit of concern that we might have just implicated Jazz's sister-in-law for murder.

Chapter Thirteen

SATURDAY MORNING CAME on sunny and warm, perfect weather for a yard sale. My friends had, however, told me that here these events were called car boot sales, a term which didn't really make sense to me since we weren't selling things out of the trunk of my car. But a phrase which, nevertheless, I used on the directional signs I hung from town to my house in the pre-dawn. Apparently, according to Gray, boot sale shoppers in the UK were the same as Americans, and they'd be out early.

Fortunately, the weather had stayed nice the day before, so Gray and I had been able to set out everything and then drape sheets over the tables to keep things dry. And when Pree pulled up in a pick-up truck later that evening, we'd helped her unload her stuff for sale and then put the sofa back into the truck.

We'd decided to do two sales, at the last minute. This one in the courtyard for all the smaller stuff, the more "garage sale"-like things that would sell for less money. Then, we were going to advertise a second sale with the more valuable items. The suggestion had come from Jay, who said we probably needed to market differently for each type of customer. I had agreed, so we were starting with the low-budget stuff with a plan to advertise in more specific publications for the next one.

Now with everything ready – including tables for Jay's, Jazz and Danielle's, Ollie's, and Scarlett's stuff - the sun shining brightly, and the first cars pulling into the drive, I felt hopeful that we'd all make a little cash and have a great time doing it.

The flurry of customers was fast and eager first thing, so none of us had much time to talk for the first couple of hours of the day. About mid-morning, though, the stream of traffic slowed, and I was able to wander over to Jazz and Danielle's spot on the premise of being interested in a set of tiny collector's spoons from the various counties in England.

"These are adorable," I said as I picked up one that said York.

Jazz rolled her eyes. "I haven't known you long, Nell, but you do not seem like the souvenir spoon type."

I tilted my head. "What do you mean? I'd like an international collection." I laughed out loud. "Alright, how are you?" I said as I sobered, looking from her to Danielle. "That was a lot the other night."

"Yeah," Danielle said as Jazz sighed. "But if Alex had something to do with the murder, we all need to know it."

"Especially Antoine," Jazz said. "He could be married to a murderer."

I stared at her a long minute as I let that sink in. "I hadn't even thought about that. I'm sorry. That's awful."

"Not as awful as him staying married to her," Jazz said with a bite to her voice. "Is Ollie coming today?"

I nodded. "He was already here to drop off his things,

but he had to go into work for a bit. He said he'd be back though." I sighed. "I hope he can tell you what's going on."

"Me, too," Jazz said. "I haven't said anything to Antoine because I don't want him to have to keep anything from Alex, but it's kind of killing me."

I bit my tongue to keep from saying that I'd felt somewhat similar earlier in the week when I'd had to keep things from her and just nodded. "So about these spoons?"

"Actually," Jazz said with a laugh. "They're already sold." She nodded toward a woman with multiple piercings and tattoos who was shopping with Jay. "She's going to turn them into necklaces."

"That might be the best use of souvenir spoons I've ever heard of," I said with a laugh and headed back to my table.

Customers kept coming in, albeit slowly, all morning and into the afternoon. At some point, I realized some of our guests were mostly looky-loos who wanted to get a peek at the house and grounds, but since I had often done much the same thing at yard sales and real estate open houses back in the States, I didn't fault them and even gave one older couple who said they were gardeners a quick tour of the grounds while Gray staffed the tables.

By the time Ollie returned around 1, sales were almost non-existent, and our tables looked sparse and raggedy. It was time to pack up. We'd all agreed that anything that hadn't sold was going to be donated, so Gray quickly brought out the totes we'd saved to pack everything up, and soon enough, Pree's truck, now free of the sofa, was reloaded and she and I were on our way to the church thrift shop with our donations.

The two tiny women who accepted our load were especially grateful to see the mismatched sets of glassware that we brought in. Apparently, inexpensive drinking glasses were a big seller for the store. I told them I thought I probably had more to give, and I'd bring them back the next week, an offer which prompted perfume-laden hugs from both of them. Sometimes generosity really does the spirit good.

On the ride back to the house, Pree and I chatted about her tough vet cases that week – a pet rat who had eaten a rubber band sounded like a particularly tricky one – and then discussed my flowers and when things would start blooming. I felt almost certain that Pree was doing the same thing I was and avoiding the topic of murder until we were back with everyone. I appreciated the silent agreement we'd made because I really didn't want to discuss anything without Jazz there. I'd kept enough secrets from her already.

When we returned, everyone had finished clean up and was reclining in a set of outdoor furniture that I didn't even know existed. They were set-up on the patio with a table, wicker chairs and sofa, and even a very festive mandala-designed umbrella over the table.

"I see you raided my fridge," I said as I sat down in a chair next to Gray and picked up a roll of prosciutto and cheese.

"And you'll see we actually put out crackers," Ollie said with a wicked smile.

The entire group laughed, and I blushed. "I presume he told you about the snafu then."

"Of course he did," Jay said. "That's too good not to pass on." He slid a bottle of beer – a Budweiser – across the table. "But we made it up to you with American beer."

I pushed the bottle back to him. "That is not a fair reparation, sir. That is beer-flavored water." I looked down at the cooler by his feet. "Pass me a cider."

A cheer went up, and I grinned. I was becoming slightly more English, it seemed, at least in my mind.

For a few minutes, we talked about the lovely, eccentric people who had come to the boot sale – that was never going to sound quite right to me, I expected – including the older man who carried a crow in a cage with him. "They seemed to have a good relationship," Scarlett said with a smile. "I'm glad they have each other."

"Me, too," Pree said and then gave us a mini-lecture on the brilliance of corvids. I actually enjoyed it, as I do whenever anyone gets hooked into talking about their special interests, but when I looked over at Jazz, her face was somber.

Pree finished with a delightful story about a friend of hers who had spent a lot of time befriending the crows in her neighborhood. But then, she'd gone out of town for two days and didn't put out their treats like usual. When she returned and resumed the practice, the birds came to the fence in her yard and stared at her before, in unison, turning their backs on her. "They can hold grudges," Pree said.

"Wow," Gray said. "Remind me not to tick ours off."

A heavy silence filled the patio then, and Jazz sat forward. "Speaking of birds," she began before glancing at Danielle, who gave her a small nod. "I'm fairly sure that feather you found, Ollie, was from my sister-in-law Alex's dress."

Ollie nodded but didn't say anything.

Jazz continued. "Actually, I'm not just fairly sure. I'm certain." She reached into her bag and pulled out a plastic bag with a white feather in it. "You'll need to test this, though, for court and such, I expect." She handed the bag to Ollie who took it somberly.

"Thank you," he said. "That's really helpful, Jazz."

She nodded and then sat back. "I can't have Antoine married to a murderer, even though I know he's going to be devastated."

The group sat silently for a long minute, but then I had to ask my question. "What are your next steps, Ollie?"

He sighed and looked at the bag in his hands. "Well, first we'll compare the feathers to be certain they match." He looked up at Jazz. "I expect that they will, I'm sorry to say."

Jazz sighed again and nodded.

"Then, we'll have enough evidence to get a warrant to look at the dress itself, and if that matches, then . . . "He didn't need to finish his sentence.

Another long moment passed, but then Scarlett said, "That doesn't necessarily mean she did it, though, right? Someone else could have dropped that feather there."

I looked at Scarlett and energy flipped around under my skin. "She's right," I said. "Anyone who had access to the dress could have had that feather."

Ollie looked from me to Scarlett. "Always possible, I suppose. But I need to be honest and say that the odds that someone else accidentally dropped this feather at the crime scene are exceedingly low."

"Right," Gray added. "Wasn't it stuck to the bottom of the sofa? Hard to just drop one and then have it float up like that, isn't it? Had to be a part of a struggle or something, right?"

"That's what our theory is," Ollie confirmed. "That Arabella and her killer exchanged words, maybe even blows and the feather was dislodged from the dress and maybe shoved up onto the underside of the couch in the struggle."

That tingle of understanding was growing in my hands.

"But that would mean that if Alex was the murderer, she'd have had to be wearing her wedding dress at the time she killed Arabella. That doesn't make any sense," I said.

Danielle sat up straight. "Right, she wouldn't have had any reason to put on her dress the night before the wedding. Besides, if you were planning to kill someone, you wouldn't want to risk ruining the one piece of clothing that everyone knew belonged to you."

"What if I wasn't planning it, though?" Pree asked. "What if I was just trying the dress on, ran into Arabella, and things happened?"

Danielle flopped back into my chair. "Right," she said and took Jazz's hand. "So she could still be the murderer."

"It's possible, yes," Ollie said. "But this conversation also tells me that we need to be thinking more broadly."

"As if someone framed the bride," I said quietly rubbing the sensation of sparks from the end of my fingers.

"Exactly," Ollie said as he stood. "I'll keep you posted if I can," he said as he moved quickly toward his car across the courtyard. "Thanks." He waved the bag in the air in our general direction and then was off.

IT'S REALLY hard to follow up that kind of conversation with anything casual, so in fairly short order, we all picked up the remnants of our food, stacked the wicker chairs in the corner, and closed up the umbrella. Soon enough, Gray and I were alone again, and I was aching to move my body. "Fancy a little gardening?" I asked.

"Sure," he said, "I was going to go home and lay on the couch mindlessly, so this is probably a better option. Keep me from perseverating on this stuff." He waved a hand around the patio.

"Oh, I agree," I said. "Since the flower gardens are in pretty good shape, what do you think about working out front here?" I looked over at the beds of trees, shrubs, and other perennials that were finally leafed out all the way. "I think we have some trimming to do."

"What, you don't want your garden to turn into a jungle? Why ever not?" Gray teased.

"Well, did St. Patrick take the snakes out of England too or was that only Ireland?" I asked.

"We have snakes here, poisonous ones, even. Adders. They're nothing compared to your rattlesnake, and yet, yeah, you don't want to get bitten. Trimming is a good idea." He pointed toward the back. "While I get the tools, do you think you could make us some of that iced tea you've told me about?"

"Are you asking me to grace you with one of the truest delights of Southern American culture, sir?" I said laying my Virginia accent on a little thicker than usual.

"Yes, please," he said.

"Coming right up," I said as I hefted the beer cooler and headed inside to swap out cider and the terrible beer for brewed iced tea. How I was going to make it from loose tea leaves, I did not know. But I was confident that Google could guide me.

Sure enough, within 15 minutes, I had a pitcher of sweet iced tea, and Gray had gathered an armload of things that looked like they could either be garden tools or some part of a torture system from a horror film. "What is this?" I said as I put the tea and glasses down and picked up a long-handled piece of metal that looked like a half-circle. "A flat shovel?"

His response was to roll his eyes so hard that I thought

he might spend the rest of his life looking at his brain. "It's an edger, Nell."

"Nope, I know what an edger is. It's on a motor and has blades that spin. The pros on YouTube use them."

The second eyeroll made me doubly worried for him. "So you're lawncare expertise comes from YouTube videos?"

I grinned. "Not exclusively, no, but mostly, yes."

"Okay, while I get started, you watch this." He took out his phone, typed something in, and then handed it to me.

I looked down to see the screen beginning to play, of all things, a YouTube video from a channel called Acres Lawn Care. As soon as the host started speaking, I had to smile. He was undoubtedly English, and sure enough, there he was edging a garden bed with that circle thing Gray was using. The video was a short, so I didn't have long to gather my thoughts before it was over and I had to admit that I'd learned something.

I said, "Well, since we are in 'jolly ole England' I suppose I'll do it the slower way. Wouldn't want to break with tradition and all that?" My English accent was not getting better with practice.

"I appreciate your kowtowing to our traditions, my lady." He handed me the edger. "I've gotten you started."

While I edged the front bed, a job that turned out to be incredibly satisfying and peaceful, especially without the engine noise, Gray trimmed up the shrubs with a hand trimmer and what looked very much like Death's scythe.

Two hours later, my muscles ached in all new ways, but the central bed in the front "garden," as Gray kept calling it, looked just the right blend of tended and natural with the shrubs in loose forms instead of balls or boxes that so many people seemed to prefer but I abhorred. "This looks amazing," I said as I stretched out my shoulders.

"It does," he said. "Funny what you can do without a motor."

THE NEXT MORNING, though, I once again renewed my enthusiasm for combustion engines when I could barely roll over in bed to turn off my alarm. I ached from skull to shin, and while I knew that moving around would loosen me up and free the lactic acid from my muscles, all I could bring myself to do was pick up my phone and scroll.

By the time I levered myself upright, my bladder was screaming, and Dante's was, apparently, too, because he was pacing little circles by the bedroom door. I jogged downstairs to let him out with a stern warning about staying close, and then I went back up and took care of my own needs before throwing on yoga pants, the loosest t-shirt I could find, and a headband since washing my hair was not going to be possible with the way my arms ached.

Back downstairs, I was delighted to hear the dog give a single scratch at the door while I made coffee, and when I let him in, he acted as if we had been parted by centuries and oceans, almost knocking me over when he jumped up to kiss my face. "Alright, boy," I said. "You did a good job."

I reached into the cabinet below the sink and took out a bone I'd been saving for him and laid it on his bed, where he immediately curled around it and went to sleep.

"Clearly that pee was exhausting," I said as I turned off the kettle and prepared my coffee. Then, I pulled another one of Aunt Jelly's puzzles out of the cupboard, set it on the kitchen table, and turned on a podcast to spend this Sunday morning in quiet bliss.

I had just managed to put the edges on the flower calendar puzzle when someone knocked on the front door. I tried to hop up but ended up prying myself from the chair to answer, expecting to see Gray and instead finding Jazz, looking a little distraught.

"Come in," I said and led her to the kitchen table. "Tea?"

"Do you have any coffee left?" She said as she glanced at my half-empty mug.

"I have as much coffee as we need," I said as I moved to the cupboard, chose a mug, and filled it before setting it in front of her. "What's up?"

She took a long sip from her mug and sighed. "I miss coffee."

"Well, I always have it here if you need some," I said.

"Thanks. Danielle loves tea, and it just seems silly to brew two pots of two different things." She sipped again and then set the mug down heavily. "I'm scared."

I reached over and laid my hand over hers. "About Alex?"

She tilted her head back and forth. "Kind of about her, but more about Antoine. What is it going to do to him to find out his wife is a murderer?"

For a split second I almost made a joke about the man having to realize the kind of woman he'd chosen but fortunately realized how inappropriate that would be before I spoke. "Yeah, what a blow," I said. "But maybe it wasn't her. Remember Scarlett's theory that someone could have planted the feather to frame Alex?"

Jazz nodded. "I know. I just can't figure out who else would have had access to her dress besides Alex herself. It's not like it was hanging in the foyer or something."

"True, but let's think about this a bit more, even if it's just to give you something else to consider, okay?"

Jazz drained her mug. "Okay, but I need more of this."

I stood, took her mug, and returned it to her full before starting the kettle for our second pot of the day. While I waited for the water to boil, I said. "Let's start with basics. Where did Alex keep her dress before the wedding?"

"I assume it was hanging in her room, in the wardrobe or something, but I don't really know."

"Well, that's the first thing we have to figure out, and that shouldn't be hard, right?"

Jazz sipped her coffee and looked out the window for a long moment. "The only people who probably know are Alex and my brother, and asking them . . ."

"Right, asking them might tip them off. Got it." I measured out the coffee and then added water. "So maybe you saw where it was hanging but didn't think to remember it? I mean did you guys get ready together?"

Jazz shook her head. "Alex insisted on her own team for hair and make-up, so the bridesmaids were in a different room altogether. I didn't see her until we went down for the ceremony, and by then, she was already dressed."

I sighed but then had a flash of insight. "Okay, but the people who did her hair and make-up might know, right?"

Jazz looked at me and nodded with a smile. "Yes, they might, but I don't know who they were. I didn't even see them, I don't think."

I carried my own mug of coffee to the table and set it down before picking up my phone. "Fortunately, we know someone who knows." I winked at Jazz and pressed the screen.

Scarlett answered on the first ring with a perky, "Hi Nell. What's up?"

"Well, Jazz and I are thinking about your theory regarding the fact that someone might have framed Alex."

"Oh yeah?" she said quietly.

"Yeah, and we had a question that you might be able to answer?"

"Um, I'll try," she said.

"Can you tell us who did the bride's hair and make-up?"

Scarlett let out a light laugh. "Of course. One sec." I could hear the turning of pages, and then she came back on to say, "Local mother daughter team, great ladies. Here's their number."

I jotted down the digits and thanked Scarlett, who sounded quite happy to have assisted. Then, I immediately dialed the number she gave me, and when voicemail picked up, I left a message asking them to call me back and leaving my number and my company name. "No need to worry them before the call," I said to Jazz. "And who knows, maybe they'll get me some business."

My phone rang just a minute or two later, and it was the mother of the pair. She apologized for screening her calls, a fact that I commended her for given the persistence of tele-marketers. "I just have a quick question if you have a minute."

"Sure, dear," I said. "What can I do for you?" Her accent was full of tumble and rolling Rs. I wasn't sure but I thought she might have been Scottish.

I asked her about Alex's dress and where it might have been stored, and when she presumed that maybe the dress had gotten stained or such because of poor storage, I didn't correct her. "Poor woman. Hard to not have your perfect day be perfect, and on top of the murder and all," I said before she told me it was actually kept in its own room with the decorations and other items needed for the wedding itself. "I know because I had to fetch it after we got her into hair and make-up."

I thanked her, let her know I was taking reservations for summer and fall weddings, and told her I'd refer her, too before I hung up.

"What did she say?" Jazz asked as soon as I set the phone down.

"She said that anyone who had a key could have accessed that dress." I told her about the room where it was stored and that the entire wedding and house staff had probably been in and out of there all day. "Our suspect list just got much longer again," I said, not sure if that was a good or bad thing in the larger scope of the situation but very glad it eased some of the pressure about Jazz's sister-in-law.

"Okay, that's good," I said. "But I guess we should tell Ollie."

"He probably already knows, but yeah, we should make sure. Want me to call him?" I asked.

She nodded, pointing out that the fact that she was snooping into a murder that her sister-in-law might be guilty of wasn't probably the best idea.

I dialed Ollie, and as soon as I relayed the information, he confirmed that they had indeed known that and were working on a list of people who had access to the room. I told him about the mother-daughter hair and make-up team and shared their number, a tidbit that he thanked me for before hanging up.

"Now, what?" Jazz said.

"Now, we do the hardest thing. We wait."

. . .

FORTUNATELY, Jazz had a thing for jigsaw puzzles, so while we listened, not quite ironically, to the Buried Bones podcast, we shuffled through the box, tested pieces, and tapped a few into place in silence. My mom and I had always done jigsaw puzzles on vacations. We'd choose a hard one, commandeer the dining room or coffee table in whatever space we were staying in, and work on it between trips to historical sites, the beach, or out for dinner. People who were intense tourists probably would have found our idea of a vacation quite boring, but for us, it was perfect. Plus, it left Dad free to do whatever he wanted, which was usually read, visit a local museum, or nap.

There's also a sort of companionable silence that comes from working on something together. You can talk or not, and if you enjoy books on audio or podcasts, they are the perfect companions to puzzles. It's a combined level of companionship, productivity, and rest that heals something up in most people who have the inner workings that make sitting still amenable.

Gray was not one of those people, as evidenced by the fact that he walked in, made a cup of tea, sat down, tried three pieces, and then said he thought the donkeys needed brushing. When he stood, Jazz rose with him. "I think I'm going to head home. Maybe take a nap," she said.

I stood up and gave her a hug. "Keep us posted if you hear anything?"

"Yep. You do the same." She waved to Gray and went out the front door.

"She okay?" Gray asked as he took our mugs to the sink.

"Yes, fundamentally. But also, no. The strain of this is getting to her." I watched as her car pulled out of the drive.

"I can see why." He finished washing up the mugs. "Fancy some time with Clover?"

I gazed longingly at my puzzle and then nodded. "Yeah, the puzzle will be here when we get back." I winked at him, and he led us out to the paddock, where Clover let me brush her for almost an hour while giving Gray the donkey stink-eye.

Chapter Fourteen

AS WITH ALL THINGS, the weighty urgency of hearing what Ollie would find from the investigation into Alex's dress faded a bit with time. By the next morning, when I woke up to the almost-completed puzzle and a long list of errands to do to publicize the business, it was only at the back of my mind.

A friend back home had offered to design a flyer and a rack card for me to advertise the business, and my order of those had arrived over the weekend. So now, it was time to start my efforts to get work in earnest. I had invested a lot in flowers, and I needed to begin making back that investment asap.

My first stop for the morning was at Scarlett's office, and she readily agreed to hang a flyer on the neat bulletin board above her desk as well as keep a stack of rack cards to share with clients. As I handed her the materials, she asked, "Any new updates?"

She spoke quietly and glanced around the otherwise empty room, so I took it as my cue to be discrete as well. I shook my head. "We spoke with Ollie about things yester-day, and he was looking into everything. But no news yet."

Scarlett nodded somberly. "Poor Jazz."

I nodded, but as I turned to go, I noted the unease that had risen up in my chest at Scarlett's words. I didn't know what to make of it yet, but I was learning to "trust my gut," as the police dramas said. Something was off.

It wasn't until I had finished my deliveries and actually managed to secure a weekly flower supply gig for a local café in town that I let myself go back to think about Scar-lett's words. There was nothing wrong with what she said, of course. We all felt terrible for Jazz since she was the person closest to us in all this stuff.

No, the issue was with how she said it. I thought back to Scarlett's face in that moment, the way she'd looked down at her desk as she spoke, shuffling her papers. That was it. She was a little shifty. I wondered why. I also wondered if I should tell Ollie, but what would I say, "Scarlett wouldn't make eye contact when I expressed sympathy for Jazz." Somehow, I didn't think that was useful police knowledge.

Still, when Ollie called a few minutes later, I found I wasn't completely shocked when he said that Scarlett had told him that she thought she had seen Alex in her dress the night before the wedding.

I took a breath and then said, "Why didn't she mention this before?"

"I asked the same thing," he said. "She said she hadn't thought it was important until she heard about the feather." He paused.

"And she didn't want to say anything in front of Jazz," I added.

"Right." I sighed. "Well, that explains why she was a little shifty with me earlier when I asked about the case."

"What do you mean 'shifty?'" Ollie asked.

I recounted our conversation and the way she'd been a little dodgy when we talked.

I could almost hear him thinking on the other end of the line when I finished. Finally, he said, "That is odd because she told me she'd already called to tell Jazz what she'd seen, said she felt like she owed her that before she told the police."

"Oh," I said with a little squeak to my voice. "Maybe I got the wrong impression." I pursed my lips. "That is weird. Why would she be worried about telling me if Jazz already knew?"

"It's a good question, Nell." He cleared his throat. "But that was only one of the reasons I called. I wanted to know if you might be able to find some flowers – just a couple bouquets – for my mom's table for the May Day Festival."

"Sure, of course. When does she need them, I scrambled in my bag for a pen and paper."

Ollie sighed. "Tomorrow night. Sorry."

I laughed. "Two bouquets? I can do that."

"Oh great," he said, and I could hear the relief in his voice. "She's the festival chairperson this year, and she wants to make it the best yet. To do that, she needs lots of volunteers. And tomorrow night is the town meeting. Her best chance to get help."

I smiled. "Oh, that sounds like fun. A town meeting – how Gilmore Girls."

Ollie laughed. "Are you Lorelei?"

"You're a fan?" I asked. "No, I'm more of the eccentric ballet teacher. Are you Luke?"

"Are you kidding? You already met our Luke. He lives at your house." He laughed again and then hung up.

As I looked up the number for the florist they'd used for

Antoine and Alex's wedding, I couldn't help but laugh. Ollie was right – Gray was Luke, through and through, but with a rake instead of an apron.

FOR A BIT, I distracted myself by casting the people I knew in Stow as characters in the *Gilmore Girls*. Obviously, Jay was the more put-together Kirk, and Scarlet was maybe Lane. I didn't have a Rory yet, but Danielle definitely made a good Sookie. Jazz was, I thought, maybe Paris Geller, but with her kindness more obvious. I couldn't even begin to figure out who Dean or Jess would be because I had always fashioned myself a Rory even though I was now clearly more in the Lorelei category. "Clearly, I need to meet some teenagers," I said out loud.

At that exact moment, Gray walked in. "Why is that exactly?"

I laughed and blushed. I mused out loud a lot, but this was the first time I'd been caught since I was a child. "Oh, nothing. Just casting a show."

"Ah, a show with teenagers. Got it," Gray said before he lifted one eyebrow and looked at me. "Are you secretly a famous screenwriter hiding behind the ruse of a flower farmer?"

An image of myself in a beret with sunglasses and a director's chair flashed into my mind, and I laughed out loud. "No, certainly not. I don't even own a beret."

This made Gray stand stock still and stare at me. "A beret? What?"

I blushed harder as I realized that what I had imagined was not a shared experience, and yet, I had assumed Gray would get it. Why?

"Um, er, don't all directors wear berets?" I said.

"I think you're thinking of The Beat poets," he said with a laugh. "But also, I said screenwriter, not director." He came over and pulled me into a tight hug. "So that clears that up."

Then, a moment later, he pushed me gently out to arm's length and said, "So then why are you casting a show?"

"I need a Rory, Dean, and Jess," I said with an embarrassed smile.

Gray dropped his hands and stared at me. "You, too? I am gobsmacked."

Now, I was the one who wasn't following. "What are you talking about?"

"You and Ollie with the *Gilmore Girls*. What is it with that show?"

I cleared my throat and looked at him from under my lashes. "Excuse me, sir. You're the one who recognized the show from the names of the characters."

He sighed. "Only because Ollie has turned our guys' nights into Gilmore Girls binge watches too many times." Now, he was blushing and moved past me toward the stove where he began making tea.

"Oh, really, and you just stayed to watch out of what, some sense of friendship or something?" I asked as laughter began to swell in my belly.

"Exactly. You don't just leave a guy to watch a teenage romance on his own. That would be pathetic."

"It's not just a teenage romance," I said a bit too sharply. "What about Luke and Lorelei?"

Gray finished filling the kettle and set it back on the burner. "What about them? Is that really why you watched?"

"Well, yes, some," I said now clearly sounding defensive.

After a long moment, I sighed and said, "No, of course it was all about Rory and her boys."

"I knew it," Gray said and raised one finger in the air. "So who was your favorite?"

"My favorite of Rory's boyfriends?" I could not believe I was having this conversation and with a handsome British man who was making tea in my kitchen.

"Yes," he said. "Dean, Jess, Tristan—"

"Definitely not Tristan," I almost shouted. "Really?"

"Well, they did date." He handed me my tea and moved toward the table.

I sighed. "Yes, they did. Sadly."

"Agreed," Gray said as he passed me the sugar bowl. "Still, you have three – Dean, Jess, or Logan?"

I squinted at him. "You know these characters fairly well. How many seasons have you seen?"

He sipped his tea and then said, "All of them. Even the new one they put out a couple years ago." He stared as if daring me to tease him.

"All of them." I stared harder. "How many times?"

"Twice," he said as he finally broke eye contact.

"I see. So you are that good a friend," I said.

"I am," Gray replied with a lift of his chin. "Are you avoiding the question?

"Are you?" I said, and we locked eyes again until we both couldn't hold back the laughter.

"Alright, fine, Jess," I said, "but Logan was a close second."

"You like the bad boys?" Gray said as he put a hand to his heart.

"I like the literary boys," I said with a grin before taking his hand in mine. "Who did you think she should be with?"

"Logan, absolutely. He was steady and good, and he could keep her in books."

The man had a point. I started to tell him that Ollie clearly had him pegged as Luke, but the thought of Ollie brought back my call with him, and the memory must have changed something about my expression because Gray squeezed my hand. "What is it?"

I sighed and told him about what Scarlett had seen and about how she had, I was fairly sure, lied to Ollie about when she told Jazz.

Gray's brow furrowed, and he sighed. "That is fishy." He looked out the window. "Do you think Jazz actually knows now?"

I nodded. "Ollie was going to talk to her, and I thought I might go over there with some dinner for them tonight. Want to come?"

"Yes," he said. "Let's go into town and pick up some fish and chips." He glanced over at my grimace, "and chicken for you, and we'll go over."

Perfect," I replied before downing the rest of my tea. "Maybe they'll have something to add to the Starrs Hollow cast."

"Oh Lord," Gray said as he smiled.

WHEN WE KNOCKED at Jazz and Danielle's door, it took a long moment for someone to come to it. Danielle opened it just a crack, peeked through, and then swung the door wide. "Thank goodness. We thought it might be Alex and Antoine."

"Oh," I said as I moved past her and then stood awkwardly in the hallway. "Why is that?"

"Because we think they are at the police station being

questioned as we speak," Jazz said as I came through the door to my right. "I suppose you already know about Alex and the dress."

I couldn't tell from her tone if she was defensive or just exhausted. I decided to err on the side of grace. "We do. Scarlett told me, and I wanted to be sure Ollie knew." I held out the large aluminum foil tin in my hand. "We brought dinner."

"Bless you," Danielle said and took the shepherd's pie from my hands and the two parcels wrapped in newspaper from Gray. "I'll get this set up. Dinner in front of the telly okay with everyone?"

"Are we watching Gilmore Girls?" Gray asked with a sly glance at me.

"No, *Bridgerton*," Jazz said with an odd glance. "That okay."

I suppressed my snicker at the idea of Gray watching a period romance, but then my mouth fell open when he said, "Which season?"

"One," Jazz said as I turned to the room I just left. "We just started over."

"Oh good," Gray said. "It's worth watching start to finish."

I could not believe him. "You like a period romance?" I said.

"Don't tease," Jazz said in his defense. "He is the best judge of male character."

"Female, too," Danielle added as I handed first Jazz and then me a plate, mine without the fish and loaded with just the pie and chips. "He pegs the couples before even we do."

I glanced over at Gray, who was looking innocently at the TV, where women in empire-waisted dresses danced some "hands in the air" spinning thing with men in long coats. "You are full of surprises," I said.

"Don't judge," he replied and then winked at me. "Last year, the women and I watched the first two seasons in the dead of winter. It was a lovely escape."

I laughed. "Sounds like it. Well, I've never seen it, so I'll look forward to it."

Danielle almost dropped Gray's and my plates when she heard me. "What? Well, then we're going back an episode, right, Jazz?"

"Of course. You have to start from the beginning," she said to me. "We can make a bed for you here if you get too invested."

I grinned. "You're true fans, I see."

"You have no idea," Danielle added.

THEY WERE NOT WRONG. I finally had to force myself up and out of the sofa as the fourth episode ended because Dante was at home, and I could not leave him there alone. "I'm going to go now. Do not let the next episode start until I am out of the house," I said. "You want to stay?"

Gray shook his head. "No, I'll drive us back. Same time next week?"

Jazz and Danielle nodded enthusiastically. "It's a date."

I laughed as we climbed into Gray's car. "You are full of surprises."

He leaned over and kissed me gently. "Wait until I show you my Jane Austen collection." He winked and then started the Rover.

For most of the ride back, my mind was filled with Anthony and Siena, Daphne and Hastings, and such, but after a bit, I remembered Danielle at the door. She had looked almost scared.

"So Alex and Antoine were at the police," I said by way of broaching the subject.

"Yeah, I was just thinking about that." He paused. "Did they look a little, I don't know, frightened to you?"

"Yes," I said and spun in my seat to face him. "Exactly what I was thinking. Why would they be scared?"

He shook his head. "I don't know. Sad, I get, but they looked pretty terrified."

"And not scared *for* them, scared *of them*," I added.

"Yes, that's weird, right?"

"Seems so to me." I turned back to the windshield and stared out of it in silence. Something was off here, but I couldn't tell what.

When we got back, Dante nearly tackled me at the door. "Oh, boy. You missed me, huh?" The dog covered my face with licks from his wet tongue. "Alright, let's go outside." I reached for his leash, but the boy was out the door before I could even touch it.

I rushed after him, hoping he was going to be as obedient as he had earlier in the day, but this was a whole different Dante. This boy was "fired up" as my uncle used to say. He was sprinting from one end of the courtyard to the next, buzzing by Gray and me, and then doing another lap. The next time he came by, Gray fake lunged at him, and Dante took off even faster. Soon, the two of them were chasing each other in zigzags all through the front yard, and I was laughing so hard my sides hurt.

Eventually, both man and dog gave out of energy and lumbered back to the house. "That is," I said as I closed the door behind us, "what we call the Zoomies." I put my arm around Gray's waist. "I just didn't know people got them, too."

"Got to get the extra energy out somehow." He looked over to where Dante was sprawled and, remarkably, already asleep. "I'm now going to be like Dante in another way." He leaned over and gave me a soft kiss. "See you in the morning."

I smiled. "Looking forward to it."

THAT NIGHT, my dreams were a mix of running dogs and running people, sometimes for fun, and sometimes for their lives. I woke up the next morning just as the sun was coming up and the dread was making me nauseous. Something was very wrong, or at least my subconscious thought so.

But since I had no idea what to do about something I didn't consciously know, I decided to let the universe work it out and show me to intervene if needed. I was kind of surprised at myself that I wasn't reverting to my old ways of trying to control everything just to feel like life wasn't spinning off its axis. But this attitude felt easier, better on my spirit, so I went with it.

After coffee, I headed out to the garden in my grubbiest of grubby clothes and started to work on weeding. We had stayed on top of things fairly well so far, but I knew that a garden that wasn't tended every day or at least every other day could quickly get out of hand. And this wasn't some hobby garden. This was my business. I had to keep up.

Gray was, not surprisingly, already out there, scrub hoeing around the seedlings in the larger field. I gave him a wave, and he smiled as I picked up my own hoe and followed suit in the smaller garden. I was thrilled to see, as I removed tiny weeds from around the starts we'd planted, a couple of small buds forming on the cucumbers and squash. We were going to have fruit in a week or ten days.

My mind turned to a possible honor-system farm stand at the end of the drive, a small booth where people could pick up produce and flower arrangements and pay what they would. My mind spun to lock boxes and signage, even as I continued to hoe away the plants I didn't want. Soon enough, I had a full-blown plan for the stand, and when Gray came over after having finished his field, he helped me with the last row of mine as I told him about my idea.

By mid-afternoon, we had constructed, from leftover plywood and lumber, a six foot by three foot by two foot phonebooth-like structure. (Gray wanted to say it looked like an outhouse, but I wouldn't have that association with my new side business, I told him.) We carried it out the lane in the wheelbarrow, and I hung my hand-painted "farm stand" sign in front with a little plaque below it that said, "Coming soon."

We set the massive box that Gray had crafted from scrap plywood onto the small shelf in the corner, and Gray screwed it in, so no one was tempted to walk off with it. I took out the combination lock that I'd had since 9th grade, and attached it to the latch before spinning in the combination one more time just to be sure that I had, indeed, been using those brain cells to store those numbers for over 35 years.

When it worked for the fourth time, I looked at Gray and said, "I think I store this information in the same place as I do the lyrics to the French Prince of Bel Air."

"Ah, yes, that section of my brain includes ABBA lyrics and my gran's recipe for blueberry scones."

"I'm making a note to do karaoke with you and also get that recipe."

When we were done, Gray and I headed into town to pick up the flowers for the Town Hall, and then he left me at the hall, where I rummaged around until I found vases, while he went back to take care of the animals for the evening. "If you and Dante get the zoomies again, I'll need a video," I said as he waved.

WITH THE FLOWERS arranged and set on the table at the front of the hall, I followed Gray's instructions and left the key in the lockbox on the parking post by the door. Apparently, almost everyone in the town had the combination for the box, so I wasn't sure it made much sense to lock up the building at all. But I had lived in enough small towns in my life to know that it wasn't wise for the new person to point out flaws in the old ways.

The evening was beautiful, one of those spring nights where the gloaming turns everything silver and you can almost see the promise of summer in the air. I was glad I'd told Gray I'd like to walk home. I needed some time to relax, and walking was one of the things that always soothed me.

Since the town hall sat on the main square, I decided to take a quieter route home and turned toward the back of the building, where I'd seen a small alleyway through the window of the hall. Normally, in an American city, I wouldn't have walked down an alley alone, even in the daytime, but this one looked like it had been built in the 14th century and was lit, as the evening grew darker, with street lights much like the main roads.

The sun wasn't yet down, but between the flow of the

lights and the slanting sun, the alley looked like a passage into a magical portal, and I let my mind wander into an earlier time as I wondered what had happened along this way throughout history. Was this ever a market? Was it a tawdry, poor place at some point? Had families owned houses along here for generations?

I was absolutely caught up in my fantasy, so when I saw a couple walking toward me, I imagined them in medieval garb, young lovers out for an evening stroll. I was trying to figure out if I knew what the dating rituals of medieval England had been when one of the people stopped and grabbed my arm.

"You're that American, aren't you? The one who crashed our wedding." The woman's voice was harsh, and she was gripping my arm so tightly that I thought I'd have bruises.

Shock rang through my body as I realized the woman hurting me was Alex Johnson, the bride, the person who might have killed her own wedding planner. "Hi Mrs. Johnson," I said, not sure if Southern hospitality would work to diffuse a volatile situation here like it might at home but willing to try anything to get this woman to let go of me.

"Unhand her" Antoine said quietly. "Our apologies, Nell – may I call you Nell?"

I looked at Jazz's brother and noted, once again, the way his voice lilted like British English but was still accented like an American. "Yes, sure," I said, not certain whether he was mimicking my own polite tendency or if this was a genuine way of speech for him.

Alex looked at him and then dropped my arm. "Sorry," she said without sounding at all like she was. "We need you to stop meddling in our affairs." She glanced at Antoine again and added a rather apathetic, "please" to her request.

"I'm sorry," I began.

Alex interrupted with a forced smile. "Your apology is appreciated. We can trust, then, that you'll drop your queries?"

I stared at her a long minute before I realized my mouth was literally hanging open. "Oh, no, I wasn't apologizing for my actions. I was going to say, I'm sorry that you think the investigation into a murder is meddling, but I will continue to assist the police in any way I can." I wasn't sure why I felt like now, in the late evening along an alley alone with two people who were obviously quite upset with me was the best time to stand up for myself and what was right, but I apparently did. Still, as soon as the words were out of my mouth, I braced for impact.

I even think I saw Alex start to draw her arm back, but then, the cheerful ting of a bicycle bell rang behind me, and I saw Jay riding up, a huge smile on his face. "Hiyo," he said as he pulled to a stop beside me. "Saw you down here, Nell, and wanted to catch up." He put out his hand to Antoine and said, "Hi, I'm Jay."

Antoine hesitated only a second before shaking Jay's hand. Jay then extended it to Alex, who stared at his fingers like they were octopus tentacles.

"Antoine is Jazz's brother," I said, "and this is his wife, Alex." I was still wary, but I felt a lot better with Jay by my side.

"Oh, it's nice to meet you both," Jay said. "Nell, I was heading your way to see Gray. Fancy a ride on the handle-bars like we're kids."

Normally, the thought of going head first into the road or shrubs would have stopped me, but in this instance, I thought the risk of traumatic brain injury might be lower than the risk to my life of standing in this alley with Alex a minute longer.

"Yes, please," I said as I clumsily hoisted myself up onto the front of his bike. "It was, er, good to see you both," I said and then held on for dear life as Jay sent us breezing out of the alley and up the road.

When we were out of the main part of town, he pulled over, and I hopped off. "You okay?" he asked as he stepped off the bike and started to walk it beside me. "That looked intense."

"Oh, you saw that," I said, suddenly feeling both relief and tears bloom to my face. "That was really scary."

"She looked like she was going to hit you."

"She might have if you hadn't come along." she paused. "And for some reason, I don't think Antoine would have stopped her."

"Really?" Jay said. "Wow."

"Yeah, that was weird." I shook my head to clear it a bit. "But anyway, thank you, my knight on a not-so-shiny BMX. Oh and I never thanked you for my saddle bags. They're great. Thank you."

"My pleasure. It was one thing to see your aunt slowly making her way down the road with that huge box on her handlebars. But I figured you'd like to have a bit more agility." Jay laughed. "I was actually headed your way. Gray and I are going to go to the trivia quiz. Want to come?"

I had never been much for trivia in the U.S., although as my mother always said, I have a head full of useless information. But here, it sounded more appealing, so for a second, I considered joining them. Then, I paused and realized I was completely exhausted and all I wanted was to settle in with a book and a big dog. "Thanks so much. Maybe next time?"

"Sounds good," Jay said as we turned into my lane. "You are going to tell Gray and Ollie what happened, right?"

"I will," I said, feeling even more weary at the thought, "but could I ask you to give them the short version tonight, that is if Ollie is going to be there. If not, I'll call him in the morning."

Jay nodded. "Absolutely." He walked me to my door. "You okay here alone? I'm sure Gray could stay if you wanted."

I shook my head. "Please don't tell him what happened until you're at the pub, and then, remind him that Dante is here." As if on cue, the giant dog bounced against the door and circled us before heading to the corner of the courtyard to relieve himself.

"Fair point," Jay said as Dante headed back over and immediately sat beside me, his head pressing up into my hand. "He clearly knows who his person is."

I smiled and scratched the wooly head. "I'm glad of that. I'll be fine. I'll keep my phone nearby."

Jay nodded and turned his bike back around to the back of the house toward Gray's apartment.

"Come on, boy," I said as Dante leaned against me, forcing me to brace myself against the entryway. "Let's get you some dinner and me some tea before we settle in."

I turned and locked both locks on the door before following my dog into the kitchen.

Chapter Fifteen

ALMOST THE MINUTE I walked into my kitchen the
following morning, there was a knock at the door, and when
I opened it, I found Gray there, looking quite anxious.
"You're okay then?" he asked.

I studied him and nodded. "I'm just fine. I take it Jay
told you what happened?"

"He did but not until it was late, and when I got here, all
your lights were off." He cleared his throat. "I let myself in
– sorry about that – but saw that Dante was asleep in the
living room and took that as a sign that all was well."

"You were that worried?" I knew that some people
might have been annoyed at Gray's forwardness, but I actually just found it touching.

"I was. Nell, someone attacked you last night. What
might have happened if Jay hadn't come along?"

I grinned and reached over to hook behind the door. "I
did have my trusty lanyard. I would have used it if
need be."

He studied the hot pink string attached to my keys. "What?"

By way of answer, I slipped the string over my neck and took a few steps back. Then, I tugged hard enough to open the latch, swung the lanyard over my shoulder and then whipped it forward a few inches in front of Gray's face. "See?"

"Bloody hell," he said as he put his hands up. "That thing could knock someone out."

"That's the point. I don't have to get too close, but I can inflict damage. Saw it in a TikTok."

He nodded. "I'm impressed. And here I thought you just needed a big pink thing so that you wouldn't lose your keys."

"That too," I said with a laugh. "But thank you. I'm just about to make some coffee. Want some?" I hung my weapon back up and stepped back to let him in.

"Yes, please," he said as he glanced over to where Dante was still sound asleep. "Maybe I shouldn't have counted on him to protect you?"

"Are you kidding? That guy's eyes opened the minute you knocked." I bent over and rubbed the sleeping dog's belly. "But he knew your scent and recognized your voice. If you had been intent on harming me, he would have taken your arm off."

"Alrighty then," Gray said with a shy smile. "Next time I might lose sleep worrying about you, I won't. You've got things covered."

"You're sweet," I said as I headed across the hall to the kitchen. "But us women have been taking care of ourselves for a long time, mostly to fend off the likes of you men. We've got this."

"So noted," Gray said as he took a seat and let his head

drop into his hands at the kitchen table. "So what did they want, Alex and Antoine?"

"For me to stop 'meddling' apparently," I said with air quotes.

"Have you actually been meddling?" he asked as I put on the kettle. "Has something happened that I don't know about?"

I shrugged. "Not that I know of. I've just been asking questions and telling Ollie everything." I smiled at him as I poured the water in the French press. "Been telling you everything too. I don't like secrets."

Gray beamed. "Me neither. So why do they think you're the problem? And why do they care?"

"My guess is that they can't exactly threaten Ollie or his colleagues, so Alex decided to bully me instead. But for why? I'm afraid the only reason I can come up with is that they have something to hide."

He nodded as he took his mug of coffee. "That's what I was thinking, too, and Ollie said the same thing."

As if saying his name had summoned him, a knock on the door was followed by Ollie's "halloo" as he stepped into the hallway. Once again, Dante opened his eyes, sniffed, and went promptly back to sleep. The dog, apparently, had astute senses and the bladder of a camel.

"Hi Ollie," I said as he came in. "Coffee? Tea?"

"No thanks," he sat down across from Gray. "Just came to get your statement about the assault last night."

I rolled my eyes. "I hardly think it was an assault."

"Yeah, those bruises on your arm tell a different story," the policeman said.

I looked down and noticed, for the first time, the four purplish finger prints on my forearm. "Oh," I said. "Well, maybe, I guess. They were just trying to scare me."

"There's no *just* about it, Nell. Alex Johnson assaulted you, and I need to know if you want to press charges." He studied me a minute. "No matter what you say, I will be addressing this with her and her husband when I go to speak with them today about the dress."

"Charges? No, I'm not pressing charges against Jazz's sister-in-law."

"Why not?" Jazz said from the doorway behind me. "She attacked you. She deserves to face the consequences."

I looked at my friend and then over my shoulder to her wife behind her. "Clearly, I have an open-door policy, huh?" I smiled and hugged them both. "Aren't you supposed to be at the coffee shop?"

"Someone is covering for me," Jazz said. "When Ollie told me what Alex had done, I wanted to be sure you were okay first thing."

Tears threatened to spill into my eyes, but I quickly turned away, cleared my throat, and got out more mugs while I composed myself. I'd never had friends like this, friends who cared this much, and it was beautiful.

When I held a mug each out to Jazz and Danielle, I was more composed and said, "Really, I am fine, despite the bruises. It was a bit scary, but I'm fine." I turned to Ollie. "And I don't want to press charges, more for my sake than Alex's. I'm just getting set up here, and I really don't have the bandwidth to handle anything more."

Gray stood up and put his arm around me. "That makes sense. But if she causes you any more trouble, you promise you'll let us know and take legal action."

I nodded. "Promise." Then, I turned to Jazz. "I'm so sorry this is happening. Your brother must be distraught."

With a tilt of his head, Gray suggested we all move to

the living room, where there was more room to sit, and so with mugs in hand, we placed ourselves in comfy seats.

Jazz took a long deep breath and said, "Please don't repeat this, even you, Ollie, at this point, but he's not. It's weird. He doesn't seem bothered at all by Alex's behavior."

We all stared at her but then I moved my eyes to my coffee. So Danielle continued. "Jazz called him this morning," She put her hand on her wife's leg, "and he told her she was overreacting, that you had overreacted, Nell. That Alex was just trying to get some peace and quiet as a newlywed."

Ollie cleared his throat. "I won't use this information from you, Jazz, but I had the same impression when I talked with him yesterday. He just kept defending her, but not passionately. Almost dispassionately so."

I thought a minute. "Forgive me if I'm overstepping here, but how are relations between police and black people here? Back in the States, a black man might have to really contain himself to keep himself safe in some circumstances."

Jazz sighed. "Things are better here, but not great. The thing is, though, that Antoine never bought into the idea that it was his responsibility to protect himself. If someone assaulted him for no reason, that was on the other person, not him."

I nodded. "I respect that, but that also erases another reason for his aloofness, right?"

Ollie was studying his hands. "I hate to say this, Jazz—"

"He's protecting her," Jazz interrupted, "which means he knows she did it."

"I fear so," Ollie said.

I was about to ask what that meant for Antoine if it was

true, when there was a frantic knock at the door. I jumped up and ran over to find Pree standing there.

"Come quickly. I need help." She ran off across the courtyard again.

"Hurry, Pree needs us," I shouted back into the living room and then took off after her.

When I reached the lane, I saw the situation. A herd of sheep was blocking the entire roadway, and a lone teenage boy was trying to herd them onto a trail that they, apparently, found utterly terrifying.

The sound of footsteps behind me meant our friends had arrived, and soon enough, we'd formed a human fence and guided the wayward animals back towards home. Once they were through the gate, they were content enough to head on down the trail, so the boy stopped for a moment to thank us.

"Minnie, my border collie, ate something nasty and needed to rest today. The sheep saw my weakness," the kid said.

"Indeed," Pree replied. "Well, we've got you Jimmy, and if Minnie needs a checkup, bring her by later, okay?"

"Thanks, Doc," Jimmy said and then headed off across the field behind his sheep, looking every bit the 18th century lad except for his Doc Martins.

"Nothing like a bit of adventure," Pree said. "Thanks for the help." She turned back to me. "I was actually headed your way. I have some news about Dante."

"Oh, really," I said. "Good news?" I was suddenly even more anxious than I had been with the sheep and the conversation about Antoine.

"Both," Pree said. "Have any coffee?" She picked up her bike that had fallen into the shrubs by the road.

"Always," I said and resisted the urge to get her to tell

me the news right there in the middle of the roadway. The six of us made our way back up the drive, and while everyone else went back to the living room, Pree helped me brew more water and make a fresh pot of coffee.

Only when we were back in the room with the coffee and all the other people, did Pree say, "Congratulations, Nell. You are now the owner of a registered, certified, full-bred Irish wolfhound."

"What?" I said. "What?" I couldn't seem to say anything else.

Pree slipped from the sofa down to the floor where Dante was, remarkably, still snoozing. "We found the owners," Pree said.

My heart skipped. "Oh?"

"They're a lovely older couple from a few miles north. They lost Gandalf – isn't that a great name for a Wolfhound? – a few weeks ago, and they had given up on finding him when one of their children saw your notices around town." I sighed. "But in the meanwhile, they had realized that the dog had been running them ragged. They live in a cottage with a small garden, and they just couldn't exercise him enough." She looked up at me.

I just stared, not wanting to jump to conclusions just yet, even though Pree had already told me the end of this story. I just wasn't ready to believe it.

"They called me because they were a little nervous to talk to the person who had found him just in case it wasn't good news, I told them that he was happy and well and living with an American who had just moved to Stow."

I watched her, my breath hitched in my chest now. "And?"

"They were delighted and asked if you'd like to keep him. I hope you don't mind but I answered for you and told them yes." Pree now looked a little nervous. "Did I overstep?"

With one quick motion, I moved to the floor and hugged her and Dante. "Not at all. Dante, boy, you're home!"

He lifted one ear, let out a contented sigh, and closed his eyes again. Clearly, he understood, almost as if he had planned this all along.

"Cheers," Ollie said as he lifted his mug. "To Nell and Dante." He paused. "Or is he Gandalf?"

I studied the dog a minute and leaned down to whisper "Gandalf" in his ear. He didn't stir. So I tried the same thing with "Dante." He let out a small bark without even opening his eyes.

"Dante it is, then," Gray said. "Speaking of which, we probably need to force his royal highness to go out, right?"

I nodded. "He apparently has great perseverance when it comes to uninterrupted rest, but I would rather not clean up the floor today."

"I've got him then," Gray said as he stood. "Who wants to see Nell's garden?"

Everyone stood and began to follow him out the door, even Dante, except for Jazz. She held back after squeezing Danielle's hand.

As soon as the room had cleared, I reached over and hugged her. "Wow, this is so hard. Are you okay?"

I held on to her for a minute longer and then said, "Yeah. Mostly. But something is up, Nell, something with my brother and his wife."

"Yeah," I said softly. "I think so, too. How do you want us to support you? What do you want us to do?"

"Find out the truth. Whatever it is. I can deal with it if I just know it." She smiled at me and then went out the front door.

I took a few moments to gather myself by rinsing out the mugs and tidying the kitchen before I joined everyone in the garden. I was spinning a little bit with the news about Dante, the sheep herding, but especially the idea that Jazz's brother could be a true-life accessory to murder. I couldn't imagine what she was feeling, and I felt a pang of sympathy for Ollie, too, because he was in a truly awkward position with all this.

Still, there wasn't anything I could do besides support my friends in the way they found best, so I stayed myself, grabbed my gardening gloves, and headed out to work. I found everyone standing around the donkey paddock. Well, almost everyone, Ollie was sitting on the ground near the paddock gate with Pree kneeling near him. He looked a little stunned.

"What happened?" I jogged the last few steps to the group.

"Oliver here thought he was the donkey whisperer," Pree said as she pulled Ollie's shirt back down. "Nothing that won't heal. No broken ribs, luckily. But you're going to be sore."

"She kicked you," I exclaimed. "Why?"

"I tried to pet her," Ollie said forlornly.

"From behind, after being warned," Gray added to me.

"Oof, yeah, she doesn't like to be touched by most people, especially men, and even I know you don't approach a donkey or a horse from the back," I said and then winced. "Sorry. I'll pay for your medical stuff."

"No way," Ollie said as he stood without taking his eye off of Clover. "I was here on police business. Workman's comp for this one," he said patting his side and then grimac-ing. "It's my fault, though. I was warned."

I walked over to Clover, who turned to me eagerly, awaiting the apple she could obviously smell in my pocket. "Bad girl," I said. "You can't just kick people."

She was now nuzzling closer and closer to my pocket.

"I'm inclined not to give you your apple today because of your bad behavior. What do you say to that?"

The donkey looked up at me and looked, remarkably, like the donkey from Shrek. It's like her eyelashes had gotten longer just so she could guilt me into giving her a treat, and of course, it worked.

"Fine, here," I said. "But next time you kick someone, it's no apples for a week."

Clover turned, still chewing my apple, and did a high kick into the air with both feet as if to say, "Oh yeah. We'll see."

"Whew, that one is sassy," Pree said. "Good guard donkey." I followed the three animals with my eyes as they made their way back across the pasture with Dante trailing beside them outside the paddock. "Dante is a smart dog."

"Indeed," I said. "So what do you think?" I gestured toward the two fields of seedlings.

"Wow, Nell," Danielle said. "You have got an entire garden here. You've done a lot of work."

"Thanks," I said. "We'll start to have flowers in a few weeks, I think." I pointed toward the cosmos whose spidery stems were already up to my ankles. "Nothing substantial until summer, but I'll be able to put out a few bouquets by the road."

"Oh yeah, I saw that," Ollie said. "You've got your busi-ness license squared, right?"

I nodded. "And it includes retail sales, so I'm all set. Thanks for checking."

"Yeah, I hate to be that guy, but it's either me or a ticket from someone else." He smiled at me. "I'd make a copy of your license and hang it out there. Just to be clear."

"Good idea," I said. "Thanks."

"Well, we best be off," Jazz said. "Thanks for being there, folks."

Everyone smiled, sadly, and when Ollie offered Pree a ride back into town, it was just Gray and me and the donkeys. "What a morning," he said. "

"I'll say." I took a deep breath. "I'm going to do a little thinning and hand-weeding. What's your morning include?"

"I was going to mow now that the grass is drying out." He headed toward the garage. "Want a tractor lesson in a bit?"

"I have driven a tractor before," I said dryly.

"Not this one you haven't. It's 250 years old and finicky." He smiled at me. "You'll master it, though. Just need me to show you the quirks."

"Alrighty then. Although I may not be as up on my industrial history as I thought, but I'm pretty certain 250 years ago, it didn't exist." I laughed.

"This is England, my dear. Everything is older than you're used to," he said and then practically skipped away.

FOR THE REST of the morning, I stayed my tiny grief over the loss of so many seedlings, as I thinned them to a spacing that would give the ones that were left an optimal opportunity. It was always the hardest part of gardening for me, having to sacrifice so many plants.

My experiment in thinning and then replanting the tiny seedlings in a new spot had failed all three times I'd tried it. The shock of the movement was just too much for the little root systems, and when I'd tried letting things just grow without thinning, everyone had come out wan and spindly. My other option was to seed more sparingly, but then I had ended up with a thin crop because of the seeds that didn't germinate. Thinning was, as gardeners for eons had proven, the best way.

Still, when I was done, I was still a little sad but found my spirits lifting when Gray pulled the tractor over to where I was drinking water and asked, "Are you ready? I left a big patch for you to mow."

"Yes, sir," I said before attaching Dante's collar to his long lead, an action he didn't even bother to shift for because, apparently, his sunbeam was that good.

Gray was right. Although I had driven all kinds of tractors, I had never driven one that required this many special movements to get it to go. Pump the gas three times before starting. Shift only from first to third, never to second. Reverse required a lifting up on the gearshift to slip it in to place. Soon enough, though, the motions were natural, and I was mowing away at the far field and dreaming of a wildflower meadow.

After riding along with me for a bit to be sure I had it, Gray hopped off and grabbed a rake to begin piling the grass clippings. Nothing was tall enough to be true hay yet, but I appreciated that he was, as I saw it, tidying the field. It turned out, though, that I didn't have the full story. Apparently, the clippings were great treats for both chickens and donkeys, so when I was done mowing, we raked everything into a pile that we pitchforked onto a trailer before hauling it to the animals. I wasn't sure that chickens had a true facial expression for joy, but their feet sure did. They were scratching and clucking away after just the first fork full.

"I have a confession," I said to Gray as we stood and watched the birds sort through their gift like it was gold.

"Yeah?" he said with a twinkle in his eye.

"Um, I'm scared of chickens." I forced a smile and looked at him. "I know it's ridiculous."

"Not at all. They're like mini-T-rexes. I get it. But they really are sweet. Want me to show you?"

"How?"

"Come on," he said as he approached a plump brown bird with ivory feathers on its chest. He bent down, scooped up the hen, and held her against his side like a football.

"They just let you pick them up?" I said staring at the chicken who seemed quite comfortable.

"Not all of them. They have personalities like all of us do." He turned toward two silver and black birds in the corner. "Those are more timid, but if you sit with them a while, they'll come over. This girl, right here, though, she's quite tame. Want to hold her?"

I did not want to hold her, but I also wanted very much to know her. So I put out my arms, and Gray placed her in them before folding my right arm around the bird so I could hold her to my chest. She didn't seem bothered in the least, and it even felt like she might have settled against me a bit.

"They're a bit like kittens," Gray said. "They like to hear your heartbeat."

I smiled, remembering the litter of kittens my family had rescued when I was about 8. Those tiny babies had laid against my neck or chest every night until they were old enough to go to their new homes.

"What's this one named?" I asked as I got brave and rubbed its back a bit.

"Oh, I haven't named them, but you could." He smiled at me.

"Okay, I will. This one is Starbuck," I said as the first name popped into my mind. "I'm going to name them all after sci-fi characters."

"Nice choice to begin with Battlestar Galactica." He grinned at me and then looked at the two silver and black birds in the corner. "Might I suggest Spock and Silar for those two?"

"Perfect," I said and before long we had names from Star Wars to Star Trek to Firefly for the birds. "I hope I can keep these all straight."

"Knowing you, you'll have them mastered by the end of the day." He smiled at me. "But I do have one question."

"Hmm?"

"Can we re-name the tractor?" he asked. "I've always thought he had a rebel spirit, more feisty than a pumpkin."

"Cody," I said, again not hesitating. I loved naming things.

"Cody?" Gray looked very puzzled.

"Like Buffalo Bill Cody. That guy has a cowboy spirit if I ever saw one." I smiled, remembering that not only had Cody come to befriend many of the Lakota and other tribes in the West but had also become a great advocate for their rights later in his life. "Sometimes," I finished, "people do their best work in their last years."

Gray smiled, and we headed toward the house with Dante following behind. I had done my best to put thoughts of Alex and Antoine out of my head for the day, but I had made a promise to Jazz. Now, I needed to think about how I was going to keep it.

While Gray rummaged through my cabinets and found the makings for curry for dinner, I told him what Jazz had asked me. I wanted his opinion about what, if anything, we could do to help find the truth.

As he mixed spices and coconut milk into the tofu he has browned, he said, "I think Ollie would welcome our help."

"Really?" I asked before I thought about his statement. I was so accustomed to the idea that the police operated autonomously that it felt a bit impossible that they would accept citizen help, even in another country. "I guess he did ask for our help before, huh?" I said as my memories caught up with my instinct.

"He did," he responded. "He can let us help where it's actually helpful and steer us away where it's not." He dished our food onto two plates and carried it over. "The question, though, is do you want to be involved. You've been threatened once already?"

I thought about his question while I took my first bite of his delicious food. "This is amazing," I said with my mouth full and then realized my rudeness and used my fingers to cover my mouth.

"Thank you," Gray said with a slight blush. "It's basically the only thing I know how to make. Never done it with tofu, but I'm glad it turned out."

"It's lovely," I said as I took another mouthful. After I chewed this time, I said, "Yes, I do want to help. Jazz told me something about Antoine this morning, that he didn't buy into civility politics, that if someone treated him badly, he held that person entirely responsible. That's how I'm thinking about this situation. If Alex comes after me again, that's on her."

Gray chewed thoughtfully, not looking nearly as solid as

I felt, but then he nodded. "I respect your decision, and I'm in all the way." He smiled at me. "Want to see if Ollie fancies a pint?"

I grinned. "Is there ever a time when Ollie doesn't fancy a pint?"

"Fair point," Gray said.

Chapter Sixteen

NOT AN HOUR LATER, the three of us were in a quiet corner of The Fox and Compass, a pint before each of us. Ollie had readily agreed to meet up, probably for the pint but also because Gray told him we wanted to help. After his first sip, he said, "Alright, so I've thought of some things you can do."

On the way over, I'd asked Gray if this was a British police thing, this willingness to work with civilians. He'd actually laughed out loud at the question. "No, most certainly not. This is an Ollie thing."

Now, Ollie was doing his thing. "First, Nell, I need some more information from Scarlett. She's still acting suspiciously, and I need to know why. Do you think you can suss out what's happening with her?"

"You don't think she's the murderer," Gray asked with a tinge of anxiety to his voice.

"I don't think so. I can't say definitively of course. She clearly gains from Arrabella's death. But no, I don't think so." He turned back to me. "This is one of those things that is going to take some finessing, maybe a little manipulation. You comfortable with that?"

I sighed. "Sadly, the Southern American woman is trained from a young age to be a master of manipulation as her most subtle and effective power, sometimes her only one. It's not my favorite thing, but I can do it. Just know, I won't do anything that would harm Scarlett, not even emotionally."

"Fair enough," Ollie said. "And Gray, I need your help with Antoine."

"Stag do?" Gray asked.

"Belated stag do," Ollie said with a smile.

"Um, stag do?" I said.

"I think you call it a Bachelor Party," Ollie said. "I don't know if Antoine had one, but if he did, we weren't invited, and that's just not acceptable." He grinned.

"Clearly not," I said, "but no women, right?"

"No, not our thing," Gray said. "Just pints and snooker."

"Oh, I know snooker. It's like pool, right?" I said with excitement.

Ollie put his hand on mine gently. "Actually, pool is derived from snooker." He gave me a patronizing smile and then continued, "Now that we have our assignments, let's enjoy these." He took a long pull from his glass.

THE NEXT MORNING, I began my part of the investigation. When I thought the word *investigation*, I put it in quotes, like I was just pretending, but of course, this situation was very real, nothing playful about it.

I had lay awake some of the night making my plan. I

could have just gone full bore with some scheme to get Scarlett to trust me completely and then see if I could get her to confess anything. But there were two problems with that plan – one, I had no idea how to get someone to confess, and two, I wasn't comfortable with that deep a level of manipulation. If it turned out that Scarlett had nothing to do with the murder, I'd have tricked her profoundly. Plus, I didn't want to ruin a potential business relationship if she was actually innocent.

So I decided to go with honesty. Not complete honesty – I wasn't going to tell her that Ollie had asked me to talk to her – but otherwise, I was just going to tell her what was going on. I hoped that would work.

As soon as her office opened at 9, I gave Scarlett a ring and when she answered, I invited her over at lunch to see the garden and make suggestions about what other flowers might be popular for weddings. I was actually eager to get a professional wedding planner's input, if not for this season since we had already finished seeding, but for next – or for when some of the annuals finished and I had more room later this year.

"I'd love that. Mind if I come a bit earlier? I have staff here until Noon, so it's easier to step away."

"Of course," I said a flush of anxiety zoomed through me. "Anytime."

"Great, I'll be right over." She sounded positively delighted, and I felt immediate guilt for what was about to happen.

Still, by the time she arrived a few minutes later, I had steadied myself into my plan with the reminder that a woman had been killed. "Hi Scarlett," I said as she stepped out of her car. "Thanks for coming."

"I cannot wait to see the gardens," she said. "And I

brought a list." She held up a white notepad with what looked to be quite an extensive list of flowers on it.

I sighed and smiled. "Great," I said. "I should warn you. I only got the idea to invite you after we finished our first seeding – my mistake. But I'd love your notes for when I can plant new things or for next year."

The news didn't even slow her down as we took the corner around the house. "Oh, that's exciting. That means you'll have flowers when? I have a full slate of weddings and want to use you, as the local farmer, as much as possible."

Guilt stabbed me because she seemed so sweet, but I, again, forced myself to remember Arabella's body and plowed forward. "That's wonderful. I'm honored. Thank you." I smiled. "I actually asked you over for another reason, too, if I'm honest."

I looked over at her with bright eyes. "Yes?"

I took a deep breath. "I can't stop thinking about who might have killed your boss," I blurted. Not the most gentle of entrances into the conversation, but here we were.

Apparently, I was more graceful than I realized because Scarlett stopped walking and turned to me. "Me neither. It's just awful."

I was not an expert at sussing out liars, but she seemed pretty sincere to me. So I plowed ahead. "I've actually been looking into her murder a bit. I know the police haven't arrested anyone yet, and I can't help but try to figure out who did it." I shrugged with feigned nonchalance. "I'm just too nosy for my own good."

Scarlett nodded. "I've been doing the same thing, and to be honest, I think I'm a suspect, too. It makes sense since I got the business and all. But I didn't do it, of course, so I'd like to clear my name. But also, most importantly, I guess, I just want to find out who killed Arabella." Tears pooled in her eyes. She was either an incredibly good actor, or she was telling the truth.

"You cared about her," I said.

"I did. She was awful. But I've learned that when people are awful it's almost always because they are hurting." She wiped her eyes. "I'm no saint, but I try to accept people for who they are."

I cleared my throat as tears threatened to form in my eyes too. "That's very gracious of you. Do you know why she was so, um, broken?" I turned to the language from Vacation Bible School because in this moment, it felt fitting.

"Not completely, no," Scarlett sighed. "But I do know that her fiancé left her at the altar on their wedding day."

That lump worked its way back up into my throat. "How awful!"

"It was, but she acted as if it was her major success, said it was what led her to arrange weddings." Scarlett cleared her throat and dropped it in pitch a bit, "'I want to design weddings so perfect that no one will want to walk away.'" Her imitation of Arabella seemed pretty good to my ear.

"Wow, that's quite a motivation, and a lot of pressure."

I started looking at the flower list again. "I told her that, too, but I don't think she could hear anything any one said to her, even the compliments. She really did plan the most amazing weddings, but I'm not sure she could ever believe that."

My encounter with the wedding planner had been very brief, but I could see the truth in what Scarlett was saying. This woman was so wounded that she could not possibly see the light if she didn't look for it herself.

I let the subject drop, though, confident now that Scarlett was not the murderer, and we spent an hour walking the garden and talking about what I would need and what I might add on a second planting. By the time we got around to greeting the donkeys, I felt more confidence than ever that my farm was going to succeed.

And I also felt like I had made a new friend. Apparently, Clover agreed because she didn't even turn away when Scarlett went to scritch her neck. Despite her curmudgeonly attitude, I trusted the donkey's sense of people. If she liked Scarlett, then she was a good one.

OUR "BUSINESS" concluded, Scarlett headed into her shop with the promise that she was going to start talking to couples about my flowers asap, and as she drove out the lane, I saw Gray step out of the barn. "How did it go?" he asked with a small smile.

I laughed. "Were you in there the whole time?"

"Well, I hadn't realized the interrogation was going to happen in the garden, and I didn't want to throw it off." He shrugged. "On a positive note, the barn is very tidy."

"Well, thank you," I said. "I didn't know barns could be tidy, but then, I don't know much about barns."

"Oh, you will learn," he quipped as he planted a kiss on my cheek. "Are you ready to tackle the great estate sale set up?"

It took me a moment to realize what he was saying, and then, it hit me—tomorrow was Saturday, and we were having the sale of our more valuable items. "Oh my word. I had completely forgotten. Yes, we need to get things out, right?"

"Actually," Gray said, as he put my hand through his arm and led me back toward the barn, "I had another plan if you don't mind."

When he opened the doors, my mouth quite literally fell

open as I gasped. "Gray, this is beautiful." I smacked his arm lightly. "And not at all just a tidy. Wow." Not only had Gray cleared the main space on the barn floor so that only clean straw covered it, but I could now see the stone walls that rose to about my waist, and with the Edison lights he had strung over the space, it looked like a wedding venue.

"Do you think this will work for the sale?"

"Um, yes, and it will be the most high-class estate sale in England's history."

He practically beamed with delight. "For a long time, your aunt and I tossed around the idea of renting the barn out for events, but her idea of an event space was very high society."

"Well, this is pretty high society where I'm from," I said with delight.

"I don't doubt it, but here, this is very informal, very casual. Think about what Antoine and Alex's wedding was like. That was high society here." Gray studied my face.

"Ah, I see. So high society means expensive and fancy. I get it." I wasn't sure I did, but I was beginning to understand the way that class still operated here in England in much stronger ways than it did in the States. "Well, I think this is perfect for events, weddings even, and it would be a great way to make some extra cash for the farm as long as we don't have to do anything but provide the space."

"Well, great," he said. "Although I don't know how many people will have a wedding here. They tend to be posh affairs."

"Got it. I'll let Scarlett come by and see it, and we can work up a price list for events." One thought hit me though. "What about bathrooms?" I didn't love the thought of a bunch of strangers traipsing through my living room to use the facilities.

"Good news. That's the first thing that your aunt did when she started thinking about the idea. Come with me." He led me out the wide barn doors and around the side to the little addition I had seen but not much attended to yet. There were just so many structures here. "These are wheelchair accessible restrooms."

He pushed open a door, and there was a pristine single toilet and a sink surrounded by white ceramic tile. "We built two and hoped that would be enough. The intention was to have a men's and women's, but maybe we make them all gender."

"Definitely," I said. "Okay, I'm ready to start renting the place then." I was bouncing on the balls of my feet.

"Alright, overly-eager Nell, let's get through the boot sale, first, okay?"

I nodded but was already planning signage and advertising and further lighting for the barn. It was going to be great.

But Gray was right, and as we walked around to the shed, where we had re-stored all the things for the sale, I forced myself to focus. "Do you think we'll have a good turn-out?" I asked as we carried the sewing stand into the barn and set it up in a corner.

"Are you kidding? Jay has pulled out all the stops for this one. I expect we'll have a large crowd.

It didn't take us long to set up our half of the barn, and when Gray brought out a couple of light stands like the ones they use on construction sites and set them in opposite corners of the space, the place looked like a perfect rustic showcase. I felt like buying something myself.

We took a break for lunch, and soon after, Ollie came with what looked to be like a million figurines. "My mom has been wanting to sell these for a long time, but she doesn't trust those 'crooked shop dealers,'" he put quotes around his mom's words, "so I told her I'd sell them for her here. She wants a pretty penny for them, so we'll price them as such and then let people bargain us down. I'll just supply the difference to make her happy."

I laughed. "That's kind of you."

"Are you kidding?" Ollie said. "I do not want to inherit these creepy things." He held up what looked to be a slightly demented clown holding a terrified puppy. "Would you?"

"No," I said. "Please put that far away from me."

Throughout the afternoon, our other friends brought by their things. Danielle had two hanging racks of vintage dresses that were gorgeous, and Jazz brought not only some great kitchen ware and a couple of gorgeous glass lamps, but also bags of coffee and single packages of baked goods for us to sell as well. "I'll have the fresh coffee tomorrow."

Pree brought two luxurious dog houses that included built in feeding and water bowls and also a very large fish tank. "My brother's. He doesn't use it, so I told him I'd sell it for him. It has everything someone needs to start."

When Jay arrived in the late afternoon with a truck bed full of old tools, mowers, and a surprising number of chains, Gray and Ollie applauded. "Some things for the men," Ollie said.

I rolled my eyes, more at the way that items were still categorized by gender than about Ollie's statement because he was right. Having tools and such here would bring out men. I'd seen it happen many a time at my grandfather's yard sales. Rusty lawnmowers were, apparently, worth quite a bit of money.

By the time we had everything set up, the barn was full

but maneuverable, and I was very, very excited for the next morning. "I can't wait until morning."

"Morning," Pree said. "Oh, no, we're starting in 10 minutes for the pre-sale." She grinned at me. "Gray didn't tell you."

"What? Pre-sale? What?" I was flummoxed.

"Oh yes, we let a few dealers and collectors from around here know what was happening. They'll be here—"

At that moment, I heard the sound of car tires on the drive beside the house, and soon enough, several car doors slammed. "They're here," Pree said with a grin. "Get ready."

I do not know how the British define "a few," but given that 25 people poured into the barn that evening as if they had just been released from Noah's Ark, I guessed the American and British definitions were quite different.

Still, these folks were serious shoppers, and by the time we "closed" an hour later, they had purchased the phonograph, several of Ollie's figurines, and a few of Danielle's dresses too. And they said they'd be back in the morning to see what was marked down.

We used one of Jay's chains and a spare lock that Gray had and locked the barn doors. And then, I remembered the farm stand. If we were going to have a bunch of people here, I needed to get something up there, seed the market, so to speak.

It was getting dark, and the only thing I could think to do was forage some arrangements, so before everyone left, I said, "Who's up for a floral scavenger hunt?" My friends looked at me strangely, but when I explained the farm stand need, they immediately joined in and spread out across the property. Soon enough, we had greenery, some wild daisies, and even some tulips that Jay had liberated –

with permission – from a neighbor's garden on the promise that she'd get into the boot sale 15 minutes early the next morning.

While Ollie and Jay ran out to get take away Indian for dinner, the rest of us pulled out all the spare vases, and soon enough, we had 10 really lovely and simple arrangements to put out in the morning. Since the arrangements would look best if they were kept chilled, I consolidated the items in my refrigerator and managed to squeeze all the arrangements into the bottom of it without squishing them too much.

When the food arrived, all of us laid into it like teenage boys on pizza, and soon enough, we were all lounging around the living room full and spent. "You're welcome to sleep here," I said groggily as I pried myself up. "There are blankets and pillows in the hall closet, and you can divvy out the guest room beds if you want."

Jazz and Danielle grinned and practically sprinted up the stairs and into the front bedroom.

"Alrighty then," I said. "The rest of you?"

"I'll take the gents to my place. They can make do with the couches," Gray said, and I wondered just how much of a bachelor pad his place was that he had multiple couches. "Meet back here at 7?"

"Better make it 6:30," Jay said. "Remember, I promised Mrs. Hodges next door a bit of early access."

"Right, 6:15, then," Gray said. "I'll get breakfast sorted."

I looked at Pree. "And you?"

She glanced at the couch. "This looks perfect." She smiled. "I could sleep on a concrete floor at this point."

"Oh my word, no. I have another guest room upstairs. Come on."

I could hear the guys squabbling with Gray about how

there were beds here, and he was making them sleep on couches, and I smiled.

THE NEXT MORNING, all of us were up and downstairs by 6, and Jazz had even made a run to her shop and brought back two carafes of coffee. "The staff will bring the rest in an hour," she said. "I figured we needed our own supply."

"You are not wrong about that," I replied as I filled the largest mug I had with the dark roast she'd brought before putting on the kettle for the crazy Brits who would only have tea.

A few minutes later Gray, Jay, and Ollie came in with a box full of what were most certainly donuts. "You have a donut shop here?"

"We are not neanderthals, Nell," Ollie said. "Of course we have a donut shop. Best one around, in fact."

"Pardon me," Jazz said. "That shop is not the best at everything."

I winced. "Competitor?"

"Only in donuts," she said. "Their coffee tastes burnt, and most of their pastries are frozen."

I nodded. "But the donuts are good?" I could eat almost anything, but a stale donut wasn't my favorite.

Jazz shrugged. "They're alright."

"They are the best," Gray said. "But the shop has nothing on Jazz's. This morning, there was only one person working, and the line was out the door."

"This early?" I said.

"It's a Saturday in the spring, Nell. There are so many festivals, fetes, and boot sales that we sell out of pastries before 7am most weekend mornings," Jazz said.

I thought about the States and realized the same might

be true there, except I had always been at work on Saturdays and hadn't even considered what other people were doing when I was busy explaining that the "green side goes up" to the woman who asked me how to plant a hydrangea bush.

"Well, then I guess we better get ready," I said as I grabbed a donut and moved it quickly toward my face.

Within a few minutes, people were filling the courtyard, and Pree quickly made a sign to point them around the back of the house to the barn, where Jay gave Mrs. Hodges her exclusive access and immediately sold her three of Ollie's mom's monstrosities.

Then, when we opened the doors to the two dozen or so people who were waiting to get in, it was all we could do to keep up with making change and helping people to their cars. Gray had stationed himself in the yard to help escort lookie-loos around the property, as we'd agreed, and to keep them from going into my house. He was walking Dante with him, so I figured that the dog looked intimidating enough to keep people from taking liberties, even if the only threat he was would be to dampen someone's sleeve with his drool.

Sales were brisk for the first couple hours of the morning and then, just as the previous week, the traffic slowed, and I could finally take a minute to use the restroom. I waved to Pree and then headed around back to the open door on the room nearest me, and I was just about to close the door when a large foot stuck in it and kept it open.

I jumped back in surprise, and that gave Alex and Antoine just enough time to force their way in and lock the door behind them. The space was ample for one person, but with three of us in there, it was outright claustrophobic, or maybe what made me lose my breath was the fact that

Alex had a coil of rope in one hand, and Antoine was holding a hammer.

"Quiet now," Alex said. "We won't hurt you if you cooperate. But if you don't, well . . . ." Her voice trailed off.

My mind was suddenly filled with the image of Arabella laying on the floor, and I knew, without a doubt, that I was in the room with my murderer, a very tiny, windowless room. "I'll cooperate. What do you want me to do?"

"Stay here, and be quiet until we come and get you," Alex said. "If you so much as let out a peep, the person we are closest to will pay the price."

I looked over at Antoine, who was holding the hammer like it might bite him. "Even your sister? You would hurt Jazz?"

Antoine paled a bit, but steadied himself when Alex said, "If that happens, it will be your fault. You understand."

I nodded slowly and then backed up a step into the sink as they stepped out of the bathroom with looks around. As he closed the door, Antoine slipped the hammer into his waistband.

"Honeymooners, for sure," Gray said a moment later, apparently surmising that the newlyweds' joint exit was from a tryst not a kidnapping.

Alex giggled. "How embarrassing."

Dante let out a loud volley of barks and then growled. "Dante," Gray scolded. "No."

Alex giggled again, and then their voices trailed off toward what I thought was the barn. When it grew silent, I heard a faint tapping on the wall to my right, next to the toilet. I listened for a moment and then presumed it was the pipes knocking, or maybe the sink next door dripping.

After using the facilities as I had originally intended, I

closed the lid and sat down on the toilet, trying to gather my wits and think. But then, the tapping got louder, and, oddly, more rhythmic. I heard, "TAP tap tap TAP TAP", and instinctively thought, "tap tap" in response. It took me a split second to realize that there was a person on the other side of those taps, but when I did, I immediately responded with two taps.

Then, just barely, I heard a man's voice. "This is Ollie. I'm locked in. Who's there?"

I wanted to shout, "It's Nell," but instead, I tempered my voice to a loud whisper and said, simply, "It's Nell. Alex and Antoine."

"Yes," Ollie said. "Stay quiet. We will be missed soon." Then, our communication stopped, and I could only assume that Ollie had received the same threat I had.

As I sat and pondered my options, I found myself – for the first time in my life – wishing that Ollie had a gun. I hated the things, but if Ollie were an American cop, he would have likely been armed, even if he was off-duty. Still, there was no use pondering what wasn't the case – Ollie had told me he didn't even have a firearm – so I forced myself to think about what Alex and Antoine hoped to get out of this situation. Clearly, they wanted Ollie and I to stop asking questions, and they must have been getting desperate if they kidnapped a police officer.

Then, as if my brain needed a diversion, I started thinking about whether was this was technically a kidnapping or a hostage situation, and I wondered what the FBI could classify it as. Soon enough, I was thinking of Dr. Reid, my favorite character from *Criminal Minds*, and in time, I let my mind skip through all the police shows I'd watched to see if any way out struck me. I had to admit the distraction was nice, but even in this situation, I was a little appalled at how many of these shows I knew well. How much TV did I watch?

I was about to slide into a series of vows about reading more and taking more walks when I heard the tapping again, just three solid knocks this time, and while I didn't know what Ollie was trying to say, I was suddenly more alert, a position which served me well when the door to the bathroom opened and Antoine was standing there.

As fast as I could, I jumped up and tried to barge past him, and while I made it partway through the doorframe, his massive arm simply wrapped around my waist and hauled me off my feet. "No, I don't think so," he said quietly and then quite literally tucked me under his arm like a football and carried me toward the shed where Aunt Jelly had kept her things.

I tried to kick and squirm, and I was drawing in a deep breath to scream when Antoine said, in a mild voice, "Alex is with Gray now. I wouldn't."

His words sucked the oxygen right out of me, and I went limp. I would not let Gray be hurt unless I could find no other way out of this situation. Antoine opened the door of the shed, set me gently inside, and then closed the door behind him. I heard the click of a lock, and knew that I'd need to find another way out. Fortunately, the building had two windows, and while I loathed the idea of breaking the original wavy glass in the frames, I wouldn't hesitate if that meant I could escape what was looking more and more like a situation that was not going to end well. In my TV-based, expert opinion, I knew that it was not a good sign when hostages – for this was clearly a hostage situation – were moved to a new location. At least I thought it was hostages, maybe it was bodies. I couldn't get my facts straight.

I turned to the first window, the one on the side of the

shed away from the rest of the farm structures and saw, with horror, that someone had nailed an x of boards across the windows and had done the same on the other side. I tried pulling the boards down, but without a crowbar or such, I was no match against nails.

Then, I thought I might get someone's attention outside, so I got as close as I could to the glass and started jumping up and down anytime someone walked by, which wasn't often at first. But then, as the day started to turn toward late afternoon, my friends were obviously out looking for us. They were wandering around the property calling for Ollie and me, but I could see that Alex and Antoine had joined the search. I wasn't about to yell and risk them grabbing the nearest person and hurting them with that hammer I could still see bulging from Antoine's belt anytime he got near the building. Plus, the light was shifting toward dusk, and I knew that in the dark of the shed I would be nearly invisible.

Soon enough, the search party moved farther afield, presumably toward the front of the house and on toward town, guided, perhaps, by false information from the newly-weds. As soon, though, as everyone else was out of site, Antoine came back around the building, opened the other bathroom stall, and pushed Ollie to the shed. I thought about trying my move to bolt past our captor when he opened the door, but when I noticed that the hammer was in his hand this time, I stayed back and let him deposit Ollie near me. The lock clicked again, and then Ollie and I were there, staring at each other in an empty room.

After a second, I leapt at him and hugged him, not sure if I was more relieved that he was still okay or that I wasn't alone anymore. He hugged me and then said, "Okay, so how are we going to get out of here?"

I pointed toward the windows. "They barred the windows."

Ollie studied the boards and gave them a tug with the same results I had. "And nothing we can use as a crowbar?"

I shook my head. "Gray cleaned out the building entirely for the yard sale."

He nodded. "Okay, then we need to find a way to signal that we're in here."

"Didn't they tell you that they would hurt our friends?"

"Yes, but they will surely kill us if we don't find our way out," Ollie spoke quickly and then looked at me. "Sorry. But we are in grave danger. We have to get help."

I pondered what options we had. Even if we could break the glass on the windows, neither of us was small enough to fit through the gaps between the boards. We could probably get an arm out, but unless someone was there to see it, that wouldn't do any good. And at this point, everyone was too far away to hear us if we shouted.

A spark of anger sprung into my throat. "If you knew they were going to kill, why didn't you scream for help earlier?"

Ollie sighed. "Because I wasn't sure until they brought us here. My guess is that they'll try to burn the building down and make it look like an accident."

A wave of panic threatened to overtake me, but I forced myself to breathe normally and focus on the situation. "Alright, then how do we get out?"

Ollie turned and ran as hard as he could with his shoulder down, but the door barely creaked when he hit it. "Ouch," he said and then examined the doorframe. "It's framed in to keep things dry and warm in here." He pointed out how the door swung out and stopped, presumably, at a rectangle of wood surrounding it on the outside. "Good construction, but bad escape route."

At that moment, I heard a bark and saw Dante pounding across the yard toward the shed. No one was with him, and I figured he must have slipped his lead and run back to find us. "Good dog," I said. "Good dog." Then, channeling all my Timmy energy from Lassie, I said, "Go get help, boy. Go get help."

The dog acted like he understood me completely and took off back toward the flower fields and the house, but at that same moment, Antoine and Alex returned with a glass jar and what looked to be one of those long lighters you could use for campfires. Ollie was right. They were going to burn the building down with us in it.

At that point, all caution was thrown to the wind, and we began screaming and pounding our feet. I found a small piece of brick that was loose from one corner of the foundation and threw it through the window facing the flower fields, and then I screamed with all my might.

Alex and Antoine were getting closer, and Ollie and I were both frantically pulling on the boards across the window, trying to get them free. But they weren't budging. We kept screaming and tugging, and yet, no one was coming, and nothing was moving. I was sure we were going to die in there.

But then, from across the field, I saw two blurs of gray running toward us with two other gray figures coming behind them. In unison, Dante leaped and took Alex off her feet just as Clover spun and kicked Antoine hard in the stomach. They were down, but they were not out. We could see them scrambling back to their feet. Dante, however, held them at bay with his growl, while Clover made her way over to the building at a rather slow lope then turned around and with one two-footed kick, launched the door open toward us.

Ollie didn't hesitate and charged out with the rock he'd found in his hand, and took one swing to Antoine's head, bringing him to the ground unconscious while Dante kept an eye on Alex. Then, within a few seconds, Ollie had Alex's hands behind her back and was asking me for rope. I remembered the rope she had been carrying early and rushed over toward the bathrooms, noticing only momentarily that Out Of Order signs had been placed on both doors. But there, in a coil between the doors, was the rope. I grabbed it and sprinted back to Ollie, who made quick work of tying up first Alex and then Antoine, who was still knocked out on the ground.

Only when both of them were secured did Dante relax and Clover, now with her two sisters who had been standing by, make their way to a particularly nice spot of grass in the corner under a crab apple tree.

While Ollie ran into the barn to get our phones, where we had left them at our tables, I sat down on the ground and pulled Dante to me. "Thank you, boy. You saved us. You saved us." I was crying freely now, and the dog kept licking my face to get the salt from my tears, and his tongue felt like the softest comfort in the world.

When Ollie returned, he had his phone to his ear and was asking for back-up at my address, "Immediately, please. We have two suspects in custody and need assistance."

I wasn't sure how immediate a response could be in the English village, but within a couple of minutes, I heard sirens and the sound of tires on gravel, and soon what seemed to be a full fleet of officers was flooding my yard with Gray, Jazz, Danielle, Pree, and Jay close behind.

"I called Gray, too," Ollie said as he slumped down onto

the ground near me and gave Dante some well-deserved pets. "That was close, Nell. How did you know the animals would come?"

I stared at him. "Oh, you thought I called them intentionally. Oh no, I had no idea they'd do that, but I'm certainly glad they did.

On the other side of Ollie, where two police officers were putting Alex in cuffs, Antoine was just beginning to stir. "I'm sorry, my love. I thought this would work."

"I know. I know," she said tenderly, the most sweetly I had heard her say anything. "We will be okay."

I wasn't so sure about that, but for now, I was content that I was okay, and Ollie was okay, and all our friends were okay. When Gray dropped down beside me and pulled me against him, I let myself give over to emotion and sobbed. A few feet away, Jazz sat between Danielle and Pree as they watched the officers escort her brother and sister-in-law away.

"Are you okay?" Gray asked when the tears subsided. "I mean, obviously not, but are you hurt?"

"No," I said. "Just scared." I reached over and tugged Dante right onto my lap. "This guy saved me. Well, this guy and Clover," I said.

"What?" Gray said as he helped me to my feet and then toward the house, where an officer said he'd be in to take my statement in a bit.

When we were all inside and Ollie, Jazz, and I had cups of hot, sweet tea, I told them all about the animals' rescue efforts. "Clover saved you," Gray said. "Our Clover."

"My Clover," I said with a small smile. "And yes, she has quite the kick."

"I'll say," Ollie added. "she took Antoine down swiftly."

He winced. "Sorry, Jazz, and sorry I had to hit your brother."

Jazz sighed. "Don't be sorry. He is my brother, but he was about to do something absolutely horrific to you. I'd like to hit him myself." Her voice was thin and worn.

"Well, I think these animals deserve a little pampering tonight, don't you?" Pree said. "Why don't I get the donkeys back in their paddock? Jay, can you help me? We might need to do some repairs if they kicked their way out."

"They didn't," Gray said. "They can jump out. They just don't choose to very often."

"Alright then," Pree said. "Still, I think I could use the help. Let's grab all the apples for those girls." Jay stood and followed her out the door to the kitchen.

"They love celery too," I added.

"They do?" Gray said. "I didn't know that."

"Ah, finally something about my farm that you don't know. It's a big day."

"In more ways than one," Danielle said before looking down at Dante, who was sound asleep on my feet. "How do we reward this guy?"

"There's some ground beef in the freezer," Gray said. "Maybe you could sauté it up for him?"

Danielle nodded before looking at Jazz who smiled just the slightest bit. "Please. Let's give this hero his just desserts."

Chapter Seventeen

THE NEXT FEW days were quiet from my perspective, but from what I heard from Ollie directly at the pub or from Gray on the nights I stayed in to rest with Dante, the legal side of things was moving swiftly now that Alex and Antoine were arraigned on charges of hostage taking. Apparently, the UK had a law specifically for that, and I made a mental note to research whether the US had something similar, just to satisfy my not-so-professional curiosity.

This arrest meant the police had some space and time to piece together the details of Arabella's murder, and the hope was – Ollie said – that they would confess, a possibility I thought a long-shot given Alex's demeanor, but I wished him luck, nonetheless.

Jazz and Danielle were quiet for a few days. Aside from running the café and maintaining a level of cordiality with their customers, including me on most mornings, they didn't come out or respond to messages. I understood, at least I thought I did. Jazz's brother and his wife had taken two people hostage, while she was nearby. That had to be a blow to the psyche in and of itself, but then add in that her brother had been hurt during our escape, that she had seen him bleeding and unconscious on the ground. . . well, that was a lot to process.

So Gray and I decided to devote our days to the farm. We had a round of weeding to do, of course, but fortunately since we'd been keeping up with it, that work was done quickly. A few patches of seeds had not germinated, so I ordered more based on the list Scarlett and I had worked up, and we reseeded those areas.

Each day, we rewarded Clover with her apple and gave the other two girls a good scratch. Gray had been right. The fence on the paddock wasn't even damaged, and so while that made me a little nervous that the donkeys might take off at any moment, Gray assured me they had lived there for at least seven years now with no trouble. "They know where the good grass is," he said.

Most of our time, in those days after "the bathroom incident," as I had started referring to it, Gray and I poured ourselves into preparing the barn to be an event space. Several people who had attended the boot sale had told us they'd love to have their parties or family reunions there, and one guest had even asked if they could have their wedding there in August.

Being an entrepreneur whose business was just beginning to grow, I told everyone yes, and then because I was also a woman of my word, dedicated myself to making sure that everything was in top shape for our first event, a young mom's tea in three weeks.

Fortunately when I'd told Scarlett about our plans, she had immediately offered to set up the booking and payment services on my very nascent website, and within a day, I could take credit cards or transfers, and I had a calendar that allowed everyone to both reserve a date and send me more information so I could confirm.

Plus, Scarlett took the liberty of coming over and snapping a few pictures of the barn once we had removed all the straw and replaced it with clean woodchips that we could recycle into the chicken coop when we were done. Soon enough, The Barn at Stow was on her website, and I had no doubt, she'd sell the heck out of it for me.

I'd decided to stage the hayloft that overlooked the main floor as I might a store window. For each season, I'd change out what was displayed there, and behind the display, we'd store extra supplies for events – tables, chairs, etc. Since our first events would fall right at the beginning of summer, I purchased some bunches of silk sunflowers from a local craft store because, as much as I preferred real flowers, these had to stand up to not only time but the heat of the loft. If we had a wedding or some other themed event, I could easily change them out to match the colors of the occasion. I used the old farm implements that Gray helped me gather from the various outbuildings, and created displays with the sunflowers and the items. A metal milking bucket served as a vase. An old horse-drawn plow had a few flowers tied to the handles. That kind of thing.

When we were done, the loft looked lovely but subtle, nothing that would take away from the main event but also enough integrated as to not feel like empty space. I was pleased.

I was also exhausted, so on Friday night, I begged off of a night at the pub with Gray, Ollie, and Jay and settled in for some *Midsomer Murders*. I had been wanting to watch it since I arrived, eager to see what my experience of England was like compared to the TV version but too embarrassed to watch with my friends. Dante had already eaten, and I'd set myself up with a plate of leftover curry with the remote in hand when a knock sounded on the door.

I sighed, put my plate on a high Shelf where Dante couldn't reach it, and went to the door. When I swung it open, I was surprised to see Jazz and Danielle there. They both looked the epitome of dour, and I immediately ushered them into the living room, where I had lit a fire to offset the chill of the late spring rain, and went to the kitchen to make tea. It had become apparent to me why tea was such an English necessary – perfect for a rainy night and the best way to provide hospitality and sometimes, solace.

When I returned to the living room with a tray holding three mugs, some English biscuits, not crackers, and a chew bone for Dante, Jazz was on the floor, with Dante's entire body in her lap as his legs stretched upward past her head. She was rubbing his stomach lightly, and he was snoring.

"Well, you have now become the favorite," I said as I set the tray on the coffee table. "You may never be able to leave."

"That might be okay with me tonight," Jazz said as I handed her a mug and tempted Dante off her lap with his bone. "We just came from the police station."

"Oh?" I said in a way that I hoped conveyed my concern and hid my overeager curiosity. "Everything okay?"

Jazz nodded and then shook my head. "In one way, yes. Antoine confessed to killing Arabella."

"Antoine?!" I said, nearly spilling Danielle's tea all over her. "He confessed."

Danielle answered. "Yes, that's why we were there. Ollie

hoped that Jazz could convince her brother to tell them what happened, and she did." She sipped her tea. "It just wasn't what we expected to hear."

I sat down and sighed. "I'd guess not. Wow." I ate a biscuit and tried to think of a delicate way to ask my question. "So did he say why he did it?" I finally said.

"To protect, Alex, apparently," Jazz said softly.

Danielle reached down and put a hand on her wife's shoulder. "I might say it was more to secure Alex's favor."

When Jazz sighed and then nodded, I said, "Like a medieval knight winning a joust?"

This made both women chuckle. "More than protecting her honor, I think," Jazz said.

Immediately images for Simon's duel in Bridgerton came to mind, but I couldn't imagine even in high society 21st century England, that anyone cared if they'd had sex before they were married. But then, another thought came to mind. "She was pregnant. I mean, she is."

Jazz nodded. "And apparently, Arabella found out somehow. She threatened to expose Alex's secret at the wedding ceremony if she didn't pay her more, and Alex was mortified. The plan, according to Antoine, had been to tell everyone after the honeymoon. They weren't ashamed; they were quite excited about the baby, but they didn't want to tarnish their ceremony."

"I can't say as I blame them, but wouldn't it have just been better to pay Arabella off?" I asked.

"That seems to have been the plan," Danielle continued, "but apparently Arabella implied that Alex was, well, promiscuous and was cheating on Antoine."

"She asked him if he was sure the baby was his," Jazz said with venom in her voice.

"Whoa," I said. "Well, that's just beyond the pale."

"Exactly, and it set Antoine off. Before he knew what he was doing, he had struck her, and she was dead." Jazz's voice was solemn now.

I sat in stunned silence for a minute but then blurted, "But then how did the feather get there?"

Danielle answered. "Apparently, Alex was waiting outside the room to support Antoine, and when she heard their voices get louder, she came in."

"And she was in her wedding dress?" I found the image difficult to form. "Why?"

"She was doing a last fitting, making sure she wasn't showing. Apparently, Arabella's threats had made her nervous," Jazz said. Her voice was very quiet, and I could see the tears in her eyes.

"I can't blame her for that," I said. We sat quietly for a few minutes, Jazz scratching Dante's head, Danielle staring into her tea, and me letting my brain catch up. Somehow, it seemed a little less awful that it was a crime of passion, one of honor, and that Arabella had provoked it. But the fact that Antoine and Alex had gone so far as to take Ollie and I hostage to keep the secret, well, that made it a whole lot darker. Then, I realized one thing.

"Their baby will be born in prison," I said without thinking and then slapped a hand over my mouth. "Oh, Jazz." I slid down on the floor to sit next to her as my tears matched hers

"Yes," she whispered. "She will." I watched a teardrop run down her cheek.

"She?" I asked.

Danielle joined us on the floor and wrapped an arm around Jazz. "A baby girl. But we have already begun arrangements to take her in. Maybe adopt her. . . depending."

I didn't ask depending on what because, well, I already knew. If Antoine and Alex were getting life in prison, then they would never again care for their daughter, in all likelihood.

"Well," I finally said, "that is a glimmer of something like hope, isn't it?" I reached over and took their hands. "You're going to be parents."

The two women squeezed my hands and then looked at each other. "We are," they said, both of them crying freely now.

AS WE FINISHED our tea in silence, I decided maybe some company would be a good idea for my evening plans, except, of course, *Midsomer Murders* was off the roster. We didn't need any more police investigations or dead bodies.

"What do you say we watch the beautiful people in the third season of Bridgerton?" I asked as the three of us helped each other off the floor. We'd made it through the first two seasons over a couple of late nights, and I was dying to see the new episodes. Plus, I thought the distraction would probably be good for my friends.

As we watched the love story of "Polin," as fans called the featured couple of the season, I thought about how much of life is about the gray moments, the ones that are both beautiful and tragic. My parents died, and I got this beautiful farm. Jazz's brother committed murder, and she and her wife become mothers. One family loses their dog, and I gain a new companion.

Maybe, I thought as I watched the way my two new friends supported each other, as I thought about the way Gray had charmed me and then kept on helping me, as I thought about the flowers and the barn and the promise of hard work and income from it, maybe the real beauty of life is the in-betweens, like a Friday evening with two friends watching the Regency elite dance. Like the way you can love your brother and find him horrifying, too. Like the way the flicker of light on a window can create both a scary fairy and the gift of laughter for millions of children.

Stitches in Crime

vinci-books.com/crossed

Paisley Sutton: single mom, salvage expert, and amateur sleuth in over her head.

Paisley uncovers more than just antiques when she stumbles upon a body in an abandoned store.

Turn the page for a free preview…

Chapter One

I cinched the scarf more tightly around my head and wedged the hard hat into place. I'd learned the hard way that not covering my hair and my head could mean a mess, sometimes a bloody one.

The doorframe appeared to be solid, and when I pushed hard against the floorboards with my right foot, they held solid, too. I walked into the Scruggs Store and crouched beneath the collapsing roof. Not much left here I could safely search through, but I was going to do my best. I'd paid good money for this salvage job, and I was going to get what I could.

I'd driven past this old gas station all my life and had mourned as the vegetation took it over and began to pull it down over the past few years. I knew, though, that no one in our rural mountain county was going to buy the place, not after someone had been murdered there twenty years ago. A single gas pump on a country road wasn't enough incentive to take on that bad mojo.

It was a loss, though, because the station had been there for almost a hundred years – first as a country store and then as a welcome fueling spot twenty-five miles from the nearest city. I was determined to not let it all disappear when the bulldozers parked outside knocked it down. My fifty dollars had gained me entry and rights to anything I could carry out before the station was destroyed, and I was going to get my money's worth while saving a bit of history along the way.

I was new at the salvage business, but I knew enough about local history and had watched enough *Barnyard Builders*, *American Pickers*, and *Salvage Dawgs* to feel like I could find the good stuff. I headed to the left toward what used to be the check-out counter and hit paydirt right away. The original counter was still there, complete with a hand-written sign about check cashing as well as a Virginia lottery sticker from somewhere in the last decade of the previous century. A few coats of poly on this baby, and it would make a great piece of wall art for someone who loved that 1990s feel or just wanted to relive their heyday.

A few good pries with my crowbar and I had the whole countertop sitting by the door ready to go. That piece alone was worth my investment, but I wanted to go a bit further in, see if maybe there was some old stock of soda or something. People paid ridiculous prices for skunked beer and flat Pepsi. The coolers were underneath some rafters, so I moved gingerly toward them. Most of the shelves were empty, probably raided before the building started to cave in, but I could see the glint of light off glass in the back. Jackpot! The overstock was still there, it seemed.

I picked and tested my way to a door that seemed to

open behind the wall of refrigerated units and prayed it wasn't locked. I didn't feel like kicking in a door and bringing down the roof. Luckily, the knob turned, and I was in. Not cases and cases of old stock, but enough to turn a good profit. As I carried out a few boxes of soda and Yuengling, I thought about how tight the margin for a store like this must have been. The owner had to keep enough supply to satisfy customers' last-minute shopping needs – gallons of milk, snacks, a few packs of diapers probably – but not so much that he couldn't make a profit on what he stocked. It was hard going.

Maybe it was easier, though, since he and his family lived at the back of the store, like a lot of shop owners back in the day. I thought about what it would have been like to grow up in that little house, to have people coming by all times of day and night to get cigarettes or pick up a sand-wich from the little kitchen in the back of the store. I might have loved it, and I knew my son, Sawyer, would have thrived with all those people to talk to. His extroverted tendencies were in diametric opposition to my introverted ones. But I thought it probably also would have grown tiring and tedious.

As I set a sixth case of Cheerwine by the door, I made my plan for a last foray into the store and then, hopefully, into the house behind. I could just make out a doorframe in the far back corner, and since I'd noted the exterior bath-room doors before I came in, I figured this must be the way into the house. The only problem was that I was going to have to crawl my way back there. My forty-six-year-old body wasn't much for crawling despite the fact that Sawyer was in a "Be a rhino with me, Mommy" stage.

Still, that little boy needed his mommy to buy him cheese crackers and milk, so crawl I did. And when it was necessary for me to be thinner than my crawling hips would allow, I shimmied my way like a snake and decided I wasn't going to suggest Saw and I try that animal imitation out.

I made it to the door, though, and I was hoping that the quick look I'd had at the house hadn't been deceptive. Luckily for me, this roof was still standing at its full eight feet. I levered myself to standing and looked around at what reminded me of the living room of my high school years. A big black television from before the age of flat screens sat in one corner, and in front of it, a couch with overstuffed arms and red plaid fabric was under a rumpled blanket and a throw pillow. It looked like someone had just gotten up from a Sunday afternoon nap.

A quick scan told me there wasn't anything worth hauling out of here, but I was glad to find that the exterior door was easy to open in case I did find anything. If only I had seen it before I covered my entire front in dust from my army crawl back there.

I made my way into the kitchen and felt sorrow hitch in my chest. A wire rack with moldy cookies was waiting next to a plastic tub designed just for cookie storage. My mom had the same one, and I loved coming home from school and raiding the freshly baked stash. Beside it, the mixer was bowl-less, and I saw the stainless-steel bowl in the sink, ready to be washed. A mug of half-drunk tea sat at the edge of the counter. Someone, probably a woman, probably a mother, had been interrupted in her work.

I took a deep breath and said a word of gratitude to that woman before I started flinging open cabinets. I only had a few more minutes before Saw or our Maine Coon cat, Beauregard, got bored of watching funny cat videos in the car or someone saw them and came to investigate who had abandoned their toddler and a giant feline in their Subaru

Outback at a derelict gas station. It wasn't my favorite choice of things to do, but Sawyer was safely in his car seat, the car was locked, and Beau was better than any guard dog, especially since he weighed in at a solid twenty pounds under his copious striped fur. The plight of a working single mom required creative problem solving, and sometimes creative problem solving involved a guard cat.

I found some vintage cookie cutters and a set of Corel dishes that I quickly loaded into the dishpan I had emptied into the sink. If I couldn't sell them, then someone would appreciate the set at Goodwill. A few pottery mugs and really nice knife block I could use at home rounded out my haul from this room.

After I deposited those items on the small porch outside the living room door, I plunged into the first of the bedrooms. I didn't think there'd be much to salvage here since the clothing wasn't going to be old enough to be truly vintage, but I hoped to maybe find some children's clothes in good shape for Sawyer and maybe a coat for me. I hit the jackpot straight off. Lots of four T pants and shirts that would fit Saw in a matter of weeks at the rate his two-year-old body was growing and even a couple of pairs of shoes. I tried not to think of the murder when I was in this room, but I prayed for this little boy. Prayed he was okay in all the ways.

There looked to be only two more doors in the small hallway, and the one at the end of the hall was likely the bathroom. I hadn't been in many abandoned houses, but I'd learned the hard way that opening the bathroom door was a bad idea. I skipped that one and went on to the other bedroom.

The curtains were pulled tight, and while the light would have been helpful, I was in a hurry. I just headed for the closet with my flashlight and rifled through the clothes before pulling boxes down in case there were antiques or any particularly great caches of photos or mementos I needed to rescue. When I had started this work, I'd made a vow that I would try to return anything personal to the owners if I could, so I always salvaged photo albums, boxes of children's art, and any other pieces of family history I could. Then, I spent ten percent of the money I earned from selling the other things to try to get those back to their owners. I couldn't afford to do more than that in terms of shipping or ads in local papers, but I figured the least I could do was try that. Sometimes, it worked. Often it didn't, and if it didn't, I tried to console myself with the fact that maybe people just wanted to leave the past behind altogether. I probably would.

I didn't find a coat for me in the closet, but I did see a small jewelry box shoved up on a high shelf. I chuckled. My jewelry box was in exactly the same place because Sawyer had developed a deep interest in wearing – and breaking – every necklace I owned. I wasn't about to let him swallow my grandmother's diamond ring, not when that was our financial back-up as well as a precious memento of my granny.

I tucked the jewelry box under my arm and turned to swing my flashlight around the room. As my light swept over the bed, I saw a lump in the corner under the window. I thought it might be a pile of discarded clothes, and with winter coming soon, I found myself praying that someone might have discarded their coat over a chair. The fact that my heart was racing made me pray even harder.

I made my way around the bed to get a closer look, and I clenched my teeth to keep from screaming. A woman was sitting in an armchair, and she wasn't moving – not even breathing.

I stepped back, took a deep breath to push down the panic because I didn't want to alarm Sawyer, and walked out of the side door of the house.

It felt awful to have to drive away from that house, but there was no cell service for a couple of miles. I threw the jewelry box on to the floor below where Beauregard reclined like the prince he was and headed north toward town. As soon as my phone showed three reliable bars, I pulled into the nearest driveway and dialed 911.

"Yes, this is Paisley Sutton. I just found a dead body in the old store on Scotch Road."

The dispatcher, used to traffic accidents and reports of four-wheelers on the roads I imagined, was a bit flustered, but he managed to tell me he was sending officers and that I should wait there. I explained I was two miles up the road and would get back to the store as soon as I could. He didn't even ask why I'd left the scene. We all knew the mountains wreaked havoc with cell service.

"What we doing, Mommy?" Sawyer asked from the back seat.

"Mommy has to talk to the police, Love Bug," I said as I ripped open a packet of fruit snacks with my teeth and handed it to him as I simultaneously swung the car back onto the road toward the store. "You're going to get to see police cars!" My son loved anything vehicular, and I was counting on flashing lights and maybe a kind officer who would show off a siren to help my toddler through this change of plans. He was going to miss his playground time, and if these police cars didn't make up for slides, it was going to be a hard fight for a nap.

My maternal worries were mostly allayed though as Saw started bouncing in his seat as soon as he saw the blue flashing lights by the store, and when I pulled over and told him to wait patiently, he said, "I will, Mama," and craned his little neck to see the police officers in uniform.

I walked to the first officer I saw and introduced myself. "I found the body," I said, and the young black woman nodded. Then, she looked over my shoulder at the car. "Your son?"

I smiled. "Yeah, I'm a single mom, so he goes with me everywhere. He doesn't know what's happening, but he sure is excited about seeing police cars."

She snapped her notebook shut with such briskness that I had a flash of fear that she was going to scold me for neglect. Instead, she tilted her head at the car and said, "Mind if I sit with him?" She pointed to the radio and flashlight on her belt. "My guy loves my toys."

I felt a flood of relief as she headed toward the backseat of my car and knocked on the door before asking Sawyer if she could sit down. When she patted her knees and let Beau settle in her lap while Sawyer squawked her radio to high heaven, I knew he'd be fine and went to see what I could find out about the woman inside.

An officer was on the front stoop of the store, and so I walked up and tapped him on the shoulder. When he turned, I recognized his face from the election posters I'd seen around the county for the past couple of months. He was our new sheriff, Santiago Shifflett, the first Latino sheriff in the area, and, thankfully, the man I'd voted for.

"Sheriff, I found the body." That was a sentence I hadn't thought I'd utter even once in my life, but here I was saying it again. "Want me to take you in?"

"Ms. Sutton, thank you for calling it in. We actually

found her already, but I would like to ask you a few questions." His voice was kind but serious.

"Of course." I had prepared as best I could to tell my story in the few quiet minutes of the drive back to the store. "Do you mind if we sit though? Sawyer, my son, got up at five-thirty, and the adrenaline is starting to wear off."

"Sure," he said. "That work?" He nodded toward the bulldozer at the edge of the lot and headed that way.

I climbed up in the seat, and the sheriff stood below. A deputy brought over two bottles of water, and I gulped mine down with gratitude. "What do you need to know?"

Sheriff Shifflett leaned against the tracks of the dozer, and I felt a little of my tension ease. If he wasn't worried about getting his uniform dirty, I felt like I could trust him. After all, I walked around with some stain – food, poop, playdough – on my clothes every day of my life. "Let's start with why you were in the house."

I pulled out my business card with "Save The Story," the name of my business, printed across the top. "I do historical salvage from old buildings. The owners gave me permission to go inside and take whatever I could." I gestured to the stack of soda and beer beside the small circle of officers on the store's porch.

The sheriff glanced over his shoulder and then back at me. "You found soda?" There was a lightness to his tone, and I could just see the start of a smile in the corner of his mouth.

I smiled. "I know, right? People pay a lot of money for old soda."

"They want the soda itself? Not just the bottles?"

"It's kind of like having old toys in the original box. Original condition means more value, I guess." I shrugged. "I don't question it. I just buy groceries with it."

Shifflett pursed his lips. "Whatever it takes to pay the bills." Sometimes people said that with mockery, but the sheriff seemed sincere.

"Exactly." I then told him about searching the house and about going into the back bedroom. "That's when I saw her. I didn't touch anything, and I'm sorry I had to leave the scene but—"

"Cell service, I know." He turned and looked at the house. "Did you notice anything unusual in there?"

I looked back up at the store and then beyond it to the attached house. "No. I mean, it was disconcerting to go into that house and see that it was like the people who lived there had been abducted by aliens. But I assume they left a long time ago, like after the first murder."

The sheriff turned back to me. "You knew about that then? And you still went in?"

"Like I said, groceries." I'd grown up nearby, and the murder had been a big deal, especially because they thought it had been someone who frequented the store. "Besides, there's a story there, one that needs to be remembered, and not just the story of the murder, the first one, I mean. Those people had lives before and after the father of that family was killed. I wanted to remember that, to help other people remember that." I took a deep breath, surprised that I'd shared that much with this man I'd just met. It wasn't really relevant to the investigation, after all.

But the sheriff didn't seem put off at all when he turned back to me. "I get it. Part of why I do my job, too. Crime happens to people and is committed by people. It's not just a thing that happens or that happens in one moment and then is gone. It's the people involved that get my attention."

I studied the sheriff's face for a second and then nodded. But then, I heard Saw's call, "Mama!" and knew my time was limited. "I hate to ask, but can I take the things I gathered from the house?"

He shook his head, "I'm afraid not. They're part of the crime scene. But if you have a minute," he glanced over his head toward the car, "maybe you could show me what you were taking. It'll help us sort out the scene but also, hopefully, I can get it to you later."

I nodded. "Of course." I took a quick look at my car and saw the deputy handing Sawyer her radio and gauged I had about five more minutes. I quickly walked him through the store and pointed out the countertop and the cases on the porch before showing him my haul outside the door of the house. He made notes and studied each pile of goods.

But then, I heard Sawyer's wail and knew I needed to go. "Thanks, Sheriff. You have my number, so call if I can help further." I waved as I jogged around the front of the store.

I hurried back to the car, where Sawyer was working up a good tantrum. I thanked the officer, gave my son a kiss on the forehead, and then climbed into the car. Eleven fifteen – it was time for a picnic lunch before my toddler went into total meltdown.

Crossed by Death Chapter Two

On days when Sawyer and I had to be out of the house early, I planned for a picnic and then a car nap. Today I was especially glad for the string cheese, tangerine, and slices of ham in his backpack because there was no way we were settling in for a nap at home after all that excitement.

I drove up the road as Saw tried to bite Beau's tail. I gave thanks for a patient cat who would walk away rather than attack.

Luckily, it was just cool enough for the farmers' market pavilion up in town to be empty, and the sole picnic table that had not succumbed to too much weather was free.

Saw was bouncing as I poured Beau a bowl of water and then unstrapped my two-year-old from his seat. "Time for picnic," he said again and again as we made our way to the table. I did a quick sweep of the area for potential hazards: pile of gravel, drop off on the other side of pavilion, water drainage behind three layers of construction fence. If I wasn't careful, Sawyer would explore all of those in the time it took for me to scarf down my own ham and cheese sandwich.

Fortunately for all of us, including the maintenance crew I might have to summon from the county office building if my son crawled into that water pit, there was a large puddle nearby, and Sawyer busied himself by throwing rocks with one hand and eating cheese with the other. That small distraction gave me enough time to think back about the morning's events.

When the murder twenty years earlier had hit the news, it had rocked our rural county. We had violent deaths, of course, but they always seemed tied to specific things like drugs or domestic abuse. Those things were horrible, of course, but this murder had seemed random, out of the blue. No robbery even. For weeks, people couldn't talk about anything else.

Now, it seemed far too much of a coincidence that a second person would be found dead randomly in that same building. It only seemed reasonable that there was a connection between the two deaths.

That hypothesis led me down a stranger thought-trail as Sawyer headed toward the rock pile. Maybe someone was hoping to hide a body there because they assumed no one would be in the building before it was taken down. If that was the case, the person must have been aware that the building was about to be demolished, and I didn't think that information was widely known, but of course, in places with few people, gossip travels remarkably fast. But that didn't mean the death was connected to the building.

Maybe, though, someone wasn't hoping to hide the body. Maybe the two deaths were linked by more than just place. Maybe someone wanted to send a message or had some symbolic reason for leaving the body there. My train of thought went very dark at that point as I pondered serial killers and cults and all kinds of ugliness. I blamed the fact that I'd binged *Mindhunter* the past two weekends that Sawyer was with his dad. That show was great but all kinds of creepy too.

Sparing me from my own macabre reflection, Sawyer made a beeline for the water hole, and I leapt into all the action my middle-aged body would allow and lifted a flailing forty-pound boy back over the orange fence he had just scaled like an American Ninja Warrior. It was time for a nap. I wondered, for a split second, how long it would be before self-driving cars were safe because that would be a true gift to the parents of small children who only napped in a moving vehicle.

Praise be to the God of parents because Saw dropped off before we were even out of town, and I had a blissful two hours to wander the mountain roads, study the way yellow trees held their leaves against the black trunks and branches of their brethren, and ponder the Scruggs store.

I didn't know much about the murder that had happened there two decades previous, just that it had been the father of the family, Luther, and that the case had never been solved, at least not that I knew of.

As we rode along the Blue Ridge, I stroked Beau's head and made mental notes about what I needed to look up. I decided I would feature the building and its history in my next newsletter. Those newsletters were one of the things I looked forward to most about my work, and as my subscriber list had grown, I'd started getting to know the people who replied. Some of my readers were genealogists with a penchant for place, and some were historians who loved the facts of a building. But most of them were just ordinary folks like me who appreciated old buildings and the stories that lived in them. They would love to know more about the Scruggs Store, and I was happy to oblige.

When Saw's father and I had split up a year ago, I had needed to find a way to work and have my son along. The research-intensive historical articles I'd been writing as a freelancer were just not feasible since they required many hours a day to dig through archives and read books, so I'd taken to a more hands-on field – salvage. In some buildings, Saw could come along and actually help me – the boy was a natural with a hammer—and when the job was dangerous, my best friend, Mika, kept Saw at her shop in downtown Octonia. He loved playing in the bins of soft yarn.

Between online sales, pop-up shops in Charlottesville, and word-of-mouth, I was building a steady income, enough that Sawyer and I had just bought a house of our own. Apartment living – as convenient as it was – just wasn't ideal. We needed history around us and nature at our door. Beau needed that too because the mouse population in our apartment complex was just not up to par.

But as much as I longed to sit on our farmhouse porch for a couple of hours, instead of turning toward home when I saw Saw was starting to stir, I headed toward town and hoped that it wasn't one of Mika's yarn group days. A toddler and women trying to knit were not a good combination, at least not as far as the knitting was concerned.

Just as we parked on the street outside her store, Sawyer opened his eyes and said, "Apple juice please," and I handed back the tumbler I had filled from a juice box while on a particularly quiet road. I had learned through a succession of sticky trials that a squeezable box and a toddler are not a good combination.

I let my slow-waking son sit and drink for a few minutes

while I wrote down the notes that I had accumulated in my mind. Everyone kept recommending those note-taking apps for my phone, but they weren't exactly ideal when a toddler was sleeping nearby.

Notes recorded, I peeked in Mika's windows and saw her and one other older woman sitting in the wingback chairs by the windows, yarn in hand. *Perfect*, I thought, and got Saw out of his car seat. Beauregard, recognizing his surroundings, hopped out and followed me to the shop door and then slid past me as I pushed it open with an elbow. He had a special bed in the back of the store, and he loved how people admired his sheer size and lustrous fur. If he could, I swore he'd be creating a line of Maine Coon-inspired yarn as a tribute to himself.

Saw wriggled out of my arms with less grace than Beau, but with equal enthusiasm, and barreled into Mika's lap, barely missing a lung puncture from a knitting needle. "Auntie Mickey," he squealed.

"Saw-Saw, I didn't know you were coming." Mika held him out at arm's length before pulling him close again. "It's so good to see you. Can you stay and help me unroll some yarn?" Mika and Saw had an understanding – he could unskein any yarn she gave him, but he couldn't do more than touch any other stock in the store. Regularly, she had him string out the yarn she was going to use for herself or for a knitting circle, and then, I'd sit around and talk with her as I rolled the loose yarn into balls that she then secured with painter's tape. It was a winning arrangement for us all.

Today, though, I was hoping Mika was okay with me skedaddling to the county courthouse. I was eager to dig into the deeds on the Scruggs store, and the presence of a toddler might just send our county clerk into cardiac arrest. She was a tad fastidious about records, a trait I appreciated unless it meant I couldn't get my hands on something I wanted. "Have time and space to keep your assistant for a couple of hours?"

Mika smiled at me as she stood and gave me a tight hug. "Sure. Everything okay?"

I nodded. It wasn't the time to talk about the murder, not with Sawyer near and the knitter still in the wingback. "I'll catch you up via text. Just need to go to the courthouse for a bit of research."

"We're totally good here." Saw was testing the drumstick quality of the various knitting needles in a barrel Mika kept by the register. "I'll text you if we need a Mommyvention."

"Thanks, Miks." I turned to the woman in the chair. "Wow, that's a gorgeous shawl. Sorry if my little tornado's presence disrupts your calm."

"Are you kidding?" she said. "I have nine grandchildren. I concentrate better when someone wants to show me something every fourteen seconds."

I laughed. This woman clearly knew toddlers. With a kiss on Saw's head and an abrupt "Bye" from him, I headed the two blocks to the courthouse. The day had stayed perfectly clear, and I studied the way a few leaves hung to the sheltered side of the maples along the way.

The county records room was one of my favorite places – big tables, heavy books, and pages and pages of history all waiting to be studied. I'd been there enough times to know just what I hoped to find, but I also knew that just because I hoped the records were there didn't mean they would be.

First, I had to find the plat number for the store then research the deeds to make a list of who had owned the property when. Then, scan any wills for those people to see what I could learn about the place. That information should be able to get me pretty far toward a clear timeline of the store, and then, with the names I gathered, I could send a few emails to ask about the people who had lived there. Soon, I'd have more than enough for a good newsletter article with links to more information.

The clerk's office was filled with the gentle thrum of office work that was typical for the space. People came here for only a few main reasons – marriage licenses, land title research for real estate activities, and historical and genealogical research. All of those were quiet activities, except for maybe the marriage license requests, which sometimes including a fair amount of giggling and, on rare occasions, loud kissing. Otherwise, the research room was a lot like a library, and after a morning tending a boundary-testing toddler, I was ready to sink into something that didn't need to be fed or washed and that could occupy my attention for more than three minutes at a time. I loved my son, but I craved space to go deep and let my brain sink into something for a long period of time.

I found the plat information on the store in no time, and within an hour, I had a full run-down on who had owned the store when, including in the 1990s when the first murder on the site had occurred. I also saw the deed of the current owners, George and Berlinda Jefferson and that they lived over in Richmond. I had known the Jeffersons owned the store because they had given me permission to salvage there once a high school friend had told me in passing at the grocery store that his crew had been hired to take it down. We had become friendly, if not yet friends, and I really liked them.

I expected the sheriff had already reached out to them about the morning's events, so I knew I wouldn't be bringing them news when I called. Still, I figured kindness dictated I wait and see what the investigation turned up before I contacted them to talk about the store's recent history. Besides, I wanted to read up on the first murder and be sure I understood the ins and outs of it before I went asking questions. In a rural community, it was best to be wise and informed before you started talking about a place's or a family's secrets.

So, I turned my attention to the early history of the store. The first time a building is shown on the plat for the land was in 1903, so I assumed – given the architecture of the building – that this was probably the year the store was built. I took the name of the owner at the time, the Elijah Scruggs for whom the store was still known, and went looking for wills.

It took a few minutes, but I eventually found reference to the store being willed to an Alice Scruggs in 1922. Alice was Elijah's daughter, and on the inventory for the will's distribution, the store and its contents are valued at two-hundred-thirty-eight dollars, which was a lot of money for a woman to inherit at the time, particularly a black woman. I felt a frisson of excitement for Alice and decided I would focus my story on her. I loved all history, but I particularly liked history that wasn't mainstream . . . which usually meant the history of women and people of color.

Then, with about forty-five minutes to go before I was due back to Mika's store, I took a quick scan of the other Scruggs wills, making notes of names and dates before carefully putting the books back on the shelves. Lifting these tomes always felt like a little bit of a workout, and my shoulders had a healthy ache as I waved a thanks to the staff and walked back out into the late afternoon.

As I strolled, my phone rang. I didn't normally answer calls from unknown numbers, but the day's events made me think it would be wise to pick up. Sure enough, it was Sheriff Shifflett, and he wondered if I had some time to talk.

"I'm downtown now. Coffee shop in five?" I said with a quick glance at my watch. "My toddler is with his auntie, so I have about fifteen minutes."

"See you in three," the sheriff said, and I picked up my pace as I crossed the street and ducked into the coffee shop across from Spin A Yarn, Mika's store. I ordered my usual late-day beverage – a steamed milk with vanilla syrup – and took a seat by the window with hopes that the late day sun kept me from being visible to Sawyer. He was great with other people . . . until I appeared. Then, it was all Mama all the time.

While I waited, I stared at Mika's shop. It had been her dream to open it ever since we were in college in Pennsylvania, but only after a really hard decade running a preschool did she decide it was time for a change. She moved down from her hometown up north, bought the storefront with the apartment above it in the town I called home, and started her bookstore/yarn shop. It had meant lots of hours of the two of us unloading boxes of used books and shipments of yarn, but I was almost as proud of that store as she was. More, though, I was proud of her. She had taken a risk, and it was paying off.

I took a long sip of my steamer and sat back and inhaled a long, deep breath just as the sheriff walked in. He waved as he headed to the counter for his own order and then made his way over with a giant cup of something coffee-based, so the scent told me.

I smiled, "Thirsty?"

"It's going to be a long night. Normally, I don't do caffeine after three p.m., but today . . . "

"Say no more. For the first eighteen months of my son's life, it was only a late afternoon coffee that got me through to bedtime." I sipped my warm milk and tried to let it soothe the nerves that had suddenly popped up when I saw the sheriff. I didn't know exactly why I was anxious, but I was.

"First, let me assure you that you aren't a suspect."

My blood pressure spiked at the words. "Wait?! What?!"

A smile teased the edge of the sheriff's lips. "Gotcha."

I glared at him until I couldn't hold back my own grin any longer. "You did get me. Too many police dramas, I expect."

"A common problem, which gives me my best gag. You were never a suspect, just to be clear." He chugged half his coffee. "No one who commits a murder first lugs out six cases of Cheerwine." He laughed.

"I'll remember that if I decide to commit a murder and want to throw you off the trail." I felt some of the tension of the day ease with the banter. "But why did you need to see me?"

A certain tightness took hold in the sheriff's jaw again, and my heartrate picked up in response. "We identified the woman in the house."

I took a deep breath. "Okay?"

"You probably know her, actually. Bailey Thomas. Name ring a bell?"

It did, but I couldn't place her. I knew, from funerals, that the bodies of people didn't look much like the people in life, but even with that in mind, I couldn't connect the wispy blonde hair, white skin, and thin frame on the woman in the bedroom with a living face I recognized. "Kind of, but I don't know why."

Shifflett nodded. "She was kind of infamous in town for

making trouble, especially at the grocery store. Some people call her, "The 'But the Sign Says' lady."

"OH, HER! Yes, I do know her. Wow." Twice I'd seen her lose it – as in screaming and even throwing things – on a clerk at our local IGA because the price on the register didn't match the price on her item. One time, the high schooler running the checkout had started to cry so hard that the manager had to take over. "She was, um, something," I said as I tried to honor the dead but not lie.

"That's putting it nicely." He cracked his knuckles one by one. "Going to make it harder to catch who did this, I expect."

I let out a long sigh. "Yeah, I guess so," I said quietly, "but how many people would really kill someone over temper tantrums?"

He shrugged. "Hopefully not many."

Now that my surprise at the victim's identity had worn off, I was again trying to puzzle out why the sheriff was telling me all this information. "Can I help somehow?"

"Well, I do have a couple more questions about this morning." He took out a small notebook.

"Shoot." I blushed and wanted to smack my forehead. "Er, sorry, poor choice of words. Ask away." I was pretty sure I'd told him everything I could this morning, but if I could help, I would.

"Did you see anyone else around the store this morning when you were there? Anyone in the woods maybe?"

My heartrate got booming again, but I tried to think, to remember what I'd seen on my way into the building. "Not that I can recall. There definitely weren't any cars there, well, except for the construction equipment." I tilted my chin up and looked at the ceiling as I scanned my memory one last time. "But no, I didn't see any people."

The sheriff made a quick note and then asked, "Anything seem out of place or weird to you as you went through the building?"

"Besides the eerie cookies and the blanket on the sofa that made it seem like people had just walked out, you mean?"

"Well, besides the cookies, yes." He scribbled in his notebook with a little too much attention.

"But the blanket wasn't weird to you?" I said. I was not going to let his careful choice of words go unnoted.

His eyes met mine, and I saw a tinge of color reach the tips of his ears. "Well, yes, but not when we found out Thomas had been living there."

It took me a second to process what he had just said, and then I was still confused. "She was living there? With all that moldy food in the kitchen?"

He shrugged. "Apparently, she didn't care much about that. But by some mistake from the power company, the electricity was still on, and so she had some food in the refrigerator and in the cupboards."

I cringed, and he continued, "Mostly pre-cooked stuff, so she didn't need the oven or stove."

"Still," I said, and then I thought about how this one steamed milk was all I could afford as a "luxury" for at least the next week and wondered if tight finances might have been why Thomas was such a bear at the grocery store. "Do you think she'd been living there long?"

"We're not sure. The electric co-op is going to pull the usage for the past few months. We'll know soon." He sat forward a bit more in his chair. "I know you have to go, but one more question?"

I nodded.

"You didn't, by chance, touch anything around her body when you were there, did you?"

My first instinct was to answer with a quick no, but I knew his question was important, even if I wasn't sure why yet. So I took a breath, walked my way through the memory again, and then said, definitively, "No. I saw she was dead as soon as I got close, and I didn't want to disturb the crime scene." I looked at the sheriff. "And dead bodies creep me out."

"That is, Ms. Sutton, the most honest answer I've ever gotten to that question. Thank you."

I glanced at my phone and saw that it was almost time for Mika to close up shop. I slipped on my coat as I stood, but I couldn't help asking one more question. "Did you think I had touched the body?"

The sheriff stood, too. "No, but since she was still warm when we got there, I was curious if you'd realized that she hadn't been dead long."

A wave of weakness ran up my legs, and I braced myself against the table. "She had just been killed? Like how long?"

The sheriff stared at me for a long minute, and I wondered if he was going to answer my question. But then, he took a deep breath and said, "Thirty minutes before we arrived."

"Oh." I shook the sheriff's hand and tried to act like this information was on par with a report on how long my dishwasher needed to run a cycle as I walked out of the coffee shop. But when I made it past the front window and out of sight of the sheriff, I let out a gasp. That woman was killed while we were there.

Grab your copy...

About the Author

ACF Bookens lives in Virginia's Southwestern Mountains with her young son, an old hound, and a bully mix who has already eaten two couches. When she's not writing, she cross-stitches, watches YA fantasy shows, and grows massive quantities of cucumbers.